Second Act at Appleton Green

Also by Kate Forster

The Sisters
Starting Over at Acorn Cottage
Finding Love at Mermaid Terrace
Christmas Wishes at Pudding Hall
Christmas Eve at Cranberry Cross
Fly Me to Moongate Manor

Second Act at Appleton Green

Kate Forster

An Aria Book

First published in the UK in 2025 by Head of Zeus,
part of Bloomsbury Publishing Plc

Copyright © Kate Forster, 2025

The moral right of Kate Forster to be identified
as the author of this work has been asserted in accordance with
the Copyright, Designs and Patents Act of 1988.

All rights reserved. No part of this publication may be: i) reproduced or transmitted in any form, electronic or mechanical, including photocopying, recording or by means of any information storage or retrieval system without prior permission in writing from the publishers; or ii) used or reproduced in any way for the training, development or operation of artificial intelligence (AI) technologies, including generative AI technologies. The rights holders expressly reserve this publication from the text and data mining exception as per Article 4(3) of the Digital Single Market Directive (EU) 2019/790.

This is a work of fiction. All characters, organizations, and events
portrayed in this novel are either products of the author's
imagination or are used fictitiously.

9 7 5 3 1 2 4 6 8

A catalogue record for this book is available from the British Library.

ISBN (PB): 9781035914685
ISBN (ePDF): 9781035914715; ISBN (eBook): 9781035914678

Cover design: Jessie Price
Typeset by Siliconchips Services Ltd UK

Printed and bound in Great Britain by
CPI Group (UK) Ltd, Croydon CR0 4YY

Bloomsbury Publishing Plc
50 Bedford Square, London, WC1B 3DP, UK
Bloomsbury Publishing Ireland Limited,
29 Earlsfort Terrace, Dublin 2, D02 AY28, Ireland

HEAD OF ZEUS LTD
5–8 Hardwick Street
London, EC1R 4RG

To find out more about our authors and books
visit www.headofzeus.com
For product safety related questions contact productsafety@bloomsbury.com

For anyone brave enough to begin again.

After losing her voice before a vital audition, West End hopeful Lily Baxter retreats to her grandmother's cottage at Appleton Green. Lily joins the local amateur dramatics society and falls for attractive nurse Nick, intending to stay only for the summer. Lily must choose between London and the village as she rediscovers her singing passion and family secrets.

Act One

One

'Morning.' Lily woke to hearing Nigel, her housemate, knocking on her bedroom door.

'Go away,' she returned in greeting, rolling over in bed and pulling the duvet up over her head. Their rescue cat, Mr Mistoffelees, was asleep at the foot of the bed, keeping her toes warm.

She heard the door open. 'Seriously, piss off,' she moaned and threw a pillow at the door but it fell short, like most things she did lately, she thought.

'Charming, you're quite the lady, aren't you?' said Nigel in a posh accent as he opened the door.

'I try me best, guvnor,' she said in a cockney accent and she rolled over to look at Nigel.

Nigel was dressed in his active wear and was doing pliés in the doorway. He was always moving, always dancing from one place to another. People like Nigel were like dragonflies, and people were captivated by them both.

'I'm heading off soon. I've got to get the train to the airport. I thought we could farewell each other over breakfast but we don't have any clean mugs. I could still make tea and we can drink it from those ramekin dishes you bought for that dinner party that time and served the crème brûlée that didn't set.'

'Don't remind me of that and don't remind me it's my turn to do the dishes,' she said as she sat up in bed.

'You haven't done the dishes in about a month, hence the ramekins,' he said with an exaggerated eye-roll. 'I have stopped doing them as an act of protest. I also haven't been here due to rehearsals but those dishes have scurvy; you have scurvy; this flat has scurvy.'

'I must,' she said. 'I just don't feel great. Even getting up is hard at the moment. I think either I'm low in iron or it's scurvy.'

'No, you're low in self-confidence,' said Nigel shaking his head at her. 'Girl, I worry about you. You have to get into it, this whole life concept.'

'I would rather stay at home. I'm thinking of applying for a new job,' she said.

'Oh? That's cool. What is it? Are you leaving the call centre or the restaurant or both?' he asked doing an arabesque.

'Neither. I'm planning on being a biscuit tester. It a work-from-home role and I just sit on the sofa and eat biscuits and give them a rating. Do you know anyone who's hiring?'

'I think that's a perfect job for you,' said Nigel and he walked into the room and picked up the pillow and threw it at her. 'Hobnob reviewer and general dilettante.'

'Thank you, finally someone can see my potential,' she said. 'More than Paul does. You know, I've left messages and he still hasn't returned my calls.'

'Paul is a shit agent. I've told you that. Unless you're a lead he's not interested. You need to try a new one, someone with a bit of hunger.'

'You're with Paul,' she cried.

'I know, but I'm a dancer; it's easier for me. You know what he's like, all about the young and famous ones.'

'Of which I am neither,' she sniffed. When Paul had first taken her on after drama school she was thrilled. He was considered the best in the business, but he had slowly started to take less interest in her as she stopped booking jobs. She knew Nigel was right but the thought of having to start again with a new agent made her tired even thinking about it.

'Now get up and go to your real job,' Nigel said firmly. 'You're not getting any younger or famous rolling around in that squalor.'

'I know.' She sighed and pulled her long dark curls up into a bun. 'I can't wait for a day of calling people to ask them if they want to join the wine club or whatever it is I'll be selling today. Who knew I'd be living this dream at nearly thirty? I mean it's amazing, isn't it? The heights I have reached in my stage career so far.'

'Don't stress, babe, you have your third callback tomorrow for *Les Mis*, on the stage no less. How exciting to sing on that stage. It's going to be amazing. I know you'll get it and then you'll be in a show and never have to sell wine or newspapers or heater servicing again, and Denise can sell the signed programmes on eBay once you're in the show.'

She sighed. Nigel knew her better than anyone and knew she came with a very intense stage mother: Denise. She and

Nigel had lived together through university and graduation and for the past eight years, but now he was going on tour with *The Wizard of Oz* and she would be left in their flat alone working, hustling, auditioning, worrying.

Nigel was an incredible dancer and strong chorus member, but Lily was a soprano and roles were harder to come by, plus with her striking looks of pale skin, blue eyes and long dark curls, she looked like she was born in another time, except she was getting older and the ingénue roles seemed to be going to the younger ones.

She had been in three choruses on the West End since leaving drama school and she was grateful for those opportunities as they'd helped her get the lead role of Marian Paroo in a tour of Europe with *The Music Man*. It was exciting to have any roles at all, as she knew how hard it was to even get an audition on the West End, but it felt like her agent had forgotten about her lately. Sometimes he would ring with a TV commercial audition or even a voiceover or narration for an audiobook but the phone had been ominously quiet in the past few weeks.

Sure, there had been a few walk-on parts on television shows and a few lines in an episode of *Holby City* but this third and final callback for *Les Mis* was everything she had worked for. All those years at college, all the singing with her gran in her cottage in Appleton Green, all the auditions and trying over and over again. She was ready for this.

With a sigh, Lily swung her legs out of bed and landed on the chilly floor. After making her way to the bathroom, she cleaned her teeth and glanced in the mirror. The bags beneath her eyes were not pretty, she thought as she leaned in closer to see the damage, but that's what happens when you work two crappy jobs with crappy hours and matching pay.

In an attempt to rouse herself, she splashed more water on her face.

'Tea's ready!' Nigel's voice sang from the kitchen. 'In ramekins, as promised!'

As Lily entered their small kitchen, she laughed at the sight of Nigel sitting on the counter, drinking from a white ramekin. With steam emerging from the makeshift mug, he gave her the other one.

'Cheers,' he said and placed her ramekin against his.

Laughing, she took a sip. Nigel always knew how to cheer her up and she made a little toast.

'To your big adventure on the road to Oz. You are going to be amazing and you're understudying the Scarecrow. That's so great – it's about time people saw how brilliant you are,' she said firmly. And she believed it. Nigel was exceptional and it was a matter of time before he was playing bigger roles in bigger shows.

Nigel smiled at her. 'And to your stardom in the future. I have no doubt that you will ace your audition tomorrow. I wish I could be here for it.'

The tour for *The Wizard of Oz* started tomorrow and Nigel would be away for two months. She wished he could be here, mostly because she knew she would miss him and because he calmed her, but she knew she needed to stop relying on him for every emotional moment she had.

She shrugged. It had felt so hard lately. As though all the dreams she had once had didn't seem to matter anymore. She was tired, and the hustle was hard.

'You're so good, Lil, please don't underestimate yourself,' Nigel pleaded with her.

Lily wished she had his level of assurance. Doubts were becoming more frequent of late. 'Nige, I'm not sure. There are a ton of gifted singers out there. What makes me so special? And I'm getting older. People know who I am now and not because I'm a star but because I keep turning up, like a musical theatre masochist or something.'

With a graceful jump, Nigel stepped off the counter and placed his ramekin down. 'What makes you special? Are you kidding me?'

He took hold of her shoulders and met her gaze directly. 'Darling, you have a voice that could make angels cry. You look like Snow White and have a voice like Audra McDonald – that's what's special about you. It's just a matter of time, I promise you. Your life is going to change with one single role.'

Lily rolled her eyes, but as he spoke, a wave of warmth went through her chest. 'You're biased.'

'I am, damn it.' Nigel winked. 'But I'm also right.'

Lily's phone buzzed on the counter as Nigel hurried about the kitchen gathering the rest of his packing. As she took a quick look at it, her stomach dropped.

The Stage Mother came up on her phone screen.

Nigel shot her a pitying glance. 'Want me to answer it and pretend to be you?'

Lily shook her head and inhaled deeply before responding. 'Hi, Mum.'

'Lily, darling!' Her mother seemed super cheerful, always a dead giveaway that she was about to start asking questions.

'Are you prepared for your big audition tomorrow? I just wanted to check in. What state are you in? Have you been working on your technique? How's the voice sounding? Do you need some of that Chinese throat syrup? You can get it at the Asian grocer near you. I rang them to check and they said they had plenty of bottles, but I got them to put one behind the counter for you anyway, under Denise.'

'Mum, I'm okay,' Lily responded, trying to remain calm. No one triggered her like Denise did. As an only child with a talent, the pressure on Lily was more than she would ever admit to people. She made jokes about it to Nigel, calling Denise 'The Stage Mother', but underneath all the questions, Lily couldn't help feeling that she was letting her mother down by not being a lead in a show yet. She couldn't offer anything to her parents that other women her age were delivering: no wedding, no grandchildren, no career.

'I've been practising. It's fine. I don't need the syrup, I promise.'

'That's good,' Denise said. 'I meant to tell you. I saw on Facebook that Sheila from the am dram group in Appleton said that her niece was down to the last three for a role in *Les Mis*. You might know her. She might be there tomorrow.'

The intention of her comment was obvious but Lily wasn't going to bite today.

Lily's throat constricted. 'There's more than one role being auditioned for, so I couldn't say, but whatever it is, that's great for her.' Staying neutral was best with Denise, she had learned over the years.

'You'll be next, darling, I just know it. You are incredibly talented. All you have to do is put in the work. Maybe take the day off and practise.'

Only Denise would encourage Lily to take a day off and practise.

Lily gripped the phone more tightly. 'I can't, Mum, I need to pay rent; that's how this whole adult thing works.' She knew she was having a dig at Denise who had never worked; instead she put everything into Lily to the point it was stifling, but sometimes her lower self won over taking the high road with Denise.

'Well, my main concern is that the jobs might be detracting from your actual objectives. Your career is what you should be putting all of your effort into. Perhaps if you practised for a couple extra hours every day...' Denise had that tone and Lily closed her eyes and mentally counted to ten. She truly loved her mother, but there were moments when the strain became too much for her.

'Lily? Do you hear me?'

After an instinctive 'Yep' Lily replied, 'Look, I have to go and say goodbye to Nigel and then I have to go to work.'

'Oh yes, how exciting for Nigel. Isn't he clever?' Denise said.

As opposed to me, Lily thought, but said nothing.

'All right, sweetheart. Tomorrow, break a leg. I'm sure you'll be fantastic.'

Lily felt her mother's expectations fall hard on her as she hung up the phone. Experiencing unexpected exhaustion, she leaned against the counter.

Nigel walked into the kitchen with plates and some glasses from his bedroom. 'How was Rose Hovick today?' he asked with an arched eyebrow.

'She's worse than Rose. She makes Rose look like she was just encouraging Gypsy. Denise is ready to start auditioning herself, I think.'

Nigel put his arm around her and squeezed her shoulders tightly. 'Avoid letting her affect you. You're doing great, thank you. You're living your dream, putting in a lot of work, and going on auditions. More than most people could say – that.'

Lily gave a little laugh. 'I know, I'm just feeling a bit fragile and she really knows how to get under my skin.' She made a sad face at him. 'What am I going to do without you? You're my live-in cheerleader.'

'Oh, you'll be fine,' Nigel dismissively stated while waving a hand. 'You'll be so busy being a star, you won't even notice I'm gone.'

Lily finished her tea in the ramekin as Nigel got his things ready to leave. Why did she feel so weird about everything lately? She felt happy for him but so terrified for herself.

Stop making this about you, Lily, she told herself as Nigel came into the kitchen.

'I've cleaned my room, so you can rent it out for a few weeks if you like. I've paid my rent up anyway, but you could rent it if you want some more cash.'

'You're a gem,' she said, meaning it.

'I would stay to clean this up, but I don't want to,' he said looking around the kitchen and living room at the mess of dishes and music and papers.

'You're such a good friend,' she said sarcastically.

'Toughen up, sunshine. I'll call you tomorrow to run through the song before the audition, okay?'

They gave each other one more hug as they stood in the doorway with Nigel's suitcases at his feet. Nigel said, 'Knock 'em dead, Baxter,' into her hair. 'And please, be kind to yourself. Do what makes you happy. Sometimes I worry you've forgotten what makes you happy.'

Lily nodded while stifling her tears. 'I know. I'll work on it. Now go, or you'll miss your train.'

Lily leaned against the door as it closed behind Nigel, taking in the sudden silence of the room. She groaned, taking a quick look at the time. It was time to prepare for yet another day of pointless calls and turned-down sales pitches.

Lily looked in the full-length mirror at herself as she got ready for work. She stopped and gave herself a serious look. Everyone seemed so much more interesting than her when she went to the auditions. Was there still a place for a classical soprano with an antique face in a world of pop princesses and belting divas?

She shook her head, attempting to shake away the negative thoughts.

But Lily couldn't get rid of the feeling that something bad was coming, like she was standing on the edge of something and there wasn't a guard rail. One wrong step and she could fall and never come back again, but she didn't want to tell Nigel that; she didn't want to tell anyone that. No, she would just get on with it. That's all she could do. She locked the door behind her and left the flat. She squared her shoulders, inhaled deeply, and stepped out into the London morning. She had promised herself and Nigel that she would try and find what made her happy, on stage or off. That was her goal for now.

Two

The lights of the Theatre Royal were blinding as Lily Baxter stood in the centre of the stage. This was her third callback for the role of Éponine in *Les Misérables* and she could feel her heart beating so loudly, she wondered if the producers and director could hear it from the stalls. She waited for the first chords from the piano for her moment to sing the iconic song 'I Dreamed a Dream' from the musical.

The first audition had been a general one. They were asked to sing in groups, and Lily had made it through; then the second was singing in a chorus and then alone for a few bars of 'On my Own' from the show, and now she was back again the next day. This was it. Her moment. She had been asked to sing alone, on the stage, ready for her spotlight.

The familiar opening bars of 'I Dreamed a Dream' filled the cavernous space and despite the heat from the lights, she felt cool and calm. She stepped forward, took a deep breath, opened her mouth, and... nothing. Not a single note escaped her lips.

What's happening? Lily's mind raced. She had warmed up in her flat that morning, ignoring the man below banging on the ceiling with a broom in objection. *Come on, voice. Work!* She'd sung this song a thousand times – in the shower, on the Tube, even in her sleep.

From the darkened auditorium, she heard the shuffle of papers, the scratch of a pen.

The accompanist stopped and she glanced at him. He frowned and then started the introduction again.

She opened her mouth... nothing. Her voice box felt closed. There was a lump in her throat that felt like the size of potato.

A male voice, tinged with impatience, came from the darkness: 'Ms Baxter? We're waiting.'

Lily's cheeks burned. She could feel the eyes of the other auditionees boring into her back from the wings. A whisper floated across the stage: 'Poor thing.'

No. No, I can do this. Lily cleared her throat, shooting an apologetic smile towards the judges' table. 'I'm so sorry. May I start again?'

Silence was the nod of approval and the accompanist, bless him, took her back to the beginning. Once more, the melancholic melody swelled around her.

Lily closed her eyes, summoning every ounce of emotion, every scrap of technique she'd honed over years of training. She opened her mouth, willing the words to flow from what she knew was her clear, powerful voice.

But her throat closed up, her chest tight with panic. The music played on, a cruel reminder of her silence.

In that moment, under the unforgiving glare of the spotlight, Lily Baxter realised that sometimes, dreams shatter not with a bang, but with a whimper – or in her case, with no sound at all.

She stumbled off the stage, aware of the looks from the women waiting for their turn to be Éponine, even for a moment, on the iconic stage. There were hushed whispers and pitying glances from some and bemusement from others, all of them feeling like pinpricks against her skin. She picked up her bag and ran away from the judgement and curiosity and took a moment in a dark corner backstage. She could hear voices coming her way.

'God, I would die if that was me,' said one voice.

'She looked so perfect for the role. All those dark curls, she would have been ideal.'

'Dark curly hair doesn't help if you're going to play the role mute,' the first cruel voice said with a laugh.

Lily bit her lip at the stinging barb and, in the cramped area, searched for an escape. There – a gap between two costume racks draped with sparkling gowns. She ducked behind them, sinking to the floor in a crumpled heap.

She put the heels of her palms up against her eyes and pressed hard, and the realities of her world swam before her, faces and lights blurring into a dizzying whir as though she was on a theme park ride. She needed this job, more than she could have explained. She had rent to pay on her flat, bills. She had bought a new dress for this audition and now she couldn't return it because she was currently sitting on the dirty stage floor. She was getting almost no shifts at the call centre, and even fewer at the restaurant where she waitressed, and she was tired. She was twenty-nine years old and was so tired that at times her bones ached. Every day was a hustle to survive and this was supposed to be the moment where she would finally break through into a role. Lily's hands shook violently as she fumbled with her water bottle, spilling half of it down her new dress.

'Deep breaths, lovey,' she whispered to herself, her ninety-seven-year-old grandmother Violet's oft-repeated advice echoing in her mind. But each inhalation felt like swallowing broken glass, her chest tight with unshed tears and bitter disappointment. She had let everyone down. Her parents had rung her that morning wishing her luck. Her best friend, Nigel, had sent her a voice memo reminding her to warm up and that he was saying a prayer to the patron saint of musicals – Patti LuPone – and Granny Violet had called last night to wish her the best for the day – and she hated talking on the phone.

'Hey, are you all right?' A soft voice burst Lily's bubble of misery. She looked up to see a very young, willowy brunette peering down at her, concern etched across perfect features. Probably the next Éponine, Lily thought, trying to keep bitterness out of her thoughts. *Don't become bitchy*, she reminded herself. Sometimes the world of theatre was so toxic.

'I'm fine,' Lily managed to croak out, the lie tasting sour on her tongue.

The girl crouched down, offering a pristine white tissue. 'It happens to the best of us,' she said, and she gave Lily a smile that might have been construed as sympathetic or maybe patronising. 'Don't be so hard on yourself. There's always next time, right?'

Lily accepted the tissue with a weak nod, knowing full well there wouldn't be a next time. Not here. Not after this disaster. This production company and this director would put her on the DNA list, Do Not Audition, and she would be persona non grata.

The brunette gave her shoulder an awkward pat before swanning off, no doubt to dazzle the judges and claim the role Lily had dreamed of since she was old enough to sing along with the original cast recording.

Alone once more, Lily pressed the tissue to her lips, muffling the sob that threatened to tear from her throat. In the distance, she could hear another hopeful's voice soaring through 'I Dreamed a Dream'. The irony wasn't lost on her as the lyrics floated backstage. Lily had never felt more alone in her life. The bustling theatre, her nirvana of magic and possibility, now seemed vast and indifferent to her pain. The show must go on, she thought as she huddled deeper between the costumes but, perhaps for her, it had stopped for a moment. What was wrong with her voice?

Once the women had gone, Lily made her way out of her hiding spot and pushed through the heavy doors of the Theatre Royal, stepping out onto Drury Lane. The bustling energy of London enveloped her like a cold embrace. She had always loved living in London but right now it felt like the enemy. It wasn't applauding for her anymore; it was a reminder that she was a no one and, for a moment there, she thought she would be a someone, at least on the West End.

Her feet began to move of their own accord. She had always walked when she needed to think. The further she walked, the further she was away from the scene of her humiliation. Walking was like her form of meditation. She couldn't sit still in a room, waiting for the enlightenment. She needed to meet it halfway and walking was where she would often tangle the mess of confusion and worry. Pounding the pavement until the solution came or her mind was soothed by the endorphins and repetitive steps. She had once thought that walking away from a problem was so she could get a perspective of it from afar, but today, not even walking to Scotland could have taken away the shame she felt from the moment on the stage.

She drifted past the vibrant storefronts of Covent Garden, the lively chatter of tourists and shoppers a stark contrast to the hollow silence in her chest. Why had her voice failed her in such a spectacular way? She walked past a bakery, the scent of the fresh bread, usually so enticing, now turned her stomach. She tried to hum and the sound came, and she tried to sing a few words under her breath. Nothing came out. A croak and then nothing, as though her voice box had run out of charge.

She cleared her throat and tried again – this time not even a croak.

She clutched her throat and walked, trying to sing every few steps, but it was gone. She spoke words aloud and they were fine; she just couldn't muster a note.

Before she knew it, Lily found herself on the Strand, the busy thoroughfare buzzing with afternoon traffic. When she had first moved to London from Carlisle to study music and drama at college, she had spent what rare spare time she had exploring London. Now she felt empty and she wandered aimlessly to the Victoria Embankment. The Thames flowed beside her, dark and implacable. She stood for a moment, looking down at the water, feeling tears fall down her cheeks. She was so close and she had frozen on stage. What would she say to her parents? Gran? Her friends? Everyone had been so excited for it.

'It's only a matter of time before everyone sees and hears how wonderful you are,' her mum had said. 'And the time is now with this audition.'

'They won't believe how wonderful your voice is until they hear it in person,' Nigel, her housemate, had told her.

'You will sing the roof off,' Gran had told her.

She had let them all down.

Lily walked until she found herself at the Millennium Bridge and she stood looking down as tourists and locals alike streamed past her. Their chatter and laughter felt like a slap to her senses and she wanted to scream at them all, 'Don't you know I just ruined my first big opportunity? I ruined it and I've let everyone down!'

She leaned forward against the railing, staring out at St Paul's Cathedral rising on the other side of the river.

'There is nothing that's broken that can't be fixed. It might look the exact way it used to but perhaps it's strong now,' she heard someone say and she turned to see an elderly man who had paused beside her, his kind eyes crinkling as he smiled at her kindly.

Lily nodded, not trusting herself to speak as she stared ahead again.

The old man reached out and put his hand on hers, which was clutching the handrail. 'You know,' he continued, and turned to gaze out at the cityscape as he gave her hand a squeeze, 'sometimes you wonder if this is the life you're supposed to live, but if you can trust the path you're on and not fight it, not try and escape it, you just never know what's waiting in the wings for you. Step into your light, dear. Your time will come again. Today is not the day to exit stage left.'

Lily gasped and before she could respond, the man had already moved on, disappearing into the flow of pedestrians crossing the bridge. His words hung in the air, mingling with the mist rising from the river.

Who was he? What had just happened?

Lily's eyes drifted to a street performer near the bridge's entrance, silently acting out an elaborate mime scene to the delight of a small crowd. Here, with no spotlight or velvet curtains, was a performance filled with more life and joy than she'd managed to summon at the audition. Was she planning to jump? She wasn't sure. She wasn't sure of anything anymore.

She sank onto a nearby bench, exhausted from the day. The last light faded from the London sky, the city's lights flickering to life around her. As the Thames flowed steadily on, Lily wondered if maybe, just maybe, there was a role waiting for her somewhere else.

Three

The key turned in the lock with a hollow click, and Lily stepped into the darkness of her flat. For a moment, she stood motionless in the doorway, letting the silence envelop her like a shroud. Outside, London pulsed with its usual frenetic energy – car horns blaring, night buses rumbling past, distant laughter floating up from the pub on the corner. But here, in the confines of her small Southwark flat, time seemed to stand still. Just this morning she had happily practised the song with no issues as she got ready.

Lily flicked on the lights, wincing as the sudden brightness assaulted her red and sore eyes, cried out so much they hurt to open. The shared flat was a study in organised chaos – a testament to two creative souls crammed into a space barely big enough for one. Sheet music littered every surface, competing for space with dog-eared scripts and a few of her half-empty mugs of long-cold tea. A garish poster for *The Wizard of Oz* dominated one wall, a glittery Post-it note stuck to the corner: *I'll bring you back a pair of ruby slippers! x*

The sight of his note made Lily's heart clench. God, she was really giving herself a pity party, she thought as she shuffled into the tiny kitchenette, filled up the kettle and turned it on. The dishes from breakfast still sat in the sink – Nigel's 'lucky audition mug' perched precariously atop a stack of plates. This morning, they'd laughed on the phone, trading show tunes and inside jokes. Now, the memory felt like it belonged to someone else entirely. He had told her she would nail it, had helped her practise the song a few more times over the phone on FaceTime, ignoring the banging on the floor from below, and she missed him more than ever.

A soft meow drew her attention to the windowsill, where Mr Mistoffelees sat watching her with knowing yellow eyes. 'At least someone's glad to see me,' Lily murmured, reaching out to scratch behind his ears.

The cat butted his head against her hand, his purr a comforting rumble in the oppressive quiet of the flat. For a moment, Lily allowed herself to be soothed by his affection, but as her gaze drifted to the mirror hanging crookedly on the wall, reality came crashing back.

The girl staring back at her looked like a stranger – pale, hollow-eyed, the spark of ambition snuffed out. Her eyes were swollen and red, her face blotched and her usually bouncy curls hanging limp and lifeless over her shoulders. Lily turned away quickly, unable to bear the sight of her own defeat.

Her gaze drifted back to the mirror.

She was seventeen again, standing on a rickety stage in the community centre, the heat of the lights making her makeup run. The final notes of 'Don't Rain on My Parade' hung in the air, and for a moment, there was silence. Then, like a wave crashing to shore, the applause erupted. Her drama teacher, Mrs Wilson, with tears in her eyes, mouthing, 'Brilliant, absolutely brilliant!'

But truth be told, Lily had once aspired to become a music instructor. She had been taught by wonderful teachers at school in piano and singing, and she had imagined herself helping people find their voice and learn to play the piano. In fact, Lily was positive that teaching was her calling. She'd even started looking into universities with strong music education departments. However, that all changed when the school's production of *West Side Story* took place.

Lily had been cast as Maria, and she was enthralled from the moment she stepped onto the stage. The brilliant lights, the rush of adrenaline, the thunderous applause – it was exhilarating. Suddenly, the concept of teaching felt... less. Less interesting, less glamorous, and less everything.

'You were born to be on stage, sweetie,' her mother exclaimed following the performance. 'You're going to be a celebrity!'

So Lily's dreams were waylaid, and she convinced herself that teaching was merely a phase, a backup plan. She was meant for bigger things, to have her name in lights on the West End.

When she started acting school, her teachers supported her new dream. One singing instructor had laughed when someone suggested teaching as a profession. 'Teaching is for those who can't make it as performers.'

So Lily had set aside her old desire, burying it behind new goals of fame and fortune. She poured herself into acting and singing, anxious to prove that she possessed the necessary talent to succeed.

But now, her voice mysteriously gone, Lily couldn't help but question if she'd made the correct decision. She remembered the joy she had felt in assisting others in finding their voice, as well as the satisfaction of developing talent. Had she been too quick to discard that option?

She shook her head and pushed the thought aside. No, she was a performer. She'd worked too hard and made too many sacrifices to quit just now. When her voice returned, she would resume where she had left off. She had to. Hadn't she?

Lily blinked, and the memories faded, replaced by the harsh reality of her dingy flat. That girl – the one with stars in her eyes and a voice that could shake the rafters – where had she gone? How had she ended up here, a hollowed-out shell of her former self, dreams lying shattered at her feet?

Her phone rang and she saw her mother's name come up on the phone screen. She had been calling all afternoon, probably thinking Lily's silence was a good sign. She noted there was a call from Paul. He could wait, she thought. The last thing she needed was her agent screaming bloody murder at her. But she did need to speak to Denise.

She would have to tell her the truth sooner or later.

'Hi, Mum,' she said, sitting down on the sofa. She was ready to tell her how terrible it had been, that maybe she wasn't meant for this life of hustle. That she really needed to stop for a moment and get her bearings.

'Gran's in hospital.' Denise's voice was tight and strained. 'A fall, they said. The woman, Mrs Harris or Mrs Douglas, I think, the one who delivers her bread and milk found her. She had knocked herself out. She's fallen out the front of the house. Badly grazed her face, needed stiches on her nose and she's put her dentures through her lip.'

'What? Oh my God,' Lily said, her misery gone with fear replacing it. All thoughts of *Les Mis* evaporated. She needed to be with Gran immediately.

'What hospital? I'll go and see her.' She stood up and started to look around for her things.

'She's in St Vincent's but she's awake now and insisting on going home. Your father tried to talk some sense into her and suggested that perhaps she might think about moving into an assisted living home, but she won't hear about it or even consider any help.'

Lily wasn't surprised. Granny Violet was the most fiercely independent ninety-seven-year-old in all of Britain. People were surprised when they learned Gran was still independent at ninety-seven but Lily said that no one argued with Gran, not even time. If she had decided something, that was it.

'I'll come up tomorrow,' said Lily realising she needed to sort her life out here and now.

'She's going home tomorrow,' Denise almost screeched down the line. 'It'll be too late.'

'Then I'll go and see her at home,' said Lily. 'Maybe I'll stay a few days.'

Denise sighed. 'Okay. That's probably a good idea. I don't want her to be alone and have another fall. You can see how she is and then let Dad and I know.' She paused and then her voice changed to something synthetic, a forced brightness. 'Now give me some good news. How did the audition go?'

Lily felt the weight of her mother's expectations on her shoulders, as though she was being pushed into the sofa, and then she thought about this moment and how much being a professional musical theatre performer meant to her mother and made a choice.

'Fine, I haven't heard yet. There were some good voices there though, so I'm okay if I don't get it,' she lied, keeping her voice bright. Who said she wasn't a brilliant actress? 'There were some real talents there.'

As she spoke, she felt the lies almost burn her tongue but now wasn't about her and the last thing she wanted to do was tell her mother that her voice had disappeared today.

'None so talented as you,' her mother said proudly. 'Okay, well we're at the hospital now and we'll take her back to Appleton Green tomorrow and maybe you can come in the afternoon, so she doesn't feel ambushed.'

'Okay, I'll come tomorrow. Bye,' she said. 'I'll drive up.' She was grateful for her little hatchback that she used when she needed to go to auditions out of London and sometimes she loaned it to friends for a small fee, which kept the insurance paid.

'Bye, love, let me know if you hear from the *Les Mis* people,' Denise said before she ended the call.

Lily looked around the flat. The need to be out of it was all-encompassing. She needed to be somewhere else to work out what was wrong with her voice and the flat in its current state was suffocating.

A few weeks in her grandmother's cottage in Appleton Green would be the perfect place to get away from London and work out what her voice and mind were doing.

She opened the iPad on the coffee table and typed into the Backstage website where performers put up rooms or flats to rent while they were on tour.

Two-bedroom flat available to rent for 4 weeks. She typed fast and found some photos of the flat when it was clean when she had put up the room on the same website before Nigel moved in. She added the price and particulars and then pressed post.

'Right,' she said as she looked around. She put the soundtrack from *Annie* on the stereo and then rolled her sleeves up and tried to sing along but nothing came out.

She turned off the music, feeling tears forming again, and she wiped her eyes with her new dress.

She would clean the flat so it was spotless, and hopefully the sun would come out again tomorrow and somehow, her voice would come back to her.

Four

Appleton Green was a small village, almost too pretty for its own good, plonked in the middle of the Derbyshire Dales with nothing around it for miles. You had to drive to the next town for any more than basics and even further to Silverton for schooling, hospitals and specialist appointments, but those who lived there loved it and had dug their heels deep into the loamy soil. It wasn't a long drive but, still, it was too far for many of the residents to bother unless they had to.

The village looked like a postcard, of which the tourists bought plenty when they came to take their picture on the old packhorse bridge across the Dove River. But they didn't stay long because there wasn't much for tourists to do in Appleton Green, besides go to the pub, and that was only open four days a week and after three in the afternoon. The village residents were middle-aged, older and old, and they all knew each other's routines.

For example, they knew when Mrs Douglas walked Wallace her corgi, or when Mrs Harris closed the post office for her lunch, which was usually cold meats and salad in summer and soup and bread in winter. They knew when Mr Sharma would be spending extra time in his garden to ensure his roses would be show-ready for the Silverton Flower Fair and when Mrs Hughes would be heading to her daughter's house in Mallorca for the winter, as her joints played up when it snowed.

The oldest resident of the village was Violet Baxter, ninety-seven years young, who refused to admit she was getting older and that she needed a cleaner in her little home, Pippin Cottage, or that she needed help with meals or a walking frame. At most, she would use the walking stick that had belonged to her husband Martin, who had died thirty-five years earlier, and sometimes she would accept meals from Mrs Harris who might have extra soup for Violet, and she would always accept shortbread from Mrs Douglas.

Now she was being taken back to her cottage by her son Peter and her daughter-in-law Denise, who were chatting as though she hadn't just taken a tumble on the path outside and didn't have a huge graze on her nose, stiches and an ugly new silver walking frame to lean on when she walked.

'The nurse said she will come by tomorrow to check the dressing on your nose and eye,' Denise said far too cheerfully for someone with such bad news.

'I don't need that. I can check it myself,' Violet said. 'I have some mercurochrome in the cupboard from when Peter was a boy – nothing wrong with it.'

Denise gasped and Violet saw Peter's hands tighten on the steering wheel.

There wasn't any mercurochrome but she liked saying things like that to stir the pot. It amused her and she knew the first thing Denise would do when they returned to her house was look for the bottle so that she could throw it away.

They were closer to Appleton Green and Violet felt her body relax at the thought of being back in the village.

The village consisted of little more than a cluster of stone houses, clinging to the banks around the River Dove. The walls of each building were made of limestone, and each one was the same but unique in its own way.

Each was named for a type of apple and Violet's home was Pippin Cottage on Dove Lane. A simple stone cottage with a slate roof, a little bit askew, like a top hat, set at a rakish angle. The exterior of the cottage was a patchwork of greys, creams, and mossy greens, with a thicket of climbing roses hiding the front door, which was painted a robin's egg blue, somewhat faded now. The door was visible through the tangle. The dogged flowers had long since asserted their ownership of the cottage, so Violet had let them have their way. It was too hard to tame nature at her age.

Every time she thought she might cut them back, then the height of summer would come and their fragrance would remind her that perhaps it was worth things being left alone.

The rest of the village had a few small shops, where she got her necessary household items delivered by Mrs Douglas. Mrs Harris ran the post office, which was also the tourist shop that opened three times a week. Other than that there was a pub and a village hall. If you wanted or needed more than that you had to drive to the village over, and Violet had let go of her car twenty years ago.

Looking out upon the lane and seeing her home again, Violet felt everything was going to be fine.

'Home,' she whispered to herself and she decided she would never leave it again, no matter what her son and his wife said.

To my sweet Lily, aged seven,

I'd like to start a new tradition as I sit here in the cottage. You left a few days ago with your mum and dad after we had a grand old time over the summer. This is the first time you stayed for the summer, and even though your mum and dad were worried you would be homesick, you told them in no uncertain terms you were home. It did make me laugh.

So I think after you have returned to your parents after each summer, I'll write you a letter. It will be something you can look back on and it will help you remember the time we spent together when you're older.

We have had a lovely summer, haven't we? It's funny how this little cottage seems to come to life when you get here, like it's been waiting all year for you. You've loved being here since you were a little baby, crawling about the floor, trying to get into the wood basket, and now you're running out the back door and into the garden with so much energy. I don't know where you get it from; it seems to be endless with you. It's as though you have sprouted wings while you are at Pippin Cottage. I know your mum doesn't like that I don't have many rules here, but we don't mind. We don't need rules during the summer; rules are for when you're at school.

I enjoyed making the new curtains for your bedroom here, and I love the little stars you put on the ceiling. What a clever idea they are. When you're not here and I miss you, I'll stand in the dark and look up at them and think of you back with Mum and Dad. I think it is a lovely room, and with the blackbirds nesting in the tree at the front, I will be able to hear them chatting as they flit about tending to their business.

I heard the owls again last night, and I know you like to hear them also. They have a soft call. It's very soothing, I think. It's a reminder to settle into bed and go to sleep. They do their work at night-time and we do ours during the day.

Little things have made this summer very special. We spent a lot of time in the garden and you have helped me plant the beans and the zinnias along the front path. You are quite the little gardener, or perhaps you just like being outside. I like watching you lying on a blanket under the apple tree, reading one of your books. It's a peaceful spot, I agree.

I enjoyed making us daisy crowns this summer and I will get the photo of us framed. We look so happy. They don't last long in the summer heat though, which is a shame.

We had fun exploring the old mill this summer and visiting the ducks. I saw a whole family crossing the bridge the other day after you had gone home. A mother and father duck and twelve little ducklings. Can you imagine having twelve babies to care for?

I've seen how much you've grown up this year. Seven is a big age, and you are very wise and love to sing and act out little plays.

You also love to look at the photo albums of when I was younger. It's lovely to see and share those memories with you again.

We still love the summer evenings together. I like to read a book or watch some television with you, listen to the radio or play cards at the kitchen table. You're very good at cards now, especially gin rummy, and you've beaten me more times than I will admit to your father.

I can hear the owls now as I write this little letter to you. I think they're saying they miss you. Where is Lily? they call. It feels like you're the only one in on the secret chat as you wait for them to call out from the woods.

The cottage misses you when you're gone.

I look forward to the next holiday, Lily, and I will continue writing these for as long as you keep coming to see me.

So, my love, here's to another summer. One day you might not remember these details, so when you do get these letters, perhaps they will tickle your memory once more and you will be reminded of the fun we had this summer.

With all my love,
Gran

Five

The little hatchback that Lily was driving grumbled in protest as she traversed the narrow lanes that led to Appleton Green. She was forced to rely on half-remembered childhood visits and the occasional weathered signpost, because the satellite navigation system in her car had long since stopped working. As the car climbed a hill, a view of rolling hills covered in lush greenery and sprinkled with grazing sheep that appeared like cotton balls spread in front of her.

She never tired of the view. She slowed the car down to be safe, as sheep where known to stray and wander on the roads on occasion, but she also wanted to drink in being back in Appleton Green.

Lily was always struck by how little had changed when she drove through the village. At the corner still stood The Crumpetty Tree, its faded sign groaning softly in the wind. She saw elderly Mr Sharma in his front garden, pruning his prize-winning roses with accuracy despite the bend in his fingers from arthritis.

As she came around into the centre of the village she saw Mrs Harris, the proprietor of the post office, crossing the road. Lily waved at her and she took a moment to see who was waving at her and then recognised Lily and returned the greeting. She had been in Appleton Green since Lily was young and was a great friend to Gran.

Lily noticed Mrs Douglas, who owned the little shop, walking her corgi, and Lily parked her car.

'Mrs Douglas? It's Lily, Lily Baxter,' she said. 'Dad told me you found Gran outside the cottage.'

Mrs Douglas had left Edinburgh thirty years ago and settled in Appleton Green with her new husband but had never quite left Scotland. Her heart was still there but her life was in Appleton Green. Today Mrs Douglas was wearing a lightweight kilt in a red tartan, red trainer and a red bowling shirt and a scarf tied around her head like Rosie the Riveter. It was an odd combination but at sixty, it worked, like an ageing punk or Vivienne Westwood.

'Oh hello, love,' said Mrs Douglas. 'How is she?'

'I'm about to go and see her,' Lily said. 'But I wanted to thank you for calling the ambulance.'

'Oh, love, it's fine. She was in a terrible state when I found her,' said the woman in her thick Scottish brogue.

The dog wagged its tail at Lily and she leaned down to pat it.

'Hello, Wallace,' she said to the dog. 'You're looking well. Last time I saw him he was a puppy.'

'He's fat is what he is. I have to walk him daily now, but it's good for me also,' said Mrs Douglas.

'Do you need anything from the shop?' the woman asked. 'I closed it for a bit but I can reopen it for you.'

Lily shook her head. 'No, I'll go and see her and see what Mum and Dad have left for her.'

Mrs Douglas shook her head in dismay. 'It's a terrible thing. Do you think she will be able to stay alone at the cottage? Sometimes I wonder if she can't get a little more help from the council. I have noticed the kitchen is a bit much for her to handle now. It does happen with age,' she said, not unkindly but instead out of concern.

Lily sighed. 'I think she needs a lot of help but I also think she would rather die than give up her independence. Mum said she's been very obstinate.'

Mrs Douglas gave her a sympathetic smile. 'It's hard with ageing parents and grandparents. I best be off but let me know if you need anything.'

'I will. Thank you again. So much.'

Lily got back into her car and continued her drive to Pippin Cottage. Despite its modest size, Appleton Green was a close-knit community where, for better or worse, everyone knew each other's business. She had no doubt that news of her return would be on the social telegraph line now. It was always exciting when new and familiar faces came to the village, and since Violet Baxter was the oldest resident, Lily's return would be worthy of the grapevine.

Lily manoeuvred her vehicle around a bend with great care, narrowly avoiding the front garden of the local vet, Stephen, which was overrun with flowers, the cosmos daisies spilling over onto the path.

As she turned a corner, she applied the brakes quickly, allowing a family of ducks to approach the River Dove from the opposite side of the road. The river, as transparent as glass, meandered gently through the village and crossed by the old packhorse bridge. She saw a few tourists who were pausing with their cameras around their necks. The ducks wandered across the road: a mother and father and she counted twelve ducklings.

Once they had safely passed, she headed off again and there was Pippin Cottage, finally visible in the distance.

Lily exhaled a breath that she hadn't been aware she'd been holding and she felt her body relax in what felt like the first time in a long time.

The cottage, much like its owner, has a certain offbeat charm. For most of her childhood, Lily had imagined she would one day live in Pippin Cottage and teach music and sing every morning in the little garden at the back. Ah the innocence of childhood, she thought as she parked her car on the road.

She and Gran had always said that the slate roof of the cottage was placed at a jaunty angle, as if it were a top hat that was worn with a hint of determination, like the Artful Dodger in *Oliver!* The blue door, a little faded now, was still a pop of colour against the grey stone. The door had always reminded Lily of her grandmother's blue eyes and now, seeing the door, she couldn't wait to see Gran again.

She hadn't seen her since Christmas when Gran came for lunch and then insisted that Peter drove her home again not long after. It had made Denise upset but Lily kind of understood. Gran had had Christmas for years in her own cottage and then, for the past few years, Peter and Denise had hosted, and it wasn't the same.

Lily sat in the car with the window down, listening to the assortment of sounds around her. She heard sheep in the distance, the gentle clucking of hens from someone's back garden, and the faint strains of Classic FM drifting from an open window. It was most likely one of Gran's neighbours,

Mrs Hughes, a retired music teacher who was the most devoted fan of classical music in the village.

Lily got out of the car, stretched and took a big breath as she did so. As the aroma of newly cut grass on the verge blended with the pleasant perfume of honeysuckle, a wave of peace washed over her. Perhaps she was romanticising it too much because she had spent nearly every summer holiday here as a child, but it was her favourite place. It was probably the place where she was most herself, and where she was completely present, not thinking about the future or the past – just being.

Lily took her overnight bag and the cat carrier and walked through the gate and up to the front door. She rang the bell.

The sound of the doorbell woke Violet from her nap in her comfortable armchair. She managed to get up to standing and then looked at the walker and sighed. She would have to use it, much to her chagrin, and she shuffled over to the door and opened it.

'Lily!' she cried.

Lily stood at the front door with a cat carrier and an overnight bag.

'Gran. Jeesh, you look like you did ten rounds down the pub,' Lily said shaking her head. 'I wonder how the other fella came out.'

'He didn't survive,' said Violet with a toss of her head. 'Come on then. Are you here because you've been sent by your parents to check on me? They only left a few hours ago.' Violet rolled her eyes at Lily.

'No, I'm here for selfish reasons only. I don't know what you and my parents are fighting about.'

Violet looked at her granddaughter closely, checking for telltale signs of her lying. When she pulled her earlobe and crinkled her nose, she was lying. Right now, Lily was still.

She looked down at the cat carrier.

'Is that yours?' she asked. Truth be told, she wasn't a huge fan of cats. They were arrogant creatures, always expecting the world to be delivered to them on a silver platter.

'Yes, you know I have a cat, I've told you about him, and I can't leave him at home alone,' Lily said looking down at the carrier. 'Mr Mistoffelees, meet Gran.'

'Silly name,' Violet said and sniffed. 'All cats should be called Puss.'

Lily laughed. 'Well he's not called Puss. He will like having a visit here, won't you?' she said to the carrier.

Violet opened the door wide for her granddaughter.

'All right, well you and Puss can come in as long as you're not trying to pack me off to an old person's home to die.'

Lily chuckled. 'No such luck, I'm here because I'm running away from home,' she said.

'Oh good for you,' Violet said and went to her armchair and sat down, trying to keep the pain off her face as she found a comfortable position.

Lily leaned forward. 'They told me you were in hospital and I thought I would come and see you, but now you're at home so I thought I would come and annoy you,' she said.

'You can annoy me anytime, darling girl, even if you do bring your cat. Now come and tell me everything.'

Soon Lily was settled on the sofa. Mr Mistoffelees was out of his carrier and in the bathroom with some kitty litter and dinner and water. Violet was in her armchair with a cup of tea made by Lily and a piece of shortbread made by Mrs Douglas.

Violet looked at her granddaughter for what felt like an eternity and then she frowned and set down her mug of tea.

'So what is it? What's happened? Why are you running away?' She could tell Lily had something on her mind, and a weight on her shoulders. She was pinched and her blue eyes were bloodshot and swollen, and her usually pale skin was blotchy and looked dry.

Lily put down her mug and sighed. 'God, I knew you would see straight through me.'

'Darling, Stevie Wonder could see it.' Violet snorted.

'Gran, you can't say that; it's not politically correct,' Lily admonished.

'Stevie would agree with me, if he were here. You don't even have to look at you, with your droopy energy. You're like a wet sock.'

Lily shook her head. 'God, you're more brutal than any theatre critic.'

Violet put her feet up on the ottoman and clasped her hands in her lap.

'Go on. Speak now or forever hold your peace.'

There was a silence for a moment and then Lily spoke.

'I can't sing anymore,' she said somewhat dramatically, Violet thought, or perhaps it was warranted. Time would tell.

'You don't want to sing or you can't sing?' Violet asked.

'I can't sing,' Lily almost cried. 'I went to the *Les Mis* audition. It was my third callback.'

'I know – your mother called to remind me,' Violet said.

'Of course she did,' muttered Lily. 'Anyway, I was fine in the morning. I did the warm-up and everything, and then I got onto the stage and my voice was gone. It just disappeared. I tried and tried to sing but nothing came out. It was like my voice had frozen.'

'And this was only yesterday?' Gran asked.

Lily nodded, tears welling up. 'And now, when I try and sing, my voice sounds like the air being let out of a balloon.'

Violet narrowed her eyes at her. 'Have you tried to sing today?'

'Yes, same as yesterday. Squeaky. I think I'll have to see a throat doctor or something. I don't understand it.' Lily sighed and put her head back and closed her eyes.

Violet looked at her granddaughter. 'Perhaps it's more of a mental voice issue in your mind rather than in your throat.'

Lily opened her eyes and adjusted an already perfectly placed cushion next to her on the sofa.

'You think it's psychological?'

'Well you look fine, and you were able to sing in the morning, so it can't be a throat infection.'

Lily was silent, her beautiful face pinched and pale.

'And it was right as you were standing on stage, for the third callback?'

Violet observed Lily across the edge of her teacup, her face a portrait of anxiety. Poor lamb, she seemed as though the weight of the earth had dropped on her shoulders.

'So you've run away because your voice has run away?' Violet joked, trying to lighten the situation. Lily's smile was subdued but it was there.

'I can't laugh about it,' Lily sighed. 'What would happen if it never came back? What if I have lost it permanently?'

Violet sighed. 'Voices do not simply vanish without a by-your-leave. They always come back when they are good and ready, just as cats do. There will be something bigger going on. I didn't get to ninety-seven without knowing a thing or two about life, and this is one of those things I know about.'

But Lily wasn't listening. 'But supposing it doesn't? What if I've wrecked everything?'

Violet shook her head. 'Lily, darling, let me tell you something. I want you to listen properly, do you hear me?'

Lily looked up at the tone of her grandmother's voice.

'Yes, I'm listening,' she said.

Violet nodded. 'Good. When I was your age, I also lost my voice.'

'Really? Or are you just saying this for some sort of life lesson moment that I'm supposed to learn from?'

'Well you should learn from me all the time, as I am a wise old crone, but yes I did, though it was never about my voice physically; it was because I wasn't telling the truth about what I wanted in life.'

Lily frowned. 'What do you mean?'

'I mean, you're not telling the truth about something. You're in denial about something, and your body is trying to tell you.'

'That's a bit woo-woo, isn't it?'

'I don't know what woo-woo is, but if you mean mental over physical, then yes, I suppose it is.'

'You've never told me this story before.' Lily looked at her grandmother with suspicion.

'There are many things I haven't told you, young lady – they are on a strictly need-to-know basis – but this one you need to know and now I am telling you.'

Lily leaned forward. 'What were you not saying that caused you to lose your voice?'

Violet sighed. It was always painful to think of old memories of people passed, but now she was ninety-seven there really weren't many memories that didn't have the dead in them. That's why she liked thinking about Lily more than anyone else.

'Before your granddad, I was engaged to another man – Raymond. He came from a nice family, was well-off, and everyone felt we were the ideal fit.'

Lily's eyebrows flew up with surprise. 'You have never told me this. God, talk about keeping secrets for ninety-seven years! So what happened?'

'Well Martin, your grandfather, he was my friend. He'd been my friend for years, always part of the group that did the theatre shows. He did the sets and the lighting. He was always rather reliable, but you know, he wasn't rich or flashy. Raymond had a wealthy family in Derby and we met there, when I went to learn typing.'

She paused, thinking. 'Raymond was respectable and safe. The sort of man my parents approved of. But when I came back to Appleton Green, to be in *The Boyfriend*, and I was cast as Polly and my voice, it just went. It was so odd and upsetting, so I do understand how you feel.'

'So what happened?' Lily urged.

'I was crying outside rehearsal one day, because I knew they would have to recast me, and then I couldn't do the show and the thing I was saddest about wasn't not performing, it was that I wouldn't see Martin. And Martin came out to check on me, and I told him. I was so clear in what I wanted and then I went back in, and I sang.'

'But what did Grandad say when you told him?'

Violet gave a little smile. 'He said it was about time I came to my senses and then he kissed me and that's when I knew I would be staying in Appleton Green. And here I am and here you are.'

Violet said, 'I lost my voice because my body was reminding me that I was on the wrong road; it was telling me what my heart already knew.'

Lily's eyes widened. 'Do you think that's me?'

'I don't know, but I do think you need to consider what you're not facing right now. It took me some time to pay attention, mind you. When I did, though, when I broke things off with Raymond and told Martin how I felt, it was as if I could breathe once again. My voice returned more powerfully than before.'

Lily sighed and took her grandmother's hand. 'I don't know that it's that simple. I don't think I'm not facing anything in my life. Truly.'

Violet gave Lily's a hand squeeze. 'My darling, the lesson is that your voice serves purposes beyond singing. It's for honouring your heart and for expressing yourself. Sometimes our bodies discover a means to alert us when we are not living up to ourselves. Pay attention to it.'

Lily frowned. 'But how did you come to know that was the right choice? Were you terrified Grandad would say no?'

'No, because whatever happened, I was being truthful. I didn't want to marry Raymond and I knew I would disappoint my parents and choose a life less safe, but do you know what was more terrifying?'

Lily shook her head and stared at Violet, her eyes wide, as though she were a child again.

'The idea of leading a life different from who I was meant to be.'

She stopped; her voice grew softer.

'I was always striving to be someone I believed I ought to be with Raymond. I could just be me with Martin. And that meant I was safe and honest, and I have lived a life I have loved, albeit not long enough with Martin.'

She thought about her beloved Martin and his gentle humour and endless support for her. He was a house painter and while it wasn't glamourous work, it was honest and he gave Violet this wonderful little cottage and a son she loved and a granddaughter she adored. It was more than enough.

'So do you think my voice will mend?' Lily asked.

Violet paused, considering her words. 'I don't know, Lil, but it seems very odd that it happened right at that moment. Maybe you need to think about it. What was stopping you from singing? I don't know what's going on for you right now, only you do, but I think this is bigger than an audition. And I think you do too. Perhaps have a little break here and work out what it is that's worrying you.'

Violet watched tears filling Lily's eyes.

Lily nodded. 'Thanks, Gran,' she said and Violet could see the relief in her only grandchild's expression.

'Righto then, I saw that you brought an overnight bag.'

Lily made a face. 'I actually have two suitcases,' she said, giving Violet a sheepish look.

'Moving in are we?' She snorted.

'Like, for a month?' Lily looked hopefully at her. 'I mean I can be your housemaid, cook, cleaner, bottle washer – anything you need – but I just need a break.'

'What about your jobs and your flat?' Gran asked.

'I have already let the flat out to a couple who are from America and doing a play in London. They move in on Friday. And well my jobs, if you can call them that, let's just say I won't miss much. I haven't really been getting many shifts. I need to look for a new job to be honest but I need to think what I can do. I don't want to serve overpriced steak and fries to drunk businessmen or call people to ask them to join a wine club when they can barely afford their heating bill.'

Violet shook her head in affirmation. 'Both of them are terrible jobs, I agree. No loss there.'

'I know.' The two women sat in silence for a moment.

Then Violet spoke. 'Well I couldn't think of anything better and between my fall and your voice, we might just be the right sort of medicine for each other.'

'I can help with things around here and just potter, you know,' Lily said.

'I don't need convincing.' Violet laughed. 'I have some silly nurse from the hospital coming tomorrow to check on me, which will be a waste of time. She will fuss about probably – you can get rid of her for me.'

'No, I won't do that. You need to be assessed, but they will feel more comfortable with me here for a bit, I think.'

Violet knew Lily was right, and she was secretly glad she was at Pippin Cottage. No one ever really understood how hard it was, getting old. It was one of those things you only discovered when you arrived at the destination. Lately

Violet had been wondering if living this long was worth it. She had no purpose anymore, getting up was a chore and each day was becoming shorter from the time she arose to the time she went to bed. She could feel the clock running slower with every day.

Six

It had been over fifteen years since Lily had last slept in this bed and yet everything felt as familiar as though she had only been away for a few weeks. She wasn't sure why she had stopped coming to stay with Gran. Life had just become busier and then there were friends, and boys and musicals and school, and slowly she had drifted away from Pippin Cottage but never from Gran. They had always had a connection, she filled Violet's heart and the empty space in her life. All the love she'd had for Martin was given to Lily.

When she looked back at her childhood, Lily was sure her mother Denise was upset by how close Lily was to Gran, but Gran understood her in a way Denise didn't and there was never any pressure from Gran. She could do as she pleased, when she pleased, and that's why summer was the best time. She tried to think of the last time she had stayed for the summer. She must have been fifteen, she thought, probably stroppy and cross because she had to be there when she would have rather been with her friends.

Now she lay in the single bed, up in the top left bedroom, listening for the owls. They would come eventually, calling out in the night about where they were and where the good mice were to be found. Mr Mistoffelees was settled comfortably at the foot of the bed, the warmth of his body heating her feet. He seemed to be enjoying his first country sojourn.

The calls of the owls would usually be heard as Lily's eyes were closing, the moment between awake and asleep where she wasn't sure if she was dreaming or hearing their sounds.

With clean sheets on the bed, Lily now lay trying to see if she could sing again. Softly of course, but the strangled squeak was still there.

Her throat felt fine, it didn't hurt to swallow or speak, so maybe it was in her mind, as Gran had suggested, but she would go and see a doctor anyway, just to be sure.

Her body ached from cleaning the flat the night before, and from the drive to Appleton Green. She had taken a shower in Gran's tiny bathroom, which could do with a deep clean, she thought, but wouldn't say that to Gran. She had always kept an immaculate home, but being ninety-seven and not as nimble anymore would make it hard for anyone to clean the shower recess. Mrs Douglas was right about the kitchen also. It wasn't dirty but it wasn't as clean as Lily remembered it, but she would have to tread carefully with that one. Gran was defiant, even in the face of the truth, and she didn't want to make her feel that she was useless.

A call on her phone startled her and she jumped.

'You're there?' Her mother didn't bother with a greeting.

'Yes, I've been here for hours. I'm in bed now, about to go to sleep,' she said.

'It's only nine.' Denise gave a little laugh.

'Gran went an hour ago; this is late,' Lily half whispered. 'She already told me she'd stayed up half an hour past her bedtime.

'What did you have for dinner?'

'I made us boiled eggs and toast soldiers.'

'How is she?'

Lily thought for a moment. 'Feisty, independent, cross with you and Dad for making a fuss, frail, tired.'

'Yes, I thought as much. You need to try and convince her to go into a nursing home.'

'Not bloody likely, Mum. She would never. I saw Mrs Douglas in the village and she said she thinks Gran has been struggling for a while, but there is no way she'll leave here.'

'She might not have a choice,' Denise said. Lily knew she was right but she wouldn't be the one to broach that with her right now.

'I'm going to stay here for a while and see how she is, just be her little lady's maid for a month or so,' Lily said casually, as though it wasn't a big deal when in fact it was a very big one.

'What about *Les Mis*?' asked Denise.

'I didn't get it,' Lily lied. 'Which was just as well. I need to be here.'

'That's a shame, darling,' said Denise, sounding disappointed. 'There's always the next audition I suppose. What about the flat?'

'Rented it out already. Nigel's not back for ages, but he already paid his rent, so I have the rent covered plus a bit extra for living expenses. Mr Mistoffelees is here with me.'

Denise paused for a moment. 'Seems you have it all sorted. But you don't want to be away from London for too long. You might miss a big opportunity.'

No one wanted West End fame for Lily more than Denise. She believed in Lily's talent to the point that it was stifling and, more and more, Lily wasn't telling her mother about the auditions she went to and didn't get.

Lily shifted in the bed, her free hand tightly clutching the duvet. Her mother's expectations felt smothering in the small room.

'Yeah, next audition,' she said, trying to feign enthusiasm.

'I saw there were auditions for *In the Heights* on the Backstage website; perhaps you could audition for that?'

'Mum, I'm not Latina.'

'That doesn't matter, does it?' Denise hadn't grasped the concept of cultural casting yet.

'Yes it matters. If you read the ad, they have asked for Latin or similar. I'm whiter than white bread.'

'Well, you won't find many in London,' Denise sniffed.

'Pretty sure there are some Spanish and Portuguese actors,' Lily sighed as she spoke.

'Don't sigh at me,' Denise snapped. 'I'm aware that—'

Lily cut in, 'Mum,' her voice strained. 'Could we not discuss this right now? I want to concentrate on Gran; and I am exhausted.'

Down the phone line, Denise was silent. Lily could practically hear her mother's disappointment crackling over the phone.

'Of course, you concentrate on looking out for Gran. Focus on her and if I see any good auditions I'll let you know. You might want to think about getting a new agent soon. Paul doesn't seem to be doing much for you.'

She squeezed her eyes closed. 'It's not like it's that easy, Mum,' she said and then regretted it. It was a constant battle to try and ger her mother to understand the machinations of the entertainment industry, and Denise's deepest faith in her daughter and pride in her talent meant she assumed Lily would be the lead in every role on the West End forever and ever.

'Anyway, thanks, Mum,' she said very differently. 'I'll let you know about Gran and how's she going. Love to Dad.' And before Denise could say anything else, she ended the call.

Lily gazed at the ceiling after hanging up, tears pricking at her eyes. The familiar glow-in-the-dark stars she had set up there when she was seven, now faded but occasionally capturing a little glow, appeared to mock her. She had fantasised once about being a star. She couldn't even tell her own mother the truth about what had happened.

Outside, an owl hooted with a clear, forceful night call. Lily wished for its assurance and confidence, its capacity to instantly become heard in the night, to go after what it wanted; but Lily didn't know what she wanted for her future, and without her voice, she didn't know what that future looked like.

She turned over and sunk her face into the pillow. Perhaps tomorrow she would find her voice. But Lily had the feeling there was something bigger she needed to admit to herself and she was too terrified to acknowledge the existence of the unspoken truth deep in the pit of her stomach.

Seven

The next morning, Lily was up before Violet. Mr Mistoffelees was outside exploring the small garden, and as Violet came carefully downstairs, Lily met her at the bottom of the stairs with her walker. The curtains were opened and Lily had straightened up the little living space, turned on the heater, and had opened a window to let a little fresh air in. As Lily pushed the walker towards her, the light hit the hard set of her grandmother's jaw as it poured through the window.

Violet huffed, her chin up fiercely, saying, 'I don't need that contraption.'

'That's not what the physiotherapist says in the report that Dad left from the hospital,' she said firmly tapping the papers on the kitchen table.

'I have managed perfectly well for ninety-seven years without it,' Violet said, 'I have my stick.'

'You used the frame yesterday,' Lily said.

'Yesterday I was being nice; today I'm not feeling so nice.' Violet pushed past Lily, using her stick as a baton.

'Gran, please,' Lily said, trying to control the frustration in her voice. Gran could be the most frustrating woman in the world at times.

'Oh, pish posh. It isn't anything I need.' Violet waved a hand contemptuously, then winced as the movement obviously hurt her. 'Those doctors don't know anything.'

Biting her lip, caught between annoyance and sympathy, Lily leaned over and whispered in Violet's ear, 'They know enough to keep you alive and kicking for nearly a century.'

Violet narrowed her old eyes at Lily.

'Make yourself useful and get a brew on,' Violet said, but the fondness for Lily came through in her tone and Lily gave a little smile at her feistiness.

'Already done,' said Lily, gesturing to the little table where Gran liked to take breakfast. She had made them both tea and there was toast in the toaster.

They ate their breakfast with gentle conversation, Lily aware she didn't want to upset Gran any more. She seemed frailer this morning. Perhaps the excitement of coming home from the hospital and then Lily coming had given her a little buck-up, but the sore bones and bruises this morning would be a reminder that all wasn't as it used to be.

Lily was about to clean up when there was a knock at the door.

'That'll be the nurse,' she said as she stood up. 'Tell her to be off and see someone who needs help, I don't need anything now I have you.'

Lily walked to the door. 'I can help you, Gran, but I can't assess your injuries so you need to do this. Just pop your big-girl knickers on and get it over with.'

'You keep my knickers out of it,' said Gran with a little laugh.

Lily opened the door and there stood a man, who was tall, with blue eyes and tousled blonde hair, dressed in blue pants and white shirt with a logo from the hospital on the pocket, and a name tag that said his name was *Nick Stafford, Registered Nurse.*

Holy bells, Gran's nurse was a dead ringer for a young Brad Pitt.

'Hello, I'm Nick Stafford,' he said. His voice had a lovely tone to it. 'I'm here to see Violet Baxter. It says she's ninety-seven but you look far too young to be her, unless you have an excellent skincare regime.'

Lily's breath caught in her throat. *Good Lord*, she thought, *Gran's nurse looks like he's just stepped off the cover of a romance novel*, and she blinked several times, realising she'd been staring.

'Hi, yes, um, I'm Lily, Lily Baxter. I'm um, Violet's granddaughter,' she managed, inwardly cringing at her stammering. *Get a grip, Lily*, she told herself. *He's just a nurse, not actually Brad Pitt.*

But as Nick stepped into the cottage, Lily couldn't help but notice how he filled the small space with his presence. He smelled faintly of soap and something woodsy, like pine needles after rain. It was oddly comforting and also disconcerting. No nurse should be that good-looking, she thought, or smell that good.

'I wasn't expecting you,' Lily said, suddenly aware of her ratty old jumper and leggings and her feet covered in odd socks. Of course the one day she looked like a complete mess, Nurse McDreamy shows up.

Nick smiled, and Lily felt her heart do a little flip. Oh no, she thought. That smile should come with a warning label like they have on medicine bottles. Do not operate heavy machinery after being smiled at by Nurse Stafford.

'They didn't tell you a nurse was coming?' he asked, his eyebrow quirking up in a way that was far too charming for Lily's peace of mind.

'No, they did,' Lily backpedalled, feeling heat rise to her cheeks. 'I just... I wasn't expecting...' *You*, she finished silently. *I wasn't expecting you to look like the perfect fantasy of a male nurse and to be so stupidly handsome.*

She turned to see Gran standing up by her chair, leaning on her frame, a knowing glint in her eye. 'Hello Nurse, how lovely to see you,' Gran said, sweet as pie. 'But there's no need for you to come. Everything is fine; Lily is here to look after me.'

Nick looked at Lily who raised her eyebrows and then gave a small eye-roll.

As Nick moved towards Gran, Lily found her eyes following him. The way he moved was graceful, confident but not cocky.

Lily shook her head slightly. She felt as though she was in some sort of weird fantasy dream. This was ridiculous. She was here to look after Gran, not ogle the nurse. But as Nick turned to ask her a question about Gran's medication, his eyes meeting hers, Lily felt a little jolt of... something. Interest? Attraction?

Oh damn, she thought. *This could complicate things.*

Taking her lead, he walked towards Gran, carrying a medical bag with him over his shoulder.

'Isn't this a lovely cottage,' he said. 'Such a cosy home – it's perfect.'

He put his bag on the ground near Violet's chair, with her reading glasses and newspaper on the little table next to it.

'It is a lovely home and would be better if you weren't inside it,' she said with a sly smile.

'Gran!' Lily was shocked at Gran's words. She was blunt but this was rude.

'I simply meant he can go and see other more needy patients than me,' she said and shuffled backwards and then sat down in her chair.

'Unfortunately I can't leave without seeing you, Mrs Baxter. Those are the rules and you wouldn't like me to break the rules and then get into trouble, would you?' Violet turned her nose up at him and Lily had to admire his approach. Gran wouldn't want anyone to get into trouble because of her.

'I don't mind breaking the odd rule, but I don't want you to be in any strife.'

'Can I get you a cup of tea?' Lily asked Nick, who was opening the medical kit bag. 'I was about to make a new pot.'

'That would be lovely, thanks,' he said as he put some ointments and medical supplies on the little table next to her.

'You're not staying that long are you?' It was Violet's turn to roll her eyes.

Lily gave her grandmother a warning look. 'Gran, let him do his job. As I said, I was making another pot anyway.'

Lily went into the kitchen as she heard Nick buttering up Violet, chatting about nothing and everything as he took her blood pressure.

She put the kettle on and then looked outside and saw some of Gran's washing on the little clothes line by the potting shed. They looked to have been out there for a few days, and probably needed to be rewashed since it had rained when Gran had been in hospital.

'Just grabbing the washing,' she said to them but they didn't seem to notice her as she stepped outside and looked around the back garden. There was a wall surrounding the space, with a small potting shed, some overgrown garden beds, long abandoned and abundant with weeds. She could do a tidy-up here while she was at the cottage. She went to the line and unpegged the clothes. She held a wooden peg in her hand, the spring rusting, and she pegged it back on the line. Gran was so old-fashioned, which was why she loved being at the cottage. The simple rituals that had marked her time at the cottage were her favourite memories as a child. The toast in the toast rack. The brown teapot and a drawer filled with tea cosies that Lily would always choose a new one from every day. All of them knitted or sewn by Gran.

The walks they used to take along the stream, picking up tiny wild violets that Lily would put in a little glass bottle by her bed, lulled to sleep with their scent.

Violet had told her the mythology of violets that came from Zeus, who was married to Hera. He turned his mistress into a heifer to hide her from Hera, and when the mistress-heifer complained she was hungry, he made a field of violets for her to eat and sent a bunch to Hera as an apology. Supposedly the flowers soothed the jealous Hera and so the Greeks began using them to calm anger and induce sleep.

Lily had always liked that story, and would lie in bed as a child and imagine being turned into a cow. Maybe if she was a cow now, she could moo her way into employment, she thought as she held the washing in her arms. She tried to sing and nothing came out again.

Lily came inside and put the washing back in the small machine under the kitchen bench and then filled the pot. Gran was having the dressing on her nose changed by Nick, who was wearing gloves and being very gentle it seemed.

She watched him work, mesmerised by the care he was talking. She watched as he gently persuaded Gran to let him do his job, his manner both professional and kind.

How long had it been since a man had been as gentle with her? Maybe she needed to fall over and graze her face for some attention. It was impossible to date when you worked in musical theatre, she always said. Late nights, and it was hard to meet people at work, since most of the male cast seemed to only want to date each other and it was sort of a weird culture of people who would burst into song at any time. Musical theatre people had a song for everything that happened in life and viewed karaoke night as an audition.

Even Lily found herself exhausting to be around at times.

'How's the tea going?' Gran's question burst her thoughts and she felt a blush rise in her cheeks.

Gran stared at her a little longer than usual and Lily knew she had been caught staring at Nick, and she turned quickly and made a pot and took out a mug for Nick.

'While you're here, Nick, can you look at Lily's throat? She said it's been a bit tricky and she's a singer. Can you see if there is anything happening in her tonsils or the like?' Gran said with that smile that Lily knew only too well.

'Of course,' said Nick with a smile on his handsome face that made her feel flustered. 'Come and sit down.' He gestured to the chair near Gran and Lily glared at Gran, who gave her a look that she wouldn't dare defy. She wished she could film this and show Nigel, because they would be screaming with laughter at the fantasies he was bringing up.

'I'm sure it's nothing. I just seemed to lose my voice when I tried to sing,' she said, knowing she was blushing.

'Oh you're a singer?' asked Nick. He changed his gloves and then took out a tongue depressor from his bag.

'She's been on the West End. She's a beautiful lyrical soprano,' said Gran proudly.

'Wow, I'm impressed. Open wide,' he said and Lily closed her eyes so she didn't have to look at him, feeling vulnerable and silly all at once, and opened her mouth. This was almost too much, she thought.

'Tongue out,' he said and she felt the depressor on her tongue as he looked down her throat.

'No tonsils, so it can't be that,' he said and she opened her eyes. 'The West End, hey?' he asked. 'What shows?'

'Just chorus, in *South Pacific* and *Legally Blonde*,' she said, feeling embarrassed and yet she didn't know why.

He put his hands on her neck and felt gently around her throat. It had been so long since someone touched her that she felt herself relax at the feeling, even though he had gloves on and was a nurse. She imagined laughing about this with Nigel when she returned to London.

'Just *Legally Blonde* and *South Pacific* on the West End.' He laughed. 'That's not a *just* situation; you should be singing it from the rooftops.'

'I would but my voice isn't working,' she quipped.

'I love musical theatre,' he said as his hands moved gently around her throat. 'Always have.'

Maybe she should introduce him to Nigel, she thought. He would love to play nurse and patient in person.

'Any pain?' Nick asked.

'No.' She shook her head.

'I have a piano here. You can try and sing now,' said Gran, nodding her head in the direction of the piano against the wall.

Lily couldn't remember the last time she had played the old thing. It would be well out of tune now, she thought.

'No, Gran, I'm not going to try and sing. And the piano will sound like an old pianola after all these years.'

'You'd be surprised,' sniffed Gran.

'Any coughing?'

'Nope.'

'You could go to the doctor and get a referral to see a throat specialist, but I can't see or feel anything. I can get you a few names if you like?'

Lily shook her head. 'No it's okay, I think it's more a weird little confidence issue,' she said.

'Singing in front of people can be hard,' he said taking off his gloves. 'Maybe you need to sing with no pressure.'

'What do you mean?' she asked.

'We're doing a production of *My Fair Lady* in the village this year. You should audition,' he said. 'Jasper, our director, has some money from the council and they're going all out – sets, costumes from the National, it's going to be amazing. I'm auditioning for Freddy.'

'Jasper Winterbottom,' Gran said. 'How is he? I heard he moved to London. He's back now? You remember him, Lily?'

She nodded and looked at Nick. 'I used to help Jasper and Sheila Trotter in the shows when Gran was still in them. Jasper was always so lovely to me; Sheila was hard work though.' She laughed.

'She still is,' Nick said with a raised eyebrow.

'I can't believe she's still in the society. I thought she would have retired years ago. She's almost eighty,' Gran said.

'She's only sixty,' Nick said with a laugh. 'And says she would rather die with her feet on the stage.'

Gran rolled her eyes. 'Always so dramatic.'

Nick gracefully ignored her jabs at Sheila and went on speaking. 'They have decided to expand and bring in four villages' societies under one, and you have the biggest village hall, in the smallest village,' he said. He took off his gloves and turned to Lily. He put the gloves and tongue depressor into a little rubbish bag and sealed it.

'I can take that,' she said to him and he handed her the items.

'Thank you.' He gave her one of those smiles that made her knees a little weak and she wondered if it was time she started dating again in London. She'd had a dry spell of late. She couldn't really use the excuse of her work in musical theatre now. It was mostly because she couldn't be bothered leaving the flat unless it was for work or an audition. Mostly she lay around on the sofa, making tea and watching reality TV shows, but it was also hard to meet people who weren't in theatre. The hours, the touring, the rehearsals. She had just given up on meeting someone.

Nigel had told her she was depressed before he left for the tour. She had told him she was just tired, but now she wondered. If her medicine was someone like Nurse Nick Stafford, she would be up and about in no time.

'You should audition, Lil. It will be good for you to practise in front of people again,' Gran said. 'It's probably all in your mind. You've spooked yourself.'

She glared at her grandmother as she stood up and made them tea.

'I'll spook you in a minute,' she hissed at Gran who looked at Nick.

'See what she says to me.' She shook her head. 'It's elder abuse.'

'I think it's granddaughter coercion and manipulation,' she joked and she looked to Nick. 'Thank you for the offer though.'

'You should audition,' he said. 'We don't have an Eliza, and if we don't get one then Sheila will take it and she's sixty and definitely not a soprano. She's more a baritone to be honest.'

Lily burst out laughing. 'She will probably knife the lead to get the role on opening night, all very noir.'

She saw Gran turn her nose up at her words as Nick kept speaking.

'Yes, she's very invested, shall we say. My ex-girlfriend, who is also her niece, and I met on the set of *Chicago*. I played Billy Flynn; Sheila played Matron, although she was insistent she could play Roxie Hart.'

Lily nodded, noting the mention of the ex-girlfriend. *That's a shame for Nigel*, she thought but she felt herself smiling a little brighter.

Nick picked up the mug of tea. 'Think about auditioning. Jasper would love to see you, I'm sure, and if it entices you, like I said, I'm hoping to play Freddy.' He laughed but somewhat shyly, and that pleased her a little. He was somewhat unaware of his looks and that, after being around people in the theatre, was a lovely change of pace. She swallowed, but the lump in her throat was gone for a moment.

'I'm only here for a month,' she said quickly.

She felt Gran's eyes on her.

'Why doesn't your ex, I mean Sheila's niece, audition for the role of Eliza?' she asked casually.

'She's actually in London, trying to make it on the West End,' he said somewhat sheepishly.

'Oh really? I wonder if I know her. Has she had any luck?'

'I don't know, we don't stay in touch,' he said, his face giving away nothing. 'I'm sure Sheila will tell me everything.'

'Auditioning is a hard slog,' she said. 'Takes a while to get going.' She thought how long it had been for her so far, with only a few breaks and no leading role on the West End.

'Anyway, we have auditions tomorrow night, if you're keen,' said Nick. 'No pressure though. Why don't I pop by when I'm coming through? I can check on Violet and see if you want to come by. At worst it's a chance to try your voice out.'

Lily thought for a moment and then looked at his face and smiled. 'Why not?' she said. 'Might be a good test.' And a chance to spend a little time with him, she told herself.

'Oh wonderful news,' said Gran clapping her frail hands. 'Now give Nick a piece of Mrs Douglas's shortbread to celebrate.'

Eight

Lily woke and wondered if she had made a terrible mistake agreeing to go to the audition. That was the problem with her and handsome men: she seemed to lose her willpower to make smart decisions.

She walked downstairs and set up breakfast for Gran, then she let the cat outside and left the back door open. It was a beautiful morning and Lily remembered how much she loved hearing nothing.

The noise pollution in London was so distracting, you couldn't get away from it. Even in the flat with Nigel, she could hear the cars and people moving about the apartment building, or music and horns and lorries.

Here she couldn't hear anything other than the garden. The tranquillity of Appleton Green encircled Lily like a cosy blanket, providing her with a sense of comfort as she leaned against the doorframe in her nightgown and cardigan. Here, in the middle of the countryside, a different kind of symphony was being played.

Lily had always had excellent hearing; she was also pitch-perfect. It was a skill not many have and she could hear all the beauty around her. The sound of the leaves gently rustling in the old apple tree was the first thing that drew her attention. The sound was so subtle that it was almost like a whisper, as if the tree was gossiping with the wind about something. Probably her return, she thought with a smile. The pattern was calming, rising and sinking with each breeze that blew through the garden.

Underneath this, Lily was able to pick up on the sound of the blackbirds singing. It sounded like an operetta singer, in contrast to the monotonous cooing of London's pigeons. She closed her eyes, and heard the chirpy trill of a robin, and the rapid-fire chatter of sparrows.

There were some cows making themselves known in the farm not too far away, a soft, low sound that appeared to roll across the fields, like a pleasant sort of baritone.

And the sound of the ever-present undercurrent of buzzing insects served as the garden's rhythm section. The hum of bees could be heard as they flitted from flower to flower, their hard labour producing a background noise that was not quite audible, but if Lily concentrated she could hear them. Occasionally, a dragonfly would whirr past, a lovely snare drum of a sound from its wings. Oh it was so good to be back.

'Morning.' Lily heard and saw Gran coming down the stairs, one at a time, using her stick. Lily rushed over and set the frame up for her to use once she came to the bottom.'

Violet tapped the frame with her stick. 'This is silly, I tell you.'

'This will keep you at home longer,' said Lily firmly.

Gran turned her nose up at both the frame and Lily and walked to the kitchen table.

'Close the door – it's freezing,' she complained.

'Sorry, I was listening to the garden,' Lily said. Gran nodded. It was something they had always done when she was small. 'A few dragonflies out this morning,' she said.

'Might have been damselflies,' said Gran.

'Hmm not sure,' she admitted.

'Damselflies are smaller; they symbolise protection. The dragonflies are bigger; they carry change with them,' she said to Lily.

Lily thought for a moment. 'Dragonflies, definitely.'

'Speaking of change,' said Gran as Lily poured hot water into the teapot, 'what will you do about the audition? Which song will you sing? I still have all the old sheet music in the piano stool for you to use.'

Lily shook her head. 'I don't think I should,' she said. 'I don't want to waste their time if I'm not staying.'

Gran sniffed at her. 'But you think Nick is handsome enough – perhaps that's enough of a reason to go.'

Lily pulled on her earlobe for a moment. 'Is he? I didn't really notice.'

'Liar, liar, pants on fire. Your tongue was as long as a telephone wire!' Gran sang.

'You're a ninety-seven-year-old child,' she said.

'You have two tells when you lie, and you just showed one of them,' Gran said.

'What are they?' Lily frowned, trying to think what she had done.

'I will take that to my grave,' said Gran. 'Now hurry up and get me some toast and tell me what song you're singing and what you're wearing. I want Sheila Trotter to be impressed by you.'

Lily sighed. She wasn't going to win against Gran today.

*

That evening Lily paced in her bedroom, trying to warm up her voice, but nothing was coming out, just a weird noise escaping from her throat that sounded like the last of the bathwater draining away.

She closed her eyes and saw a flashback of hiding in the costumes in London after the failed audition, and her eyes stung with unshed tears. What was wrong with her? The shrill sound of the doorbell made her jump.

'Nick's here,' she heard Gran call from downstairs as the doorbell rang.

This is a stupid idea, she thought as she went down to answer the door.

She was dressed in a plum-coloured dress with a scoop neck that showed off her creamy skin and her hair was down, a cascade of glossy brunette curls. She had put on a little makeup and simple silver earrings.

'Hi,' she said as she opened the door to Nick. He was in jeans and a navy jumper and looked even more handsome out of his nursing clothes. His hair was messy and he gave her a wide smile.

'All ready?' he asked.

'Come in,' she said and stepped away from the door for him to enter the cottage.

'Hello, Mrs Baxter, how are you feeling?' he said.

She waved her stick at him. 'Now don't you be calling me Mrs Baxter; I'm Violet to you.'

Nick laughed. 'Well I won't argue since you're using a weapon. I'm coming back on Friday to check your dressing on your nose and leg.'

'I look forward to it,' she said with a twinkle in her eye.

'And I hope you're using the walking frame, not the stick?' he said with a raised eyebrow at her.'

'Of course,' said Violet with sweet smile.

Nick looked at Lily who put her hands up. 'I am saying nothing, because she might whack me with the stick in her sleep.'

Nick turned to Violet.

'If you use the frame, it will be easier to steady yourself and then you won't fall and break a hip and end up in a nursing home eating stewed apples three times a day.'

Lily saw her grandmother's eyes flash and her jaw set.

'I hate stewed apple,' she said as though that was the deciding reason.

'No, it's not my favourite either,' said Nick and he went the few short steps to the frame, then carried it back and put it to the side of her chair.

'Best to be safe, Violet,' he said and she gave an almost imperceptible nod.

'You ready to go?' He turned to Lily.

She sighed. 'Listen, my voice is still playing up. I don't think I can do it.'

Nick looked at her and frowned.

'Well you're all dressed up, and at worst you can try again in a different space, and nothing lost. At least come and see the other auditionees. It will be fun.'

'This isn't the West End, Lil. Have a nice night and listen to some singers and see how you feel,' Gran said.

She thought about the night ahead with Gran. Listening to the radio or watching some television and then heading to bed early, waiting for the owls to call and wondering where her voice was. At least it would be a change of scene in which to feel wretched about her future.

'I'll be back to help you to bed,' she said.

'No, please, I can do that myself. I'll use the frame down here. I'll be fine,' Violet said sternly.

'I'll bring you one for you to use upstairs on Friday,' Nick said. 'We have lots of them at work.'

'Goody, I can't wait,' Gran said dryly and Lily shook her head.

'Night, Gran.' She kissed her grandmother on the cheek.

'Goodnight, have a lovely time,' Gran said and then she and Nick were out the door and into the cool night air.

They walked out of the cottage and through the gate and to Nick's work car. Nick opened the door of the car for her, as she read what was written on the side.

'Derby Homecare,' she said. 'A company car no less. All the bells and whistles.'

Nick laughed as he closed the door and came around and got into the driver's seat.

'If you ever need a bandage or some gauze, I'm your man,' he said and he started the car and then drove up the road and into the heart of the village.

They passed the nearby cottages, the lights on inside, looking cosy and warm.

'I do love it here,' Lily said. 'This village makes me feel calm.'

'It's lovely, probably the best village in the area,' Nick said. 'Have you thought about living here? Be nice for your gran to have you around.'

Lily gave a little laugh. 'I don't think I could have a career and live here – bit hard to commute after the shows.'

They drove past the shop, run by Mrs Douglas, from which Gran had her small selection of groceries delivered every week, and the post office, run by Jean Harris, which was only open Mondays, Wednesdays and Fridays. The Crumpetty Tree pub was open but it looked close to empty as they passed it by. Everything was on half time in Appleton Green, she thought as they drove.

As a child she had dreamed of living in the cottage when she was an adult. There was a safety and security there that was unlike anything she had at home. Not that her childhood was terrible; it was simply lonely, even though being an only child she did lots of activities and she had school. But when she was at Pippin Cottage, she never felt lonely. Gran was her best friend. She had Gran and the villagers who all knew her name, though many of them had gone now; she had the owl who called at night; she had the stream she walked along and sang beside; she had the little garden and a sense of peace she had never really known anywhere else.

If she could live in the cottage and then go to the West End every day she would be as happy as a lamb, but that wasn't possible.

Her phone pinged in her bag and she took it out.

A text from Nigel.

What's happening? Voice better? Run has been extended. Won't be back for an extra eight weeks.

She texted back.

> No voice yet. Am going to try and sing tonight at the am dram audition. Don't ask. It's an experiment. I might stay with Gran for the summer. She's frail.

Nigel sent back a sad face and some hearts and she slipped the phone back into her bag.

'That's my housemate. He's on tour with *The Wizard of Oz*. He's a swing and in the chorus,' she said proudly.

'That's great,' said Nick. 'Did you two do a show together?' he asked.

'No, we met at university. He's an incredible dancer. He does the big dance sort of shows, whereas I try and do the acting with singing shows or light opera,' she said.

Nick turned the corner in the car. 'Like *The Secret Garden* or *Light in the Piazza*?'

Lily half turned towards him in the car. 'How do you know those shows?' she asked. 'Knowing that is more than just liking a bit of *Hamilton*. That's, like, serious knowledge.'

Nick laughed. 'My secret is out. I'm a massive musical theatre nerd. I try and go to shows as often as I can and have a large collection of soundtracks. I'm a bit of an MT tragic actually,' he said. 'Which is funny, because people make assumptions about men who like musical theatre but I'm just a straight guy who loves a great sing in the car and on an amateur stage.'

Lily remembered her own thoughts and felt a little embarrassed about them.

'And you said your ex-girlfriend was also into musical theatre?'

'Oh yes, very much,' Nick said as he parked out the front of the village hall. 'She's a great singer, beautiful soprano.'

Lily wasn't sure why that jarred with her but it did, and her competitive streak came forth.

'Oh that's nice,' she said and wondered what Nick would think of her voice.

'What's her name?' she asked as she got out of the car.

'Jessica,' he said as he closed the car door and they walked up to the hall. 'But she's in London, so I think Eliza will be all yours if you want it.'

'I'm just practising; I'm not staying,' she said. 'It's just for a test,' she said again but she wondered if she was trying to convince herself. A summer with Nick, singing and staying at the cottage with Gran, could be just the distraction she needed. Or was she simply wasting hers and the societies' time?

Nine

Nerves flooded Lily's body and she wondered if she could escape. What was she doing here? This was so stupid. She had long passed by amateur theatre and her voice wasn't working anyway.

Nick opened the door and she heard a piano playing, and talking and laughing as she stepped inside. Lily hesitated for a moment at the doorway while Nick kept the door open. Her heart hammered in her chest.

There was that lovely energy she remembered about being in a show in the room. It didn't matter that it was an amateur show, everyone was there for the same goal: to be a part of something. Along with the happy gathering of people and music, the warm glow of light spilt out into the street. Breathing deeply, she steadied herself and entered.

Unlike the calm lanes of Appleton Green that led them to the village hall, inside was a hive of activity. Coffee and tea were set up and some cake and biscuits were on a trestle table to the side, all beautifully laid out on a pretty blue tablecloth. Lily could smell the cinnamon cake, along with the subtle mustiness that seemed natural in all community facilities. To her left, a makeshift café with mismatched seats surrounding unsteady trestle tables had been set up. Sitting around hot cups of tea and coffee, a small group of people chattered, their eyes curious at this interloper to their auditions. She smiled at a few and they thankfully smiled back at her.

A dilapidated upright piano stood boldly in the middle of the room, its keys being fiercely pounded by a portly man with a shock of white hair. Lily started to recognise the melody; it was 'On the Street Where You Live' from *My Fair Lady*.

'Nick, you're here, thank goodness. Where is Jessica?'

She turned to find a big table piled with scripts, pens, and what appeared to be sign-up sheets. Rising above the noise, a harried-looking woman with frizzy red hair was trying to sort the anarchy by calling names and distributing paperwork.

'In London, last I heard,' said Nick to the woman. 'Sheila, this is Lily Baxter. She's said you two know each other?'

Lily smiled at Sheila who nodded. 'Nice to see you again, Sheila,' she said.

Sheila peered at Lily. 'Oh yes, Violet Baxter's granddaughter. How is she?'

Lily smiled. 'She's fine, still at the cottage. She sends her best,' she lied.

Sheila gave a pursed half-smile. 'I'm sure she did,' she said and turned to Nick.

'Let me know when Jessica arrives. She's my Eliza.'

'Isn't she in London?' he asked, confusion clouding his handsome face.

'She's back, didn't she call you?' said Sheila looking smug for knowing something Nick didn't, and she walked away like a cat swinging her tail.

Lily leaned to Nick. 'Well if it's already cast then I don't need to worry,' she whispered with a smile.

'I didn't know she was back,' Nick said and Lily heard an edge in his voice.

'Did things end badly between you?' she asked, knowing she was being nosy but wanting to know everything about her competition.

'Let's just say we won't be catching up for coffee anytime soon,' he said and he handed her the sign-up form and went to speak to Sheila.

Lily wandered about the room looking at the fading posters of earlier productions – *The Importance of Being Earnest*, *Guys and Dolls*, *A Midsummer Night's Dream* – each one homely and unpretentious and reminding Lily of why she loved the theatre so much.

But the anxiety of having to sing still loomed.

She glanced around the room looking for Jessica, her supposed competition. Even though Lily knew she most likely wouldn't commit to being in the show, she wondered what the girl's voice would be like. There was always someone better in London, and sometimes she would stay back after an audition to listen to the others sing their songs and wonder why she even bothered. Everyone was so talented on the West End.

'Hello, to the most glamourous ingénue. Miss Lily Baxter, how are you?' She turned to see Jasper, looking much older but still very fabulous in his black fedora and an electric blue overcoat draped over his shoulders, stood in front of her, as Nick came to her side.

'Hello, Jasper.' She beamed at him. He had always been so kind to her when she was a child. 'I can't believe you remember me,' she said.

'I've been watching your career from afar,' he said with a smile. Jasper smelled of mints and orange peel and maybe the faint smell of tobacco. He wore a rose gold pinkie ring and under his arm was a tiny Pomeranian dog.

'It's not much of one,' she said with a shrug.

'It more than most, darling. Now are you coming to sing for Eliza?'

'I thought I might just have a little sing.'

'This is Bernadette,' he said to Lily, pushing the dog slightly forward for her to see as Nick came to her side.

The dog looked at her as Lily put her hand out for the dog to sniff.

'No,' said Nick and Jasper in unison, but Bernadette licked Lily's hand with her tiny tongue.

'Well that's a sign,' said Jasper. 'Last year she bit Sheila's webbing between her thumb and pointer finger, and now she has a floppy thumb.'

Lily looked at Nick who nodded. 'It's true, I applied pressure and they stitched it, but it's not been the same since according to Sheila.'

Jasper smiled at her. 'I do hope you will bring Violet to the show. She would have been a wonderful Mrs Higgins.'

'Yes, we will come,' she said to him and he wandered to the tea table where he took a piece of cake and fed it to Bernadette, and then went to the group sitting in the chairs.

Nick looked around and she wondered if he was nervous about Jessica's arrival. 'Come on, we need to get a seat and wait our turn to audition,' Nick said to her.

The room hummed with obvious excitement, as any audition space did, and she tried to push the memory of her failed audition out of her head.

There is no pressure here, she reminded herself. *There is no need to worry, just sing the song and enjoy yourself*, she thought. She wouldn't let herself get carried away; she couldn't. This was a test for herself, not a real audition.

'We sing in front of each other?' She looked around.

'Of course.' He smiled and she wondered how a man this good-looking could be single.

Lily nodded and inhaled once more, trailing Nick as they went to the chairs.

'Everyone, this is Lily. She's from London. She's a West End singer, and she's here to practise and audition,' he said to the group. She nudged him.

'Shhh, don't,' she hissed but he ignored her.

'West End? How marvellous. Why are you here, dear? Will be you in the show?'

The questions tumbled from the people around her and Lily didn't know which one to answer first, when the door opened and everyone turned.

'Jessica,' said Sheila and she rushed up to a young woman who looked uncannily like a very tall Audrey Hepburn and who glanced at Nick and then at Lily and raised an eyebrow. She wore a black cape over a white dress and had her hair in a perfect French roll. She wore black heels with stockings and carried an elegant clutch purse. The only colour was a perfect red lipstick and the red on the soles of her heels that Lily captured a glimpse of as she stalked into the hall.

Sheila turned to the group who were all sitting on the chairs.

'Everyone can relax, our leading lady is here,' she said, her eyes holding Lily's for a moment too long.

Jessica came to the group and looked at everyone and then leaned down and kissed Nick on the cheek. 'Hello, darling,' she said to him.

'Hi,' he said, seeming a little awkward, 'Jess, this is Lily. She's new in the village.'

Jessica stared at her for a longer than usual moment and then a slow smile spread over her face and she laughed.

'Hello, Lily, how nice to see you again,' she said. 'You're helping your grandmother. How sweet, like little red riding hood. Be careful of the wolf,' she said with a coquettish bat of her eyelashes.

Nice to see you? She couldn't remember ever meeting her before.

But before Lily could ask anything of Jessica, Sheila clapped her hands.

'Okay, everyone, time to get ready. We are casting for all roles,' said Sheila and she gave Jessica a wink.

Jessica preened and it annoyed Lily more than was reasonable. There were other younger women in the group who might be right for the role of Eliza. Why did Jessica assume it was hers? Was Sheila making the casting decisions and not Jasper?

'Listen, I might not audition,' she whispered to Nick. 'It's a silly idea. I'll wait for you to sing and just watch.'

'No, you have to sing. This is just to see how your voice is, okay? Look at me the whole time and just focus on the singing and nothing else,' he whispered back.

There was a calmness to him that soothed her but still, she thought, it wouldn't be right to waste everyone's time.

'Lily Baxter?' She heard her name and looked up to see Sheila standing with the call-out sheet.

'Um, yes,' she said. Sometimes she hated having a name that started so early in the alphabet.

'Just sing and see what happens,' Nick whispered and she looked at him and made a face. 'Go,' he said and pushed a little with his hand on her elbow.

Lily walked to the piano and realised she hadn't brought any sheet music.

'I forgot my music,' she said to the portly accompanist.

'That's okay, Andrew knows everything. Just tell him what song and in what key and you can start,' Sheila instructed with a toss of her teal and purple paisley pashmina over her shoulder.

Lily stood still, thinking of what song to sing.

'"So in Love" from *Kiss Me, Kate* in G# major?'

She glanced at the rickety upright piano where Andrew sat, poised to begin. His fingers hovered over the keys, waiting for her nod. Lily's mouth felt dry, her palms clammy. What if her voice failed her again? What if she opened her mouth and nothing came out, just like that disastrous day in London?

He nodded and started to play the introduction.

She knew the song so well. It was one she used to sing with Gran when they would put on the *Kiss Me, Kate* movie soundtrack when she was small, and she would sing every role, but she loved the role of Kate the most.

The chatter of the room had died down to an expectant hush, and she could feel every pair of eyes boring into her. Her heart hammered against her ribs, threatening to burst free. *Please don't let me down*, she silently asked her voice.

Taking a shaky breath, she looked out into the audience. Most faces were a blur, but one stood out clearly: Nick. He sat in the front row, his kind eyes fixed on her, a reassuring smile on his face. He gave her a subtle thumbs up, and something in Lily's chest loosened just a fraction. Why did he have to be so handsome? At least it was distracting enough to make her stop worrying about what might or might not come out of her mouth.

Lily closed her eyes, allowing the familiar melody to wash over her. When she opened them again, she fixed her gaze on Nick, using him as an anchor in the sea of her anxiety.

As the moment for her to begin approached, Lily felt a flutter of panic. But then Nick mouthed, 'You're fine,' and somehow, impossibly, she believed him.

Lily opened her mouth, and to her amazement, her voice emerged – clear, strong, and full of emotion.

The words flowed from her, each note ringing true. As she sang, the world around her faded away. There was no audience, no judging eyes, just the music and the story she was telling.

Her voice swelled with the crescendo, years of training and passion pouring out of her. In that moment, Lily remembered why she had fallen in love with singing in the first place. It wasn't about the applause or the bright lights of the West End. It was about this – the pure joy of losing herself in a song. She remembered singing it in Pippin Cottage to Gran, who told her she had something special, that she could do something few others could do, that her voice brought Gran joy.

As she hit the final note, holding it with a control and power that surprised even her, Lily realised that tears were threatening to fall and she ducked her head as the last piano notes faded away, and for a moment, there was absolute silence.

Then, the hall erupted in applause. Lily blinked, coming back to herself. She saw Nick on his feet, clapping wildly, his face beaming with pride. The rest of the room followed suit, a standing ovation from this small but appreciative audience.

Except Jessica and Sheila who sat, slightly smiling, clapping somewhat less enthusiastically.

Lily felt a smile break across her face, a real, genuine smile that reached her eyes. For the first time since leaving London she felt confident again. Her voice wasn't broken, she'd just needed a break.

Ten

Violet sat in her armchair after Nick and Lily had gone. The cat was sitting on the sofa, staring at her.

'What are you looking at?' she asked the animal with a raised brow. The cat turned its back and settled into the seat with a flick of his tail.

Plans were afoot, she thought.

Lily was at the audition.

Violet traced the lip of her mug of tea with her fingers as she grinned quietly to herself. Her voice wasn't lost, she was lost. There is a difference, she thought. It was a shame Lily had lost herself and her inner knowledge. As a child she'd had such a strong sense of self. When did she lose that, Violet wondered? Was it before college or after? Was it Denise or was it someone else? She knew how much Denise wanted success for Lily but it would only come if Lily wanted that for herself.

Lily had always been an entertainer, a singer. Even as a little child, she could not resist playing music, her voice carefree and bright. However, life has a way of fading that brilliance and making people doubt the things that came so naturally when it becomes a burden.

But things were changing.

Violet had noticed the shift in Lily's demeanour when Nick came into the house. Oh there was chemistry there, real chemistry.

It made her think of Martin. Nick reminded her of Martin and his kind ways. She didn't dabble in romantic affairs, but she had seen enough in her life to recognise when two people were meant to be together.

She had been feeling in her bones for some time now that her days were getting shorter, and she wasn't sure how much longer she had left. Not that she would have said that to Lily or Peter. No one needed to hear such things. It was better that life was full so when she went there were other things to distract them.

Nothing worse than when people can't get over the death of someone. Life goes on, no matter what, she always said.

But she knew things needed to be arranged in a way to ensure that Lily would be happy in her life when Violet died, despite the grief she knew Lily would experience. She needed to have a life she thought was worth living, and Violet wondered if the one Lily was living now was something she wanted to be a part of.

Perhaps a little gentle push here and there would help, she thought.

She'd had a good life, a full one, and before she died, all she wanted to see was Lily finding her true path wherever that might take her.

Violet went to her little bureau and pulled out a bundle of letters in envelopes. None of them sealed yet. Yes, she would have to write another one soon, but not yet. Things weren't in their right places yet.

She leafed through the letters, reading them and smiling at the memories. The last would be wonderful, a final chapter in her story but only just beginning for Lily, and Violet couldn't wait for everything to come together finally.

Eleven

The curtains in Lily's bedroom opened wide, letting the early morning light illuminate the ceiling's fading glow-in-the-dark stars. She woke with a start, as though she had forgotten something and then she remembered the night before.

The events of the night replayed in her mind like a movie dream as she lay there, gazing at the familiar plaster cracks.

Jessica had sung after her and it seemed as though she was she was furious with Lily for going first. Jessica sang a song from the musical *Waitress*, which was pleasant, but she had a thin voice, cracking a little and without any passion or emotion, and Lily wondered if Jessica's voice would make the week-long run of the big musical. It was a musically sound voice but she needed some good voice lessons to let the sound come out, and some decent performance advice, she thought, but it wasn't her job to help Jessica.

However, she was very beautiful, Lily thought – more Audrey Hepburn in the movie than Julie Andrews, the original Eliza on West End, but the interpretation was missing the heart and soul that Eliza Doolittle required. Lily couldn't help but think of Julie missing out on the film role to Audrey because Audrey was considered more beautiful.

After she had sung, Nick had a little furrowed brow and his applause seemed more muted than enthusiastic for Jessica's performance, and then a few auditions later, Nick sang his piece.

Lily closed her eyes and let his tenor voice wash over her. As he passionately sang 'On the Street Where You Live', Lily had felt a chill run up her arms. His comments resounded throughout the entire hall, causing Lily to forget she was in a village town hall and not in a theatre in London.

He was so good he could have been on stage professionally, she had thought to herself as he'd finished the song.

After everyone sang, they had more tea and cake and a chat, but Lily noticed Jessica only spoke to Sheila, while occasionally shooting poisonous looks at Nick and Lily.

Nick had driven her home and they hadn't talked about Jessica because she didn't want to know. That was one night and it showed her that her voice still worked, that *Les Mis* was an anomaly, and that was more of a relief than she could express.

'You up, dear?' She heard Gran's stick knock on her bedroom door.

'I am now,' she said to herself and got out of bed and opened the door.

Gran was dressed in her blue floral robe.

'I'll have a shower, and then we can have breakfast and talk about last night. How was Nick?' Gran said, a sparkle in her eye. 'Did he serenade you?' She clutched the front of her robe as though in love.

Lily couldn't help but laugh at Gran's cheek.

'Gran, don't be smart with me, young lady. He's just a new friend while I'm here.'

'Get a brew on and tell me everything,' Gran said as she shuffled to the bathroom.

'Do you want a hand?' she asked but Gran waved her away.

'No, I'm fine thank you very much,' she said. 'If I can't bathe myself, then I will know it's time to call for my maker to take me the big stage in the sky.'

Lily pulled on a sweater over her nightgown and slipped on a pair of thick socks and padded downstairs. It was still fresh for late May and she hoped the sun would come soon and warm up for summer.

She set about making tea and toast as Mr Mistoffelees came sauntering downstairs and sat on the back of the sofa.

'I suppose you'll be wanting breakfast also,' she said to the cat who looked at her expectantly.

She sang a few lines from the song last night and thankfully her voice was back.

'That was a scare wasn't it?' she said to the cat who flicked his tail at her.

She fed the cat and made herself some tea and drank it with the back door open as she looked at the garden and a small blackbird busy digging for worms.

'Close the door – it's freezing,' said Gran as she came down the stairs.

Lily did as she was told and got Gran a mug for her tea and settled her in her chair at the little table.

'So how was it? Did your voice come back?' Gran asked, always straight to the point.

While holding the hot mug in her hands, Lily slid into the chair across from her. She said slowly, thinking before she spoke. 'It was... unexpected.' Her lips curved into a smile. 'I sang, Gran,' she said. 'My voice sounded better than ever.'

With a wide grin that emphasised her fine lines, Gran's face softened. 'I'm so pleased, Lil. Now tell me everything. Was the horrendous Sheila Trotter there?'

'Gran, you can't call her horrendous.'

'I can call her horrendous and I just did,' Gran said firmly as she sipped her tea. Her hand had a slight tremor, Lily noticed, and she thought she should mention it to Nick. 'I've known her for years, jumped-up wannabe politician with her ridiculous red hair. You know it's dyed. She tried to run for council for the area, wanted to bring a McDonald's into the region. Not bloody likely.'

'I never knew this,' Lily said. 'Good gossip though. Jasper's dog, Bernadette, everyone described it as Cujo – the evillest dog in the world – but it liked me. Gave me a little lick. It hates Sheila, apparently bit her and gave her a floppy thumb,' she said as Mr Mistoffelees came and rubbed up against her legs.

'I won't even ask what that means, you and your slang.' Violet shook her head. 'So tell me all – what happened at the audition? Are you the new Eliza?'

From Nick's encouragement to the tsunami of applause that she had experienced, Lily told Gran everything that happened the night before and then she got to Jessica.

'Who is Jessica?'

'Sheila's niece, who used to date Nick. She came swanning in. She's very beautiful. She auditioned. Sheila seemed to think she was their Eliza. She was weird with me, as though she knew me but I've never met her. She was kind of fixated on Nick and me throughout the auditions but there's nothing happening there. I don't know what she's so paranoid about.'

Gran gave a dismissive sniff. 'She can sense the chemistry.'

'Gran, there is no chemistry.'

'And I'm about to turn twenty-five. Go on,' Gran said.

'The looming issue is... Jess, she's... well, she's not making it easy. She has some sort of weird vibe about her. I think she would make this really awkward for me if I do it, which I probably won't,' she said.

Gran let out a laugh. 'That brings back memories. Have I ever mentioned Beatrice Hawthorne to you?'

Lily shook her head.

'When I was first in the am dram society, before I was even engaged, Beatrice was the star of our local theatre group.'

She paused and raised an eyebrow at Lily. 'Well, she was talented and so beautiful, stunning in fact, and she was well aware of it. I was no great beauty but I did have stage presence and was helpful and kind and had a lot of energy. Beatrice seemed to suck the energy out of a room. She made every scene about herself, and would always try and pull focus when she was on stage, even if it wasn't her line.'

Lily made a face. She had seen her fair share of that before.

Granny's eyes gleamed. 'So that summer we were doing *A Midsummer Night's Dream* and Beatrice was irate because I was cast as Hermia. She was determined to play the part. She tried everything to get rid of me, cajoling the director, bad-mouthing me to everyone.'

'So what did you do?' Lily leaned forward and asked.

'She was cast as Titania, which was perfect for her. She was so beautiful but she wasn't happy. She wanted a lead. So at first, I did my best to make her happy. I tried to befriend her and make things right, like offer to run lines and give her compliments and applaud her performance as Titania in rehearsals, but it didn't work. She was mad and she was making my rehearsals so awful that I began to get stressed and anxious before they even began.'

Lily nodded as Gran went on.

'Then the dress rehearsal came and Beatrice "accidentally",' she said using quotation marks with her hands, 'tripped me up backstage and I badly wrenched my ankle.'

'Oh my God, that's terrible.' Lily gasped. 'What did you do?'

'I did the show, with a walking stick,' she said and she glanced at the walking frame, 'although I could have used that also.' She laughed. 'And I incorporated it into the character and everyone gave me a standing ovation and Beatrice was so furious, she left the society and joined a new one over in Stoketon.'

Lily laughed uproariously at the outcome.

'So I have to wait for Jessica to maim me or hope she goes away in a huff for her to leave me alone?'

'My point is, don't give up because she doesn't like you or want to even get to know you. Stand your ground,' Gran said. 'Now tell me more about Nick. Did he have a good voice?'

Lily smiled and hugged herself for a moment. 'Nick has a lovely voice. I'd love to hear him sing Marius from *Les Mis*. He would be perfect.'

Gran raising an eyebrow at Lily who laughed. 'Perhaps he might be what the doctor ordered for you?'

'Don't try and set me up with your nurse, Gran. I'm only here for the summer.'

'The summer? You said only a month.' Gran clapped her hands.

'Is that okay?' Lily asked. 'I mean I don't want to overstay my welcome.'

'Is that okay?' Gran beamed. 'It's excellent news. We can have a wonderful last summer.'

'Last summer?' Lily asked, but before Gran could answer the doorbell rang.

Lily went to the door and there was Nick in his nursing shirt and pants, carrying his bag and with a shower chair and another walking frame.

'Morning, Violet; morning, Lily,' he said with his eye catching hers, and she felt those silly butterflies rise in her stomach again.

'Oh, I didn't know you were here today,' Lily said, aware of how she was dressed and wishing she didn't look like she had slept in a charity bin.

'I'm supposed to be here tomorrow but I thought I'd drop these off,' he said, 'to help make Violet's daily living easier.'

'What's all that rubbish?' Gran asked from where she sat at the kitchen table, glaring with narrowed eyes at the equipment. She was suspicious of anything new, having told Lily when she suggested a coffee machine for the cottage, that she would sooner drink pond water than that newfangled muck.

'It is an assortment of things to keep you out of hospital or a nursing home.' Nick was kind but firm. 'I call them a compromise.'

Lily couldn't help but admire how he handled Gran's prickliness with such ease, because she was testing her patience right now.

Lily bit back a flickering smile. 'Gran, it will help you remain independent. Surely that is worth a little bit of a compromise?'

'Independence? Funny! I was climbing trees and chasing sheep when you were both but twinkles in your parents' eyes,' Gran said, but Lily observed her glare softening somewhat as she once more stared at the tools. 'I just don't think it's necessary. It was one fall, and we're already cramped in this house, without adding more contraptions.'

Lily was ready to tell Gran exactly what she thought when she heard Nick speaking in his kind and gentle way, which was never condescending but always respectful.

Nick patiently went over the purpose for every object. 'The chair is for the shower; this frame will enable you to go about more safely. Mrs Baxter, these are not restrictions. They are pieces of equipment to enable you to keep doing what you love, which is be independent.'

Gran huffed at him. 'Well, if it means that it will keep those busybodies from the hospital and my own son and daughter-in-law from suggesting a nursing home, then I will try your contraptions. I won't guarantee I'll enjoy them, though.'

'You don't have to enjoy them, Mrs Baxter, but I expect you will enjoy the ongoing independence.'

Lily turned to Nick and both of them suppressed grins. Although it wasn't exactly acceptance, from Gran it was a settlement between them. Lily felt a warmth in her chest as she watched Nick keep talking with Gran, softly nudging her into walking a little further with the frame, his hand hovering at her back to guide her. Finally Gran was back in her chair, after doing a lap of the room, while Nick rearranged a few small items of furniture to make room for the frame.

'I'll pop these upstairs,' said Nick. 'And then I'll give you a quick check-over.'

'Cup of tea?' asked Lily as he carried the items upstairs.

'Yes please, if it's made, but don't go to any trouble,' he said as he went upstairs.

'Go on, get your leading man a mug,' teased Gran as Lily shook her fist playfully at her.

'Shh, or you'll be popped in the shed with the old pots,' Lily whispered as she made Nick a mug of tea.

'That's elder abuse that is,' said Gran loudly for Nick's ears as he came back downstairs.

'What's elder abuse?' asked Nick as Lily set about making the tea.

'Lily said she'd pop me in the shed with the old garden pots.'

'Don't forget to use your frame on the way there,' Nick said as he sat down at the table, and Gran and Lily burst into laughter.

'So the upstairs is ready. I've popped the frame at the top of the stairs, and I've placed the chair in the shower.'

Gran gave him an expression of despondency and resignation. 'That's depressing. Getting old is so frustrating. It really does sneak up on you.' She shook her head at herself. 'But enough about that sad stuff. How were the auditions last night?' Gran asked him as though she hadn't heard a thing from Lily.

Nick smiled at Lily. 'Your granddaughter is a marvel. I don't know why you're not the leading lady in every show in London,' he said to her and she felt herself redden with his praise.

He leaned over to Gran. 'Lily really does have an incredible voice. Apparently Sheila and Jasper were fighting about you after we left.'

'Oh that's not good,' Lily said quickly.

'Why?' asked Nick.

'Because I can't be in the show. It was just a test to see how my voice went,' she said.

'Do you think you're too good for the Appleton Green Amateur Drama Society?' Gran asked, and Lily wasn't sure if she was being serious or not.

Lily felt her cheeks flush at her grandmother's question. 'It's not that, Gran,' she said, stirring her tea absentmindedly. 'It's just... this isn't the West End. And after everything that's happened... I don't know. It feels like a step back. Now I know I can sing again I should be thinking about auditioning for shows, after I've got you on the mend again.'

Resting in her chair, Gran's gaze remained as piercing as before. 'You said you would stay longer and it's not as though I need waiting on hand and foot; perhaps see it as a chance to practise and have something to do while you're in Appleton Green.' Sipping her tea, she stared fixedly at Lily's face. 'It doesn't matter where you are, if you want to sing, sing. You see, my dear girl, talent has no boundaries. Unless you really do think you're too good for the show.'

Sighing, Lily shook her head. 'No, Gran, I told you I don't think I'm too good. I think I'm just a bit confused and besides they haven't offered me anything anyway. Sheila was adamant she wanted Jessica in the role. I think she has more say than Jasper in the casting.'

'Oh piffle to Jessica and Sheila thinks she has more power than anyone. Are you happier chasing that dream in London or rediscovering why you loved it in the first place, right here for the summer?' Gran asked with a kinder tone.

Lily hesitated before responding, unable to think of anything to say. A few straightforward words from Gran could always clear her head, but with Nick here, she felt confused.

Leaning back, Nick's face betrayed his seriousness. 'Lily, you were just amazing. It is evident that you have accomplished much with your training and commitment to your voice, and I know it's a bit silly doing an amateur show but it would be wonderful for us, and I already know I'm playing Freddy – Jasper rang me this morning – so we could be playing opposite each other. It would be such an honour to sing with you and we would have a blast.'

Lily knew she was blushing now.

'That's exactly what I've been advising her,' Gran said. 'I said to myself last night that you would be a lovely Freddy.'

She felt Gran's hand on hers as she extended across the table. 'Lily, I would love to see you sing again on stage. I can't get to London anymore and having you here and then performing in the village, well I couldn't think of anything better for my summer.'

Tears irritated Lily's eyes and her gaze fell to her hands, where her grandmother's weak hold remained. Could it be that easy? Could she simply stay with Gran over the summer, and stop worries about auditions and competition and her voice and just sing for a while?

'I would love to sing for you again, Gran,' she said in an almost whisper. 'But I haven't been offered anything so let's not get ahead of ourselves. And I still don't know if I can trust my voice.'

'Your voice is fine. It's rich and powerful; it's wonderful and I know this show is not professional or the West End,' Nick said, 'but maybe it's time to reset your expectations for a while and see what it feels like to sing without all the pressure from doing it professionally on your shoulders.'

She wasn't sure why but his words felt soothing, like a balm, and she closed her eyes and let them envelop her. Imagine a whole summer of not running from audition to audition, working at the call centre and the restaurant for the rent. Trying to juggle her social life, dating, the chaos of the flat with her and Nigel working different hours, always trying to be quiet when he was asleep and trying to manage the shopping and eating properly and looking after her voice.

Perhaps they were right. Perhaps there was more at stake than a stellar career or the West End. Possibly, this was all about rediscovering her voice in the most basic, uncomplicated way.

'I can see why you're a nurse. You just healed me in many ways,' she half joked to Nick.

'Speaking of which, I need to give you a check-over, Violet, and that dressing on your nose needs to be changed.'

'Anyway, I don't know what you're both worrying about, I haven't even been offered chorus.' She laughed as she stood up from the table to clear the plates when her phone rang.

'Destiny's calling,' said Gran wryly as Lily picked up her phone.

Lily went outside to take the call.

'Lily Baxter?' she heard a man's voice say.

'Yes?'

'Jasper Winterbottom. and you, my dear, are our new Eliza Doolittle. Congratulations!'

'Oh wow,' she said, feeling the rush of success through her body. It never mattered how big the role; being chosen was always a special feeling.

'Yes indeed, we start tomorrow night for a read-through, so don't be late,' he said and before she could say a thing, the line went dead.

Lily walked back into Pippin Cottage, where Nick and Gran both turned to look at her expectantly.

She shrugged. 'I guess I'm playing Eliza for the summer,' she said and then did a spin.

Nick grinned at her and Gran clapped her hands.

'Oh wonderful, I'll have to stay alive for a little bit longer now to see my girl sing the role of a lifetime.'

Nick laughed at Gran's words but Lily saw a flash of something else in her grandmother's face, just for a moment, that sent a shiver of something unfamiliar through her bones, and as much as she didn't want to face it, she wondered if this really would be Gran's last summer.

Twelve

Lily stood outside the village hall, staring at the weathered wooden doors. Her heart pounded as she wondered what lay on the other side. She could hear the faint sound of piano keys and chatter filtering through the cracks. This was supposed to be simple, just a local production in a small village, but it didn't feel simple at all. In fact, it felt enormous. She took a deep breath and pushed open the door.

The room was a swirl of activity, with people bustling around. Sheila was standing next to a pile of scripts, writing on a clipboard, while Jasper was pointing out lighting on the makeshift stage. Bernadette, his tiny Pomeranian, watched with mild indifference from a pillow in the corner. Lily hesitated at the entrance, feeling like an outsider in a place that should have been welcoming.

'Oh, look, everyone, it's our Eliza.' Jessica's voice cut through the room like a knife. She stood by the piano, a script in one hand and a smug expression on her face. 'Our West End darling has graced us with her presence.' Jessica was wearing black cigarette pants, ballet flats and a striped Breton top, and her dark straight hair was in a high ponytail with a black ribbon in it, making her more Audrey than Audrey herself.

Lily forced a polite smile, her stomach twisting. 'Hi, Jessica,' she replied, moving further into the hall. She could feel eyes on her, some curious, some expectant. She tried to keep her focus ahead, on Nick, who was setting up chairs in the front row.

She wished she had worn something better than her jeans and rugby top and trainers, but then she remembered she never wore clothes like Jess and why would she start now? She was comfortable and that's what mattered.

'Good to see you, Lily,' he said, his smile easing some of her tension. He leaned and whispered to her, 'Ignore Jess. She's a bit put out. She'll get over it.'

'What role is she playing?' she whispered in return, glancing at Jess who was talking to Jasper, while Bernadette snarled at her.

'Mrs Higgins,' he said and made a face.

'The mother?' Lily turned to Jess and looked at Nick. 'She is far too beautiful to be the mother. No wonder she hates me. Who told her about me being on the West End?'

'I mentioned it, so people would have told her.' said Nick. 'I mean it's not exactly a secret. People talk. Besides you should be proud of yourself.'

'You sound like my mother,' she said and gave a large sigh.

'Is your mother very proud of you?' asked Nick as he adjusted the chairs.

'Stupidly, undeservedly so,' she said. Explaining Denise to people was hard because everyone thought it was great to have a mum so invested and supportive, but they didn't realise the expectations that came with it.

Sheila clapped her hands. 'Everyone, take your places. It's time for the read-through.'

Gathering around the trestle tables that had been set up, the cast members took their places, as Sheila handed them each a script, a highlighter and a pencil.

Lily sat down next to Nick, nerves rising as she took her script and saw her name – *Miss Eliza Doolittle – Lily Baxter*.

Nick nudged her with his elbow. 'It's exciting isn't it? I love a new script.'

He gave her an encouraging look that made her feel, if only momentarily, that everything would be good, perhaps even lovely.

She looked up and sitting straight across from them was Jess, her eyes narrowed as she stared at Lily, her mouth in a thin line. Lily was sure she could feel the poisoned darts being sent her way.

Jasper clasped his hands. 'Righto, let's start with Act One,' he said, his voice resonating off the old walls of the hall.

Lily opened her script after a long breath, her fingers shaking just a little. She looked at the lyrics, the well-known Eliza Doolittle lines, and urged herself to sink into the part. Her voice started off a little wobbly, but as the words came out her confidence grew. She felt her cockney accent running off her tongue as smoothly as if she had spoken that way her whole life. She felt herself sinking into character. She sensed a spark, a flash of the passion that had defined her, for the first time in months. God, she had missed this.

As they worked through the script, the voices of the characters bounced around the room.

David Caruthers, the local primary school principal, was playing a very good Henry Higgins and Stephen Waddell, the local vet, was playing a more than suitable Colonel Pickering.

A man called Sean Wilkins, who was an accountant from two villages over, was playing Alfred P. Doolittle, Eliza's father, and what he lacked in accent he made up for in enthusiasm for the role.

'He sounds more Indian than cockney,' Nick whispered to her.

'I'll help him with the accent.' She smiled at Nick, as they came to the end of Act Two. 'They're easy enough once you get the hang of it.'

'Everyone, time for an intermission. There's lemon drizzle cake and some cheese and biscuits. We have a sturdy cheddar and a lovely blue, if you're keen,' Sheila called out.

Lily pushed back her chair and stood up. 'If every rehearsal is like this, I'll be the size of a house,' she said to Nick as Jess moved around to the front of the table where Lily and Nick were standing.

Jess's voice sliced across the room like a razor: 'Lily, I was thinking, you might try to tone down the accent a bit. It's sounding a bit forced.'

Lily gasped at the note from Jess. No one would ever say that in the first read-through on a professional run. It was nasty and uncalled for and, more than that, it was rude.

She looked down at her script, the words blurring just slightly from anger and embarrassment.

Then she heard a low growl and Jasper's voice next to her: 'Actually, I think Lily's interpretation is spot on,' he added, staring at Jess with a look that brooked no argument. 'If you have notes, you speak to me, not directly to the other actors.'

Bernadette was in his arms, her lip snarling at Jessica, who turned and walked towards Sheila.

'Oh God, this is going to be awful,' she muttered to Nick as they sat with their mugs of tea. 'She hates me.'

'No it will be fine. She won't do it again; Jasper popped her back into her box in no uncertain terms.'

'I can't imagine you going out with her. Was it serious?' she asked him.

'No, not really,' he said vaguely.

'How long did you go out for?' she asked.

'About six months,' he said.

'That's not a short time,' she said.

'Well I did spend the last three trying to end it, but she was sort of… ' His voice trailed away.

She looked at Jessica who was flirting with an uncomfortable Higgins and Pickering.

'I get it, I think. She's very charming.'

'She's also very manipulative.' He sighed. 'Boundaries are things on a map for her and not to be honoured in everyday life.'

'Well she definitely hates me,' she said. 'She's going to make this so awkward for everyone.'

'No, she'll settle down; she's just trying to prove something right now. Ignore it, rise above it,' he said. 'Now come and try the cheese with me. I love cheese. Do you love cheese?'

After the tea and cake, everyone was back at their places at the table ready for Act Three.

Jasper clapped his hands and walked around the centre of the U-shaped tables. 'Opening of Act Three. The scene unfolds in the elegant drawing room of Mrs Higgins, where the atmosphere is charged with anticipation as she prepares to welcome her esteemed guests.'

Jasper spoke passionately as he walked. 'Eliza and Mrs Higgins are to meet, and Eliza and Freddy are to finally meet, which sets off a chain of events, so let us begin.'

Jess began the scene, reading her lines with a tinge of contempt.

When she had to interact with Lily, she stared at her across the room, as though Lily was something to be pitied.

She missed a line and she felt Nick nudge her. 'Your line,' he said pointing at the page.

'Sweetie,' Jess pounced, her voice soft but condescending. 'Please try to keep up. Moving from the great West End stages to our modest production must be challenging, but we do like to keep the show moving.'

'I have it in hand, Jess. But thank you anyway,' she said smoothly but then she bit the inside of her mouth, tasting blood. The sting of Jess's comments were worse than she had anticipated. It was like returning to school, with that never quite fitting in sensation. She looked at Nick, who rolled his eyes at Jess's actions, his face a mix of irritation and encouragement, but it hurt and Lily swallowed the blood where she had bitten the skin.

Inhaling deeply, her shoulders drooping, she felt exhausted, every bit of her enthusiasm sapped by Jess's continuous undercurrent of hostility and obvious hatred.

Nick leaned into her side. 'You're doing great.' His breath was warm against her ear. 'Don't let her get to you.'

Lily nodded, but it didn't take the sting away. They managed to get through the rest of the read-through but the fizz of excitement had left the room with Jess's words.

'I'll drive you home,' Nick said to her as Lily put her script into her bag.

'Lily, dear.' She looked up to see Jess standing in front of them, her voice loud enough for everyone to hear and tinged with phoney worry. 'I hope you're not finding this too... provincial for your tastes. It's just am dram after all. I mean I've recently been in London, so I know how different this all is.'

Lily felt the rage swell up for a minute, a scorching flash building over her cheeks. She considered Gran, the summers spent in this very town, the cosiness of community theatre, the love of the shows and music and all those years she sang to Gran in the back garden of Pippin Cottage.

She inhaled steadily then turned to Jess, her face cool.

'Actually, I'm having a great time,' Lily said, her voice clear and calm. 'Community theatre is unique and so important, don't you think? The enthusiasm, the friendship.' She gestured to the room. 'It's incredibly special, and as the professionals I work with on the West End say, there are no small roles, only small actors.'

She paused, knowing the rest of the room was listening. This was her chance to show Jessica she would not be bullied. 'I just wanted to be a part of it all, after Nick told me about the auditions. I would've been happy to be chorus, just so I could sing this marvellous score, but I think only small-minded people believe any show or role is beneath them, don't you?'

Jess's smile stumbled a little, her eyes flickering with annoyance. This was not the answer she was expecting and she mumbled something about understanding and absolutely she was pleased to be a part of it and no role was too small for her either. Lily looked at Nick.

'Shall we go?' she asked him sweetly.

'Absolutely,' he said. His eye caught hers, and she saw pride there. He gave her the smallest of winks, and Lily had a flutter of hope in that instant, a feeling that perhaps this summer production might be just what the doctor ordered.

Thirteen

Nick drove Lily back to Pippin Cottage in silence. Lily wasn't sure what was happening with Jess, but it felt more than just the production and she knew Nick could read the room.

'Are you okay?' he asked as he turned off the car and they sat in the darkness.

'I don't know. I mean, she's actually acting so terribly,' Lily finally said. 'It feels like it's more than the role. It's not really about me, is it?'

Nick sighed. 'She's just a bit insecure. She's upset because we broke up and she didn't get the role and she's threatened.'

'But it's not very nice to be around and it's awful for the other actors and crew. I know I stood up to her tonight, but I don't know if the drama is worth it.' She paused. 'I mean I think you need to work out what Jess is trying to say and maybe speak to her, because she's taking it out on me and that's not okay.'

'I know,' he said with another deep sigh. 'I honestly didn't know she would be back. She said she was staying in London.'

'I get it but honestly I need to think about the show, because I don't want to have every rehearsal like that. It's not worth my mental health and everyone was so tense after her rubbish tonight. It changes the energy in the room and it won't make for a good show.'

Nick stared ahead, his hands on the wheel. 'If I talk to her, will you stay?' he asked.

She opened the car door. 'I need to think about it. I'll call Jasper tomorrow and let him know I'm having second thoughts; besides, rehearsal isn't until Saturday afternoon, and today is only Thursday. Gives me time to think and them to prepare.'

She got out the car and leaned down. 'Thanks, Nick, you're great and have been so wonderful with Gran. I appreciate it, and I know she does also.'

'Goodnight, Lily,' he said. 'I'm sorry.'

'Night,' she said and she walked through the little gate to the cottage, as Nick waited in the car to ensure she got inside safely.

With great care not to create too much noise, Lily opened the cottage's front door. The living room was semi dark, softly illuminated by one lamp in the corner and the television on, the sound almost too low to hear. Gran never left the television on, she thought, and when her eyes adjusted to the darkness, she noticed Gran was still in her armchair. She usually would be in bed by now and Lily tiptoed closer to check on her.

Gran's peaceful breathing mixed with the low sound from the television, creating a hum in the room. It was so cosy, Lily thought, as Mr Mistoffelees greeted her with a low meow and spun around her ankles in search of attention.

Finding solace in the warm, familiar weight of him pushing against her legs, she stooped to stroke behind his ears.

'Hello, trouble,' she said softly to the animal, as the cat purred loudly, his eyes half-closed in satisfaction, and she picked him up in her arms.

Quietly setting her bag down, Lily went to the window and peered out into the dark garden, seeing nothing and thinking about tonight. The read-through today had been truly awful, worse than any university or professional production, and Jess's criticisms were so nasty and so clearly pointed squarely at Lily but also directed at Nick. Nothing was worth this, and certainly not an amateur drama production in a little village.

She glanced over at Gran, and Lily wondered what Jess's anger seemed to be based on – something more than just professional rivalry?

Her ideas swung back and forth: should she approach Jess one on one, dismiss her, or just leave the show altogether? She had come to care for Gran, and work out her own life, not to participate in this silly heated drama for the summer.

Mr Mistoffelees leapt from her arms and onto the windowsill, his gaze tracking hers across to her grandmother, and he walked confidently along the backs of chairs and landed on the back of Gran's armchair. He nestled there, on the old patchwork comforter, curling into a tidy ball, claiming his space.

Lily went over to the little side table and picked up the framed picture. It was of her and Gran from their early years, both of them smiling for the camera, Lily with a crown of daisies that Gran had made for her. Everything about being with Gran as a child was magic, from the daisy chains to the little songs they would sing, from watching old musicals on video and Lily spending hours listening to Gran's old records of musical soundtracks.

Lily softly put the picture back and walked to the bookcase. She knew she should wake Gran and help her to bed, but she was drawn to something. Nestled among a stack of papers and paperback books was a big, dusty photo album. Lily hadn't looked at it in years, perhaps ten or more. She carried it carefully to the sofa, opening it gently.

Inside were black-and-white pictures of a young Gran, vivid and full of life, posing in several theatrical costumes. There she was as Lady Macbeth, a malicious glitter in her eye and knife in her hand, wearing a lot of tartan. Another displayed her in a chorus line from *South Pacific*, arm in arm with other players, all of them laughing. A decaying playbill dropped out between the covers, and Lily delicately picked it up. 'Amateur Dramatics Society Presents: *A Midsummer Night's Dream*,' it read. The role of Titania played by Violet Baxter.

Lily developed a lump in her throat. It was in her genes, she thought, so why was everything so hard? Why had her voice failed her in London? Why was Jess making it so uncomfortable at the first rehearsal? Why was it so difficult for Lily at the moment? Why couldn't she just enjoy it like these pictures of Gran, who had given her heart to the stage for pure joy and nothing more.

She looked across at Gran, still asleep, her face calm. Gran had often told her stories of those days, of the excitement of opening evenings and the friendship of the actors. It had never been about perfection or honours. It had been about the love of creating, about living totally in the moment, about passion. Lily knew that this summer was about rediscovering that feeling of delight and purpose, not only about looking after Gran.

Mr Mistoffelees jumped down from the back of Gran's chair, padded over and jumped onto the sofa next to her. He drew her back from her thoughts by pushing his head into her arm. She reached out to massage him absentmindedly, a calm resolve growing inside her chest. This had nothing to do with Jess or the theatrical tension or her voice or wondering if she was worthy enough. This was about honouring the passion of theatre her grandma had passed on. Gran wanted to see her sing the role of Eliza in her village and she would. Nothing would be better than Gran seeing her sing again. Jess could throw all the arrows she wanted. This wasn't about her; it wasn't even about Lily. It was about the ninety-seven-year-old woman sleeping across from her. She needed to make her proud.

Rising from her seat she kneeled down beside her grandmother's armchair and softly held her hand in her own. Gran shook slightly, her eyes flickering open.

'Sorry to wake you, Gran,' Lily murmured.

Gran spotted Lily and blinked slowly, a gentle grin crossing her lips. 'Good, darling. You arrived back late. How was the rehearsal?'

'Fine but you should be in bed,' Lily admonished gently.

'I wanted to stay up to hear all about it,' she said, her voice croaky with sleep and age.

Lily hesitated then started to grin. 'It was... a challenge,' she said. 'But you know what they say: the show must go on. Come on, up to bed and I'll help you get ready and we can have a long gasbag about it in the morning.'

Gran's eyes gleamed, a spark of the old theatre lover still blazing inside them. 'A challenge hey? I can't wait to hear about it. I bet you held your own.'

Lily nodded and tightened her grip on her grandmother's hand. 'You bet I did. I learned it from an old lady I know who loves the theatre.'

Gran caressed Lily's hand and her smile grew wider. 'That's my girl. You're a trouper.'

'Righto, let's go to bed. I'm knackered,' Lily said and slowly she and Gran climbed the stairs together.

To my sweet Lily, aged ten,

Once again, summer is coming to an end. I'm writing you this letter at the kitchen table while the last of the apple sauce cools on the windowsill. I hate apple sauce, but I might give it to Old Mr Campbell up the road. He's likes it on his cereal.

The cottage still smells like apples and nutmeg and cinnamon, a lovely scent as the air becomes crisp as autumn draws closer.

This year's apple harvest was really excellent, wasn't it? There were so many apples on the trees that their stems almost touched the ground. I can still picture you out there with your basket, gathering the drops and tiptoeing up to reach the ones that were just too high.

I think I might be done with apples now though. We made pies, crumbles, chutneys, jams and cakes. We tried everything! I know that making the apple tarts was your favourite part. I can picture you carefully putting the slices in order and layering the pastry.

It's been lovely having you here these past few weeks. When I think about all the summers we've spent together, I've noticed that you've changed. This year, I've heard your singing voice in a way I haven't heard it before and even though we've always sung together, sitting at the piano, something feels different now. I think your voice is maturing, and it's lovely to hear.

Lily, I know you're starting to understand that your voice is unique and stands out, but I want you to remember something important. Yes, your voice is a gift, but it's your gift. You don't have to use it if it doesn't make you happy, not even if it makes someone else happy. I know your mum has been saying you need lessons and the like, but hang off until you're sure you want them.

Things we love can become duties in this world, but I don't want that for you. If singing makes you happy, go ahead and sing your heart out. But if you don't feel like it some days, that's okay too. You own your voice.

Being aware that you're able to choose is a very important thing to know. I remember that when I was younger, I felt like I had to do certain things because other people wanted me to, and that took away some of the fun. That is not how I want you to feel at all, not about something as important as your voice. People will always have their own thoughts, but only you can choose what makes you happy.

You've always been a girl who knows what she wants, even at ten years old. I saw it this summer in the way you worked on our baking projects – you were so set on making each dish perfectly. You give careful thought to everything you do, which is great, but I hope you won't be too hard on yourself. The most important thing is to enjoy the process, whether you're singing a song or making apple tarts.

Hasn't this summer taught you a lot about being creative? We had a lot of fun coming up with new ways to use the apples and making up songs while we worked together in the kitchen.

Even though you're not here anymore and the cottage is a little quieter, I can still hear your laughing and singing, and I know you'll be back here again soon.

One more thing, people may start to notice your voice as you get older and tell you all sorts of things about what you should do with it. But remember this, my love: you can use your voice however you want. Let it fly if it makes you happy. You can put it down if it feels like too much. Do what makes you happy and stay true to who you are.

With all my love,
Gran

Fourteen

The next morning Lily stood in front of the slim, old-fashioned pantry next to the refrigerator, her hand hanging over the doorknob. She had opened Gran's door so she could hear her get up and now she could hear Gran's soft snores floating down the stairs. Gran had fought her tooth and nail to not have the nap, but Lily told her it wasn't to be argued with and she knew Gran needed it. She had stayed up too late the night before and was very tired today.

She drew a deep breath, as if about to open Pandora's box, and pulled the door open. She knew there was a muddle of things in the pantry but this was something else.

'Oh, good Lord,' Lily mumbled, her eyes widening at the sight in front of her.

The shelves were a genuine museum of past culinary eras. She reached for a tin of baking powder, glancing at the expiration date: '2010? I was still in secondary school,' she said to herself as she shook the tin, half expecting to hear the fossilised remnants of what was once baking powder.

Feeling more confident, Lily began her archaeological search through Gran's cupboard. She brought out a pickle jar with a faded label that resembled a Cold War relic. 'Best before July 1985,' she said loudly, repressing a giggle. 'These pickles are older than me. They could go on Antiques Roadshow!'

She then spotted a packet of jelly, the brilliant red colour having faded to a mournful pink. 'Oh, Gran,' Lily groaned and turned the packet over. 'Win a trip to the 2000 Olympics! I believe we missed that boat by around two decades.'

A tin of condensed milk attracted her attention, concealed beneath a jungle of antique spice jars. Lily delicately withdrew it, as if it were a fragile artefact. The expiry date had long passed, yet the price sticker proudly read '75p' in fading lettering.

As Lily dug deeper, she discovered a packet of crackers so old that the cellophane had turned yellow. She probed it cautiously, half expecting it to collapse to dust with her touch.

This was ridiculous. She picked up her phone and walked outside.

'Dad? Hi.'

'Hello, love, how's Mum?'

'She's okay but honestly, Dad, did you and Mum see the state of her pantry when you were at the cottage?'

'Do you think she would let me look in her pantry? It was enough she even let us through the door,' he scoffed. 'You know how independent she is.'

'I do but it's terrible. I need to go to town and do a proper shop for her, some meal planning, I mean, she's got things in that pantry from 1985.'

'I'm not surprised,' her father said. 'Do a clean-out and I'll transfer you some money; get anything else she might need also.'

'Thanks, Dad,' she said and she walked back into the kitchen where the mess of jars and packets were on the benches.

She started to place the items into rubbish bags and went back into the pantry for another look.

Finally, at the back of the top shelf, Lily curled her palm around a small, enigmatic tin. She pulled it out, brushing away a layer of dust thick enough to write on. Her eyes widened when she read the label.

'Spam? Is this actual Spam?' She turned the tin over in her hands, admiring it as if it were the holy grail of expired food. 'I thought this only existed in Monty Python sketches and wartime stories!'

Just then, she heard movement upstairs. Gran was awake. Lily quickly threw all the bags into the pantry, resulting in a dangerously balanced stack of ancient groceries. As she heard Gran's slippered feet on the stairs, she hastily shut the pantry door, leaning against it and pretending to be innocent.

Gran entered the kitchen, looking at Lily suspiciously. 'What are you up to, dear?'

Lily smiled. 'Oh, nothing, Gran. I thought I'd do some baking. But, yeah, I guess we might need to go shopping first.'

Gran nodded in approval. 'A good idea. While we're there, remind me to get some more pickles. I believe we might be running low.'

Lily bit her lip to avoid laughing. 'Sure thing, Gran. We would not want to run out of pickles. Not for the next century or two, at least.'

'What do you mean?' Gran moved with her walker into the kitchen. 'And why are you propping up the pantry door?'

Lily stepped away slowly. 'I'm doing a clean-out,' she said waiting for the barrage of protest about the state of her pantry and that Lily should keep her nose out of her Spam.

But Gran took a look inside at the bare shelves and the bags on the floor and nodded.

'About time someone did that. I was going to but it seemed too overwhelming, so I kept adding to it.' She laughed.

Relief came over Lily and she reached into a bag and pulled out the can of Spam.

'Spam? Really?' she asked her grandmother with a laugh.

'I don't even know where I got that from. Your grandfather and I loathed Spam. Maybe we won it? In a pub raffle or the like.' She shuffled back to her chair. 'Now do I get a cup of tea or have you thrown the tea leaves out as well? I'm lucky my chair is still here,' Gran muttered as she sat down and Lily rolled her eyes as she went back to the kitchen bench.

'I saw you rolling her eyes then,' called Gran from her chair.

'Impossible,' said Lily, laughing into the kettle as she filled it up.

Lily had Gran settled at home with the classic musical *The Band Wagon* playing on her ancient DVD player, a cup of tea and some shortbread. Lily was off to restock the kitchen.

She drove to the bigger village, parked at the supermarket and walked into the store.

Pushing a trolley, she started to make her way around the aisles.

'Lily?' she heard and she turned to see Nick standing at the end of the aisle with a small basket in his hand.

'Oh hi,' she said, feeling odd to see him outside of the cottage or the village hall. He wasn't at work today and was wearing jeans and a white shirt, which did nothing to make him seem less attractive. He looked so like Brad Pitt it was unnerving, as was the way his forearm flexed holding the basket with the heavy items in it.

'You buying a few things for dinner?' he asked.

She laughed. 'A few things? No, I just cleaned Gran's cupboards out, and let's just say it was like being in a kitchenalia exhibition of the past thirty years. I need to restock everything. She had products older than me. It was like she was hoarding for the next nuclear scare.'

Nick laughed, and put his basket into her trolley. 'Why don't I push and you put things in it and we can chat?'

Lily paused and then pushed the trolley towards him.

'Okay, let's go.'

She started selecting the necessities. Some fresh vegetables, fruits, meat, bread and a few indulgent delights that she was certain her grandmother would enjoy.

'I spoke to Jessica,' he said as she stood by a display of cakes.

'Oh?' She picked up a packet of madeira cake.

'She said she would apologise to you.'

'She doesn't need to, she just needs to stop it,' she said as she put back the cake.

'Did you speak to Jasper?' he asked as they walked along the biscuit aisle. She picked up some crackers for Gran to have with some cheese and some digestives for them when shortbread was in short supply.

'Not yet. I was going to but I got sidetracked by the pantry of yore,' she said with a laugh.

Nick stopped wheeling the trolley and she turned around to see what he was looking at.

'Don't leave, Lily. You're so fabulous and we can have fun. Ignore Jess and stay in the show.'

A woman walked past them and glanced at Nick and then she smiled at Lily as though she had done well for herself.

She sighed and gestured around her. 'This is the real reason I'm here though: to help Gran. Not deal with rubbish in the village hall twice a week for June and July and then a week of shows in the last week of August.'

'I know but it will be better and it's a great chance to keep your voice in check and sing for your gran,' he pleaded.

They kept walking as Lily put some cleaning supplies into the trolley.

'Okay,' she finally said. 'But I'm not taking any rubbish from Jess and you need to work it out with her, because her behaviour is not that of someone who is okay with the break-up. She's acting like the spurned ex-wife.'

'I'll get it sorted, I promise,' Nick said, and she saw a look of worry cross his face. For a moment she nearly felt sorry for him, but if he couldn't stand up to Jessica and their relationship hadn't been serious, then that was his problem.

Fifteen

Inside the village hall, the familiar scents and sounds of the theatre group welcomed her. The quiet buzz of performers chatting as they waited for rehearsals to start, Jasper's loud voice calling for Sheila to change the set up for the rehearsals on the small stage, the clatter of items being moved.

There was the familiar cinnamon cake scent and some coffee, which made Lily's stomach rumble, and she looked around to try and see Nick. She saw Jess speaking with another cast member at the far end of the room, her back straight, arms folded. Jess's eyes darted to Lily, then narrowed momentarily before she turned aside to carry on talking. Lily straightened her shoulders, not allowing the icy reaction to stop her. Today's rehearsal was about the show, not about Jess.

Nick finally entered, still in his nursing top and pants, and waved at Lily. She had put on a pretty sun dress this time, white with yellow roses on it and a matching yellow cardigan. It was perhaps a little formal for the rehearsal but it made her feel pretty and she needed the little dose of confidence around Jess, who was in all black and looking like a panther.

'How are you?' Nick asked as he came to her side.

'Nervous,' she admitted.

'Righto, let's go. We're blocking Act One, Scene One,' called Jasper.

'I need Mrs Eynsford-Hill, Freddy, Eliza, Colonel Pickering and Higgins on stage please.'

Sheila walked on stage with Nick and the others following.

'You're playing Mrs Eynsford-Hill?' Lily asked Sheila. 'I didn't realise, how lovely.'

'I was to be Mrs Higgins but since you are now Eliza that threw everything out of whack.'

Lily stared at Sheila for a moment, summoning up her grandmother's courage.

'I can leave and you can have the role back if you like. It's no skin off my nose.' She smiled as she spoke and saw Sheila's mouth drop.

'I mean…' Sheila tried to reverse her comment but it was too late; Lily was on a roll.

'I know you wanted Jess as Eliza but Jasper chose me, because I can sing the role and because Jess is very beautiful but doesn't have the voice. It's that simple and it's not personal, but for some reason you and Jess seem to have made it personal. I don't care either way, but if you're going to act like Jess and be passive aggressive and rude for the rest of my time here, then I will leave and I will tell Jasper exactly why.'

Sheila clasped her script to her chest. 'No, we don't want you to leave and I agree, you do have the better voice. So

I'm sorry I spoke that way to you and it won't happen again.'

Lily saw Nick's head bouncing between them as though he were in a tennis match.

'Great, so we'll move on and pretend this never happened,' Lily said with a sweet smile.

'Everything all right?' asked Jasper from the floor as Bernadette the dog toddled off to her velvet pillow to sit on and review the work.

'Absolutely – just discussing character,' said Sheila with a forced smile.

Jasper started to block the actors while the rest of the cast looked on as they worked through the opening scene.

Jasper's direction was sensible and straightforward, and Lily was glad she didn't have to do anything too fancy. It was very clear Jasper had this well in hand.

Lily threw herself into it with fresh enthusiasm as Higgins sang the first song: 'Why can't the English?'

Gosh she had forgotten how much fun it was and David, the local school principal, was an excellent Higgins, she thought.

After the scene was blocked and Jasper called a break, Nick came to her side as she made a cup of herbal tea for herself.

'How did the pantry restock go at Gran's?' he asked.

'Fine. She claimed she wasn't interested but seemed to have a lot to say about the placement of items,' Lily said with a laugh. 'You know what she's like.'

He nodded. 'I do and I bet she had a lot to say. I'm back on Monday to see if we can take the dressing off her nose now, so I can have a look and pass judgement on your work with her.'

Lily chuckled and then blew on her tea to cool it down.

'I have been meaning to say that I've noticed a tremor in her hands. I mean more than usual.'

Nick frowned. 'Okay, I'll take a look but she's getting on in age, you know; tremors are a part of it all.'

'Lily, what a pretty dress. I had wallpaper like that as child.'

Lily looked at Jess from over the top of her mug that she was about to sip from.

'Did that comment make you feel better?' she asked.

'Pardon?' Jess blinked her eyes innocently.

'I thought you spoke to her about this,' she said to Nick.

'Spoke to me about what? You're so sensitive, Lily. It was a compliment on the dress; you have chosen to take it another way.'

'I'm not sensitive, and I'm not stupid. I really don't know why you're like this, Jessica. It's just so uncomfortable for everyone.'

Jessica rolled her eyes and walked away as Jasper clapped his hand loudly.

'Scene Two, the pub – and we will sing through "With a Little Bit of Luck",' he called.

Lily went up on stage with Mr Doolittle and the rest of the chorus. As they started to block, she saw Jess staring at her, a small smile on her lips as though she were waiting for Lily to trip. It only steeled Lily further and she did everything Jasper asked and reminded Mr Doolittle of his blocking also.

'Lily, you are a lifesaver and such a professional,' said Sean, the accountant playing her father.

Lily smiled. 'My pleasure. We don't want anyone to be left behind,' she said and she meant it, and she saw Jessica shoot a death stare at her.

Nick came up on stage after the song and shook his head at Lily.

'You're marvellous up there. You have real stage presence,' he said and she smiled at him.

'Thank you and so do you. All the girls will be in love with you as Freddy.' She smiled and he gave her a shy smile in return.

'Oh I don't think about that sort of thing,' he said and he scuffed his shoe on the floor.

Looking behind him she saw Jess observing them from across the room.

'I think Jess still has feeling towards you,' she remarked softly. 'You really do need to sort it out.'

'I don't care what Jess thinks, to be honest,' he said and he smiled at her again. 'She doesn't want me, she just doesn't want anyone else to want me.'

Lily felt herself blush. Was he saying he thought she wanted him or was he sending her a message about himself?

He paused. 'I know we see each other here and at the cottage, but I would like to see you outside of your gran's and rehearsals. Do you think you'd like to have dinner with me?'

Lily paused. Dinner. With Brad Pitt, the nurse?

But if it went weird then they had to do the show together and it was already awkward enough with Jessica.

'Um, I don't think that would be...'

'I mean just as friends,' he said.

'Oh great, then sure,' she said, feeling a little disappointed it was just as friends, but she also knew it was for the best for the show.

'Excellent. Do you like Indian food?'

'Of course,' she said. Nick smiled at her and she bit her lip as she smiled back.

Who was she kidding? She had a crush on Nick and she was pretty sure that he had one on her, but what was a little breaking of poppadoms between friends? It couldn't hurt; they could work on their chemistry on stage. Nothing serious, she told herself, just a summer friendship.

Sixteen

Lily and Gran settled into a slow-paced routine that was working and, at times, Lily even wondered if Gran wasn't just a little bit less tired and a little feistier than when she had first moved in.

The mornings were the busiest time of day. To avoid waking Gran, who slept a little later, Lily would get up early and make her way around the property in a quiet manner, opening curtains, opening the back door and allowing Mr Mistoffelees to go out into the garden. Depending on the weather first thing, she would turn on the heater to warm up the room for Gran and then she would make a pot of tea.

She snuck out of the back door as the first light of dawn rose over the horizon. She had always been an early riser and it was even better watching the sky lighten at Gran's house. She held a warm mug of tea in her hands as she made her way into the garden and moved the old metal chair that gave a scrape on some bricks. She winced, hoping that the sound wouldn't wake Gran.

She sat down in the overgrown garden, the wet grass soaking the hem of her pyjama bottoms, and surveyed the space. She really did want to tidy it up for Gran but between the rehearsals for the show and caring for Gran, there was little time for anything else.

It was a shame, because she could remember when the flower beds had once been meticulously maintained instead of the tangled mess of weeds and wildflowers they were now. She felt a dull ache in her chest at the sight of it, reminded of Gran's age. She knew Gran couldn't live forever but she hadn't thought about what it would be like when she died. It was too much to bear to even think about.

A small blackbird jumped onto the branch of the gnarled old apple tree where the fruit was starting to form. Once she and Gran used to pick the apples, but she doubted they had been harvested in ten years or more.

Mr Mistoffelees appeared out of the thicket like a shadow that had been given form and, in his elegant manner, he jumped onto the little table next to her, fixing her with his golden gaze as if to say, 'Where is my breakfast?'

Lily mumbled, 'I'm sorry, Your Majesty,' as she scratched behind his ears repeatedly. While he was curled up against her leg, he uttered his contrition for her.

Before taking a look around the garden, Lily took a sip of her tea, a strong builder's tea with a splash of milk, feeling it warm her as she swallowed it down.

Even though the garden was wild, there was a certain charm about it, she thought as she looked around. There was a trellis that was broken, and honeysuckle climbed over it in a random manner, but the sweet perfume of honeysuckle mixed with the earthy smell of damp dirt surrounded her with its heavy scent.

The blackbird had a friend now, she noticed, as it hopped about with a worm in its mouth, then it flew into the thicket and she could just hear some birds chirping.

'You stay away from the nest,' she told Mr Mistoffelees, but he seemed uninterested in anything as his eyes closed in the morning sun.

She watched the morning rise in the garden, with some butterflies busy with the dandelions and a little bee looking for somewhere to land, and she began to imagine what she could accomplish with the space there. In one of the garden beds, she could replant the vegetables or some tomatoes. Gran had always had a taste for fresh tomatoes – she made a beautiful chutney – and maybe she could add some herbs in that sunny nook. It would be more than possible for her to clear a path and possibly install a small water feature for the birds if she had time.

Mr Mistoffelees stretched into a languid pose across the table, as though showing off for an invisible audience.

She envisioned Gran sitting out here on warm afternoons, ordering Lily about with a pleased smile on her worn face as she instructed her granddaughter on how to weed properly or how to stake up the tomatoes.

The sound of a window opening on the upper floor broke her daydreaming. Gran was up. She would want to shower and dress and then be down for her own cup of tea and breakfast. In most cases, it consisted of something straightforward, sometimes porridge with a touch of honey or scrambled eggs on toast. As Gran's appetite had diminished, Lily focused on good food in small portions so Gran didn't feel overwhelmed.

Lily drained the dregs of her cold tea and she rose up and walked inside with Mr Mistoffelees following her.

Lily's resolve grew stronger as she made her way back inside, thinking what a lovely project this would be. She turned before she shut the back door and took one last look at the overgrown paradise. She was already mentally preparing lists of the seeds she needed to purchase and the tools she would require.

She ran upstairs and knocked on the door.

'You need me to help you?' she asked cheerfully.

'No, dear, I'll be down soon,' Gran said and Lily went downstairs to get things ready for their breakfast. She had some crumpets and honey this morning, which would be a lovely treat, she thought as her phone rang. She saw Nick's name and a little thrill ran through her. It was silly, she knew, but it was nice to have a distraction.

'Morning,' she said to him.

'Morning to you too. How's things in Appleton Green?'

'Busy, busy, you know, rushing about, all of the things that need to be done.' She laughed. 'How are you?'

'Great, about to visit a patient, but do you want to do dinner tonight? I can pick you up around seven?'

Lily paused. 'Can we make it earlier? I don't want Gran to be alone too late. I came home the other night and she had sat up for me and fallen asleep in her chair and was a bit rickety the next morning.'

'Of course, actually, why don't I bring dinner over? I can pick it up on the way to you and the three of us can have something to eat. It might be nice for her to have a change in cuisine. That's if she likes Indian food? I can bring her anything to be honest. Whatever the queen desires.'

Lily smiled. 'She's fine with a little butter chicken and rice. She eats like a bird so don't bring too much.'

'Okay, I'll come over at six with the food. How's that?'

'That's perfect, and thank you for being so understanding,' she said.

'It's not a big deal. I'm looking forward to it,' he said. 'Got to run, got to check on a broken arm.'

'Bye,' she said with a smile as she put down the phone.

Not long after, Gran was downstairs and at her seat, buttering a crumpet.

'So what's news this morning?' she asked Lily, who was already on her second crumpet.

'Well Nick is coming for dinner,' she said cheerfully.

'Is he? How nice. What will we make?' Gran asked, looking pleased at the news.

'Well, he's bringing Indian takeaway, if that's okay? A bit of a treat for us all.'

Gran nodded. 'That sounds lovely. What a nice thing to look forward to. He is turning into a lovely friend, isn't he?' She gave Lily a knowing look, and she laughed in return.

'Don't get any ideas – it's not like that. I'm only here for the summer,' she said and she crinkled her nose at her grandmother.

Gran laughed. 'You really are a terrible liar,' she said. 'And besides, summers turn into autumns that turn into winters and then into springs. Don't say no to the possibility for love. It doesn't come around often,' Gran said. 'I thought your grandfather was just a friend to go to a dance with and we ended up dancing for many years after.' She paused, thinking. 'I wish it had been more years though. I didn't realise it would be so short in the scheme of my life.'

Lily reached over and took Gran's hand. 'It's very unfair for you. I wish I had met him.'

Gran nodded, a glaze of tears in her old eyes. 'He would have loved you, Lily,' she said and then she shook her head, as though shaking away the memories. 'Oh well, enough about that. What else is news?' Gran brushed her hand off and with it her mood.

Lily met her grandmother's change of topic with her own. 'I was thinking I should fix up the garden.'

Gran took another bite of her crumpet and chewed slowly with her eyebrows raised quizzically at Lily.

'What? I thought I could weed it all and plant some vegetables and some tomatoes, maybe pick some apples?'

Gran swallowed and took a sip of tea. 'Why?' she asked.

'Why what?' Lily was confused.

'Why do you want to plant the garden up?' Gran asked again.

'I just thought it would be nice,' Lily said, feeling a little less sure of her decision now.

'Having a cup of tea is nice. Building a garden is work.'

'I know. I'm not afraid of work.' Lily frowned as she spoke.

'I know, but you won't be here to harvest it,' said Gran. 'And I can't be out there. That's why it's in the state it's in.' Gran's tone was matter-of-fact, dismissive perhaps; Lily wasn't sure.

Lily was silent. 'I suppose,' she said.

Gran shrugged. 'Don't plant anything you don't plan on staying to harvest, my girl.'

Lily thought about Nick and their growing flirtation. Perhaps she needed to think a little more sensibly about it all, especially with Jess back home. And besides, she had no idea how he thought of her; she was probably delusional, she thought, and she set about cleaning up breakfast.

When Gran was settled in her chair after breakfast, Lily sat outside in the sunshine. The very fact that Gran said she didn't want her to start anything she wasn't planning to finish seemed to tease her even more, and she looked around and pulled a weed from the path, and then another, and soon she had weeded around the area where she was sitting.

Pulling out what you don't want in your garden isn't a bad thing, she told herself as she looked around. It wasn't as fun or interesting as planting, but it was still good to see where the room was for new possibilities.

Seventeen

Nerves had somehow made their way to Pippin Cottage and Lily found herself fussing over the kitchen table before Nick arrived. She brushed out imaginary wrinkles in the faded embroidered tablecloth, which had seen better days but was still Gran's favourite. Gran had also insisted the fine china be taken from the chiffonier and washed and set out for their takeaway Indian dinner.

Lily had put her foot down at Gran's suggestion of the old brass candlesticks.

'He'll think he's walking into a seance,' she said to her grandmother.

'He might be. You never know what ghosts are around these cottages,' Gran said. 'I've been seeing your grandfather more often lately. He's often standing in the garden, just by the apple tree near the fence.'

'Okay, well say hi to him from me,' said Lily jokingly. She seemed to be moving things for no reason and checking the wine in the fridge was cold enough. 'It doesn't feel cold,' she said as she opened the fridge again.

'It can't get cold, as you keep opening the refrigerator. Please, Lily dear, stop fidgeting,' Gran said from her armchair. 'It's only Nick, not the Queen of Sheba.'

Lily felt her cheeks warm. 'I know,' she said. 'Sorry, I'm overthinking.'

'I'm sure he'll think the table and its setter are lovely, no matter what.' Gran's voice had a knowing smugness to it, Lily thought, and before she could react, the doorbell rang, setting her heart racing.

She had worn a white linen skirt and a simple silk T-shirt in a lovely cornflower blue and her feet were bare. Her hair was pulled into a bun and she had tiny daisy earrings in each ear. She adjusted her T-shirt, took a deep breath, and went and opened it.

Nick stood on the doorstep, holding a bouquet of wildflowers in one hand and a large carry bag of food in the other. His hair was messy, as usual, and he was in jeans and a button-down shirt in a pale lemon. Lily's stomach flipped slightly as she saw him and his smile.

'Hi,' she said, suddenly feeling like a tongue-tied teenager. She had been fine around him until now and suddenly she was being pathetic.

Nick's effortless smile lit up his handsome face. 'Hello yourself. These are for you,' he continued, presenting the flowers. 'And this,' he explained, holding up the bag of food, 'is our dinner.'

'It's perfect,' Lily replied, smiling as she accepted both. 'Come in. Gran's excited to see you.'

As they walked into the living room, Gran looked up from her newspaper as though she hadn't been waiting for him to arrive all afternoon, her blue eyes beaming. 'Nicholas, it is nice to see you. What a lovely idea this is.'

Nick bent to kiss Gran's cheek. 'Hello, Violet, you're looking well. I can take that dressing off tomorrow.'

'You're back tomorrow? You might as well move in,' teased Gran. 'We'd like that, wouldn't we, Lil?'

Lily shot her a look but Gran's smile was so serene, Lily was sure Gran was batting her eyelashes in innocence.

Lily took the food from the plastic containers and transferred it into serving bowls, which she placed on the table.

'Dinner is ready,' she said theatrically to the other two.

'Let me help you, Violet,' said Nick, assisting her up to standing and then walking the short distance alongside her walking frame.

Soon they were seated, wine was poured and plates laden and they tucked into the delicious, fragrant food.

Dinner was lovely, with Nick entertaining Gran with stories from the hospital and asking her many questions about Gran's youth. As Lily listened she realised that there was still so much she didn't know about her grandmother.

Most of the time, Lily found herself watching Nick. How his eyes crinkled when he chuckled, the delicate way he replenished Gran's water glass without being asked, and the warmth in his voice as he chatted with Gran. It was all wonderful. Comfortable. He seemed very at home in this cosy little cabin with her and Gran.

Gran regaled them with stories from her youth, and her marriage and raising Lily's dad and having Lily stay for the holidays.

Nick, for his part, listened intently, laughing at the appropriate moments and asking just the right questions to keep Gran engaged, but after dinner and a cup of tea and a shortbread biscuit, Lily could see Gran was fading.

As the evening progressed, Gran's yawns increased. 'I think it's about time this old lady turned in,' she said, struggling to her feet.

Both Lily and Nick moved to assist her, but Gran turned them away. 'I'm not completely decrepit yet,' she admitted with a wink. 'Goodnight, dears. Nicholas, it was nice to have you over for dinner. Thank you for bringing such a delicious assortment of delights and I will see you tomorrow,' she said and she moved with her walker to the stairs.

'Goodnight, Violet,' Nick murmured, gently. 'Thank you for having me.'

Once Gran had climbed the stairs, the room fell silent. Lily busied herself clearing the table, acutely conscious of Nick's presence as he insisted on helping.

'You don't have to do that,' Lily objected as Nick started scraping plates into the rubbish bin.

He smiled at her over his shoulder. 'I want to. Besides, if we do the dishes now then you won't have a mess when you wake up.'

They settled into a comfortable rhythm, Lily drying while Nick washed. The domesticity of it all didn't escape her, and she found herself wondering what life would be like with a man like Nick. She had dated in London, and had a boyfriend while at college, but the performing world wasn't conducive to long-term relationships.

'Penny for your thoughts?' Nick's voice interrupted her thinking.

Lily blinked, realising she had been staring at the same plate for about a minute. 'Oh, just... thinking about London.'

'Do you miss it?' he asked as he rinsed off a plate.

She thought for a moment. 'I don't actually. I mean I've been busy here. In London I have more time but I do nothing with it. I work two jobs but the shifts are becoming few and far between and then there are auditions.' She paused.

'Actually, and this is a secret...' she said. Nick put down the scrubbing brush and leaned against the sink. Dammit, why did he look so handsome?

'I have been teaching singing and piano at home. That's how I've been supplementing my income.'

Nick frowned, his face confused. 'Why is that a secret? It sounds like an entirely sensible thing to do.'

Lily sighed, 'There's this idea, that to resort to teaching means you've failed. It's weird, and hard to explain but you're supposed to be doing it, not teaching other people how to do it.'

She picked up a bowl and started to dry it with the checked tea towel.

'Yes it's weird,' said Nick. 'But it's also a bit elitist. I mean how else are people supposed to learn?'

'I know,' Lily said. 'And the worst thing about it...' She paused. She hadn't yet admitted this to anyone and here she was spilling her secrets over sudsy water to her grandmother's nurse. 'It's the most rewarding and fulfilling thing I do in London. I can't explain why but I love it. I love encouraging people and seeing their faces when they learn the tricky bars in the song or hit the note I knew they could reach.'

'That's amazing, Lily; maybe you should do it full-time and give up the other jobs you have. Is it worth it financially?'

She nodded. 'Yes, it is, but my mother would be furious and most of my college friends would think I had failed.'

Nick rinsed the last dishes and then cleaned the sink the way a health professional would, so it was shining and whistle-clean.

'Let me understand this. Your mother and friends would rather you drag yourself around London for horrible jobs on a minimum wage than teach what you're good at in the safety of your own flat and make more money for less work?'

Now that he said it out loud, she realised how stupid it sounded. 'Well Nigel my housemate knows, but when I told my mother I didn't want to take the place at the college to do performing, I wanted to be a music teacher, she told me that I was wasting my talent.'

He stared at her for what felt like a lifetime. 'Thank you for sharing that with me, Lily,' he said. She swallowed, aware the energy between then had changed. Lily became acutely aware of how close they were standing and the warmth emanating from Nick's body.

'Lily,' she heard Gran's voice say from upstairs. 'Can you bring me my heartburn medicine? The butter chicken seems to have stayed in my chest.'

'Of course,' she said and smiled at Nick. 'I should go and check on her.'

He picked up his car keys and wallet that he had left on the bench.

'Thank you for the dinner,' she said. 'It was lovely.'

Nick nodded. 'It was a great night. Thank you for hosting.'

'See you at rehearsals,' she said, and he nodded and then left her alone in the cottage, wondering what would have happened just before Gran called down. Perhaps she was imagining it all; it had been a while since she had any sort of flirtation with a man.

Get it together, Baxter, she told herself. *You're acting like a silly lovestruck ingénue and he is just being nice. You've been attention-starved for too long. Time to grow up and stop acting like a teenager.*

She picked up Gran's tablets and turned off the lamps and locked the doors.

Act Two

Eighteen

For a week Lily had dreamed of trying to kiss Nick, but every time they got close Jessica was there. It was becoming uncomfortable at rehearsals, as she was sure she was red every time she spoke to him, and Jessica wasn't letting up with her overtly friendly manner with Nick and her snide asides to Lily.

In the morning one week after their dinner, she went to the bathroom, washed her face and applied some skincare and cleaned her teeth and then grabbed her script and went downstairs to set up breakfast.

When Gran was downstairs, they were sitting in silence as they ate, Lily learning her lines and Gran reading the newspaper, when her phone sounded a text.

Feel like running lines? she read from Nick. I'm behind.

Lily smiled as she typed back.

'Who is that?' asked Gran, peering over her glasses frames at Lily.

'Nosy Nora,' said Lily with a laugh.

'I have to be. I don't get texts. All my friends died before they could even work out how to open a phone, let alone send a message.'

Lily made a sad face. 'That must be hard, seeing your friends pass before you.'

Gran nodded. 'It's lonely,' she admitted.

Lily reread the message. 'It's Nick. He want to run lines for the show,' she said.

Gran pretended to bat her eyelashes.

Lily ignored her and typed back: Sure, you working today? I'm home with Gran all day.

I'm off today, so I'll come by mid-morning.

Come for lunch, she typed back.

Done, see you at 12.30.

She put down her phone.

'He's coming for lunch and then to run lines,' she said. 'We can run them in the garden.'

Gran smiled. 'I used to love learning a script. Now I can't remember my own birthday some days, which is just as well because then I don't have to think about how old I am.' She cackled to herself and Lily laughed.

'If you didn't know how old you are, like take away the old bones and aches, how old do you feel in your heart?' she asked Violet.

The old woman paused, thinking for a moment.

'Probably thirty-four. I was happy, pregnant, living here. Martin was alive; it was all so lovely and perfect.'

Lily smiled. 'That's gorgeous.'

'What about you?' asked Violet.

Lily sighed and closed her eyes. 'I think, to be honest.' She opened them. 'I feel about twelve in my heart, when I was here with you and everything was so simple and easy.'

Violet reached for Lily's hand. 'You know it can still be simple and easy.'

'Being a grown-up is hard.' Lily sighed. 'I'm twenty-nine, no real career success, no boyfriend or family. I don't even own a house and I'm in a local village show, which is the only leading role I've had in a year. I'm a bit of a failure.'

'Don't speak about the person I love like that,' Gran admonished. 'You're not a failure; you're just a little bit lost. Stay the course, see where this path takes you.'

As Lily cleaned up after breakfast and prepared a plate of meats and salad for lunch, she thought about Gran's words. *See where this path takes you.*

For the past twenty-nine years she had been on a path that hadn't given her much joy. Everyday felt hard and as though she were dragging herself through a field of rocks and potholes. Nothing had really grown in it and here she was wishing she was twelve again. What would she have done differently? she wondered.

It was a scary thought to even consider she might have had another path than the one she had taken. Her talent had forced her on this path, to say she didn't want to pursue singing felt like she was ignoring the god of music and singing, who had bestowed it upon her. But who was the god? If she was honest with herself, it was her mother who had pushed Lily on this path. And Lily, being the only child, was afraid to try anything else. Denise wanted this for Lily more than Denise seemed to want anything for herself.

At twelve thirty, Nick arrived with some fresh cherries from the roadside stall and a bottle of lemonade.

'You are a keeper,' said Gran to him as she stole a cherry from the punnet.

'How are you feeling, Violet?' he asked, sitting down on the sofa.

'Fine, I'm excellent – feeling thirty-four again.' She laughed.

Lily leaned against the doorframe to the kitchen. 'She's wicked, I tell you that much,' she said with a smile. Nick looked up at her and she felt her stomach flip.

'Like grandmother like granddaughter,' he said and she nodded.

'Bring your script?' she asked. 'I thought we could work in the garden so we don't annoy Gran.'

After Lily entered the garden, Nick followed her out while carrying the lemonade and cherries that he had brought with him. As the bees settled down at the iron table and chairs that Lily had put up in the shade, the afternoon sun was warm but not oppressive, and the soft hum of the bees floated on the air. After she had poured each of them a glass of water, she moved the punnet of cherries in the direction of Nick and thumbed the wet condensation that was already forming tiny droplets on the sides of the glasses.

After popping a cherry into his mouth and tossing the stem into the plate that Lily had brought out, Nick smiled. 'It really is lovely. No wonder you enjoy being here so much.

While staring out across the garden, Lily gave a slight nod. The heavy heads of the hydrangeas were swaying gently in the breeze thanks to the fact that they were in full bloom. 'To me, it has always seemed like a safe haven. I can be completely myself here.'

'And you couldn't at home?' Nick questioned when he was reclining in his chair. He had his gaze set on her, and she could sense the way his eyes searched her face.

After a moment of hesitation, Lily looked down at her glass. 'There are times,' she said carefully. She paused. 'That it feels like life has already written the script for me, and I am merely playing along.'

Nick cocked his head to the side, a crease appearing on his forehead. 'What exactly do you mean?'

She let out a sigh as she reached for a cherry. 'I mean, do you ever get the feeling that you're unable to change the direction that you're heading in? Consider the following scenario: you are adhering to a plan that was devised for you by another individual, and you are too afraid to deviate from it because... what if there is nothing else?'

Nick thought for a moment and then he leaned forward and rested his arms on the table. 'I think everyone has experienced that at some point in their lives. The question for you is, can you rewrite your own story now?'

'Have you always wanted to be a nurse?'

He shook his head. 'Nope, I actually thought I wanted to be a doctor but I didn't get the marks, so I thought I'd try nursing and then try and get into university for medicine. And then I started nursing and haven't thought about being a doctor again. I think I get to do more in this role, and I love talking to people and the change of patients and being able to zip about and help people in their own homes. Like Gran – helping her has been a highlight.' He smiled at her and she felt her stomach flutter, but she also felt a faint sinking in her chest. It was obvious that Nick had everything figured out. At all times, he gave off the impression of being so stable, so confident in himself, as if he was completely aware of his place in the world. In comparison, it made her feel even more disorientated and confused. He probably thought she was a flake.

She sighed. 'I wish I had that kind of certainty. I can't help but feel I'm on the wrong road. Nothing is really happening and I can't continue like this. I don't even know if I still enjoy it or if I'm just doing it because… well, because I don't know what else I'd do and this was all I was told I could do.'

Nick gazed at her for a brief period. His blue eyes seemed brighter in the light. 'I don't think it's ever too late to change paths. You always have the option to try something else if you find that something isn't making you happy. Change doesn't have to be bad but, Lily, this is your life. The choice of what you want it to be is entirely up to you. I mean who else is pushing you?'

She wondered if she could explain her mother to him without sounding completely pathetic.

'My mum, she really wants this for me. I would disappoint her, and probably Gran. I mean she adores the theatre.'

Nick shrugged. 'But they've had their turn; this is your turn. You can do something different. It won't make the world stop, I promise.'

It felt as if his words were hanging in the air between them, laden with possibility. What would it look like if she changed her life? She wanted to believe him, but the idea of beginning over, of abandoning everything she had worked for, seemed inconceivable to her; yet he made it seem so simple, attainable.

A slight grin formed on Lily's face as the sincerity in his voice pulled at something that was buried deep within her. 'It sounds easy when you say it, but I don't know how to do anything else.' There was a small lack of confidence in her voice. She couldn't explain how raw and exposed she felt as she sat with him, yet it also felt safe to tell him she was questioning her future.

When Nick leaned forward once more, this time with his elbows resting on the table, the space that separated them felt electrified and electric for a brief instant. 'So what would you do if you could do anything? Would you want the big career on the stage? Eight shows a week for a year or more for the rest of your life? Or what else would you want? How does your life look if you didn't have that?'

'I don't have that now.' She laughed ruefully.

If she was truthful with herself and Nick, she would admit she had never even dared to think about what her life might be like if she deviated from her road to the West End.

'Perhaps... I mean, I might decide to remain here. Work in the garden, help Gran, and consider teaching singing rather than performing. I do love teaching but like I said some people see it as failure. But most of all...' She paused, watching a bee hovering about a geranium in the sun. 'I think I want something less complicated.'

'That doesn't sound like failure to me,' he said. 'It sounds like a nice life, and I for one would be thrilled if you stuck around.'

Lily felt her cheeks blushing and the butterflies weren't just in the garden. She opened her mouth to speak, but the way he was looking at her, with such a low-key intensity, caused her words to become stuck in her throat.

They both fell silent for a considerable amount of time. It seemed as though the world was getting smaller, with the sounds of the garden receding into the background until it was just the two of them, seated at that small iron table, the space between them being filled with many possibilities for the future.

Then Nick was the one who broke the stillness. He picked up his script and cleared his throat.

'I think we better get on with the lines,' but his tone had been more subdued and somewhat reluctant recently.

Lily couldn't shake the feeling that something had changed between them as they began to read their lines. She wasn't quite ready to describe it, but it felt lovely, like the sound of the orchestra warming up before words on the page became jumbled together, and her concentration began to waver as her thoughts continued to dwell on Nick, thinking about the way he had looked at her and the way he had spoken to her, as if he had recognised her for who she truly was.

But he had given her something else other than a crush; she had the tiniest glimpse of hope for the very first time in a long time – hope that something else was waiting for her. She just had to be open to it, and if Nick was by her side, she might even find something truly special.

Nineteen

Another week passed without Lily seeing Nick other than at rehearsals. He seemed distracted but still attentive to her when she spoke to him, but she noticed Jessica and he didn't speak at all; in fact, they seemed to be avoiding each other.

But she wasn't about to ask and Jessica was leaving her alone, which was a relief, but she wondered what had happened.

After rehearsals on Saturday afternoon, Nick came to her side.

'You around tomorrow?'

'I think so, why?' she asked with a smile. 'Need more help with your lines?'

'I'm nearly off book, I think.' He laughed. 'Do you want to go on a picnic with me?'

She was surprised by his offer. 'A picnic?'

'Yes, I know it sounds twee, but I have a lovely spot I wanted to show you. It's fine if you can't – no stress,' he said and she noticed a red flush up his neck.

'That sounds lovely,' she said firmly. 'I can't wait.'

Nick's face burst into a wide smile and he nodded. 'Excellent, wonderful, I'll pick you up before midday?'

'Picking up? Where are you two off to?' Jessica's voice interrupted them.

Nick turned to her. 'I'm taking Lily and her grandmother to an appointment,' he said.

'On a Sunday?' Jessica narrowed her eyes.

Lily watched his face change as Jessica spoke.

'I'm going. Have a nice night, everyone,' she said and she walked out of the hall, wondering why he had lied to Jessica about their picnic and if this was going to be a problem.

Lily wore her sundress with the little daisies on it, which Jess had said looked like wallpaper, and, at the last minute, she pulled a denim jacket on and tied her hair up in a bun as she looked in the mirror in her bedroom. She felt a mix of excitement and nervousness. She had agreed to the picnic, but what did that mean? And why didn't he tell Jessica? She understood that Jessica was hard work but this felt far too duplicitous for her. Maybe he just wanted to protect her?

The doorbell rang, interrupting her thoughts. 'Lily?' Gran called. 'There is a nice young man at the door. Should I send him away?

Lily couldn't help but laugh. 'No, Gran. Tell him I'll be right down.'

When she descended the stairs, she noticed Nick and Gran talking happily in the living room. Gran in her chair and Nick on the sofa.

As Lily walked in, he looked up and smiled warmly, making her heart skip a beat.

'Ready?' he questioned.

Lily nodded and quickly kissed Gran on the cheek. 'Don't get into too much trouble while I'm gone,' she warned.

Gran waved them off with a knowing smile. 'You two are having fun. And, Nick, make sure you get her back at a reasonable hour or she will turn into a pumpkin. It's a genetic thing,' she joked.

Lily kissed her grandmother goodbye. 'You're incorrigible,' she said.

'Good,' said Gran. 'I plan on remaining that way. Now off you go.'

Soon they were driving through the countryside, in Nick's work car.

'Why did you lie to Jessica about today?' she asked.

'Wow, okay, straight into it,' he said as he drove.

'It made me feel uncomfortable,' she said.

'I know, me also,' he replied. 'But the less Jessica knows about me and you the better. She's got a way of twisting things and I didn't want her to ruin this, because I like you, a lot,' he said and he glanced at Lily.

She felt herself blush again, and she nodded. 'I think I understand.'

'It's just this is new, and I like you and I don't want it being ruined before it's started.'

She wanted to ask if he meant friendship or more but said nothing. There was enough tension in the air.

'So, where do you live?' she asked him instead. 'I don't really know anything about you. Give me the Nick life's story.'

He laughed. 'Okay, I'm thirty-three, parents still married. Dad works in government and Mum is a nursery school teacher. I have two sisters, both older. One is a nurse – she influenced me to be a nurse, she loved it so much. The other sister runs the foodbank in Silverton.'

'Gosh, your whole family is so community-minded,' Lily said.

'Maybe, I mean we're a normal family, it's just I suppose we like helping people. It's how I grew up; it doesn't mean everyone has to do that,' he said. 'We can't all do one thing; everyone brings their special something to the world.'

Lily thought for a moment. 'You're right, that's true. Sometimes I used to wonder that my pursuit of being on the West End was shallow, ego-driven.'

'I get it,' said Nick. 'But probably it's because you love to sing and act and dance and wanted to share it with audiences. Because my family and others are the ones in the audience; it gives us the relief from the hard day or difficult jobs. Everyone matters.'

'I like that,' she said. 'So do you live at home?'

'No.' He laughed. 'I bought a little flat in Silverton, close to Mum and Dad but not too close.' He gave Lily a look and she nodded.

'Yes, my mother would have me live next door if she could, but still ensure I was close to the theatre.'

'It's a nice flat; I bought it last year. I mean it's nothing flash – nurses' wages, you know,' he said.

'Do you like living in Silverton?'

'I've lived there all my life. I don't know any different,' he said. 'I mean it's okay, not much community, you know but it's nice enough. I don't think I would stay there forever. I'd like to live somewhere like Appleton Green, doing district nursing like I do already; but the cottages are few and far between,' he said. 'Tell me about your place in London.'

'It's a nice flat, not big – it's just Nigel and me. We don't own it or anything; we rent it.'

Nick nodded and they drove for a bit.

She looked out the window, mentally comparing the scene to her life in London. The rolling hills draped in emerald, sheep like little white dots in the distance, and then there was London, all severe angles and steel and so many people on the streets.

There were no tall buildings around her here; rather, there were ancient dry-stone walls that crisscrossed the landscape and told stories from ages before. And the sounds. London seemed to have a continual soundtrack, day and night; but here, well it was silent, apart from the bleating of sheep, the rustling of leaves, and the soft babble of some secret streams.

Lily thought about her return, and if she and Nick turned into something more. No, there was no point thinking about that when she was going back to London and he didn't like it. Friends they would have to be, she decided.

As they drove through countryside, Lily felt a sense of belonging that she hadn't experienced in years as they travelled through lovely villages. She turned to gaze at Nick, whose profile was highlighted by the warm sunlight. She pondered the possibility that she had been pursuing the wrong goal the entire time. Lily had always considered London to be a symbol of success; however, while she was in this location, with this man, she'd started to wonder if she had been wrong all along.

As soon as they turned off the main road, Nick led the vehicle down a short lane that appeared to disappear into the countryside.

'So, where are we going?' she asked, hoping to relieve the gnawing feeling inside her of doubt and worry.

'We were almost there.' he said. The car bumped gently off the narrow country road and into a small roadside parking area near the entrance to Lathkill Dale. A simple wooden gate led to the footpath.

'Right, short work but it's worth it.' Nick said as he stopped the car. They got out of the car and Nick went around to the boot and opened it, pulling out a picnic basket.

'Wow, I can't believe you have an actual picnic basket.' She laughed as they walked. 'Or did you buy it for this occasion?'

'That's for me to know,' he said, 'It's actually my mum's.'

They settled on a little grassy area that was tucked away between limestone cliffs and was hidden from view by ash and hazel trees.

'Oh this is lovely. I haven't been here in years,' Lily cried, looking around. 'And there's no one here.'

'It's a Thursday, not a popular day for picnics,' Nick laughed as he opened the large basket, took out a rug and shook it out for them to sit on.

Their quiet hideaway was accompanied by the calming sound of the River Lathkill's gentle gurgle.

Lily felt her anxiety subside as she sat on the rug and looked around.

'I don't think I've ever been on a picnic where the man did everything,' she said. She could see some wildflowers scattered across the grass and remembered their names from Gran's lessons. Bluebells, cowslips and harebells that were nodding in the gentle breeze, as though offering their approvals to Nick and Lily's plans.

'It's very beautiful.' Lily exhaled as she lay down, her hands over her eyes. The sun was warm on her body and she sat up and took off her denim jacket and folded it and put it under her head for a pillow.

Nick stretched out beside her on the blanket and she became acutely aware of him.

She put her hand down next to her and put her little finger out and felt his hand and he took hers in his. The electricity between them, even holding hands, was powerful and she leaned up on her side to face him.

'You know we're supposed to be friends,' she said.

'Friends hold hands,' he said rolling over to face her, lying in the same position.

'Oh? And what else do friends do?' she teased, feeling the butterflies back. This was a bad idea, she told herself, but she couldn't seem to stop; she was so drawn to him.

He leaned forward and kissed her cheek.

'They do that,' he said in a low voice.

She nodded slowly, as though considering what he had just done.

'And what else?' she asked, biting her lip briefly, as her eyes searched his face.

'They do this,' he said, his voice low, and he leaned forward and kissed her on the mouth.

She wasn't sure if it was the outdoors, or the sound of his voice, or the isolation, but she had never felt as much desire as she felt on that blanket with the sound of the water and the birds surrounding them.

'We shouldn't be doing this, but don't stop,' Lily said as they kissed on the blanket. He had pulled her on top of him and she felt his desire as she ran her hand under his T-shirt, her finger tracing over his stomach.

'Jesus,' he moaned and he flipped her onto her back, pulling the straps of her sundress down and kissing her skin.

'God, you're so sexy,' he said to her and she laughed.

'What?' He stopped for a moment. 'You don't think you are? Because I can tell you, you are – so gorgeous,' he said and his hands moved down her back.

'You said just friends. I insisted on just friends and we can't keep our hands off each other. We're useless,' she said and laughed and he joined in.

'You can't fight chemistry,' he said and she sighed.

'I just know I'll get feelings towards you besides lust and then I'll be sad and it will be weird and difficult when I leave. I'm a very sentimental person,' she said.

'What if I already had feelings besides desire?' he said, rolling onto his back and closing his eyes.

Lily hadn't expected that and she sat up and looked at him. 'Well that's different,' she said.

'How?' he asked.

'I don't know but it just is.' They were silent for a while.

'Is there anything in that basket or is it just for show?' she asked finally. 'Because I am starving.'

Nick grinned and sat up and opened it. 'Roast chicken, some cheeses and dips, a baguette, Greek salad and, for dessert, some brownies and strawberries.'

'Oh wow,' she said peering into the basket.

'And wine,' he said brandishing a bottle, and he opened it and poured them each a plastic glass of wine.

'On my days off, I enjoy exploring. It helps to clear my mind.' He paused and softly stated, 'I love it here, but I only ever come by myself.'

Lily felt a warm sensation flow through her, unrelated to the wine. 'What did you mean about your feelings, Nick?' she asked as she picked up some chicken and ate it. 'We don't have to discuss anything if you're not ready,' she said quickly.

Nick shook his head. 'No, I want to. You know I was with Jess, well it wasn't serious. She thought it was but I never was. She and I are very different. So when we broke up I told myself I would only pursue anyone who had the same values and interests as me. It's not like I usually meet people at work. I honestly thought I wouldn't meet anyone. I mean I work with old people most days,' he said with a laugh.

Lily smiled.

'And then I met you. I mean the first time I saw you at your gran's you were just so vibrant.'

'I was in a nightgown, a rugby top and odd socks,' she reminded him.

'I don't remember that. I just remember your energy and smile and your gorgeous hair.'

Never before had any man spoken to her this way and she put down the food and wiped her hands on a napkin.

'And the dinner at your gran's. God you are just so incredibly kind and patient. It's beautiful and it took my breath away. Kindness is an underrated quality; it's really beautiful,' he said.

Lily groaned.

'Too much?' he asked. 'I'm sorry.'

'No.' She shook her head. 'It's not too much.' She paused. 'I've just never felt so deeply about somebody so quickly before, and it scares me,' she said.

Nick reached out and clasped her hand in his. 'Why does it scare you?'

Lily took a deep breath. 'I came here for the summer to help Gran while also figuring out my life. I did not expect this. You. And now I don't know what to do. I thought I would spend my entire life in London.'

Nick nodded, drawing circles on her palm. 'Can I tell you something?' When Lily nodded, he said, 'I've never felt this way either. I've had relationships obviously, but meeting you, it feels different. It's as if I've been waiting for you without knowing it.'

Lily felt tears build in her eyes. 'But what happens when the summer ends? What about my career in London?'

Nick was silent for a minute, considering. 'I don't know all the answers, Lily. But I understand that what we have is unique. Perhaps instead of worrying about the future, we could just be present, right now. Maybe we just focus on getting to know one another and seeing where this leads.'

Lily looked at him closely. His gentle glance, the way the sun shone on the golden strands of his hair, the way his finger traced her palm. She thought of how much he cared for Gran, how he made her laugh, and how at ease she felt with him. It was almost too perfect.

'Okay,' she said gently.

Twenty

Lily slipped on her lightweight cardigan over her T-shirt and jeans and adjusted it as she stood before the mirror at Pippin Cottage. She and Nick were supposed to see a movie in Silverton and then have dinner. She ran downstairs to set Gran up for the evening.

Gran was organised with some delicious cold meats, salad and some cold hard-boiled eggs and a glass of white wine for dinner. Lily had got her a little tray table so she could eat it in her armchair and watch some of her favourite quiz shows while she ate.

'It's like I'm in first class on a plane,' Gran said when Lily had arranged everything.

'Have you ever been in first class on a plane?' Lily asked her with a smile.

'I've never been on a plane.' Gran giggled. 'But it's not too late. I might put it on my bucket list for when I turn one hundred.'

'Excellent,' Lily said as she saw Nick coming up the path through the window.

'Okay, Nick's here,' she said. 'I won't be late.'

Nick came into the cottage and kissed Lily on the cheek and then Violet.

'How are you, Violet?' he asked.

'Still alive, which is good news, I think.' She cackled to herself.

'You look beautiful,' he said to Lily and she felt the familiar flutter in her stomach when she was around him.

Soon they were on their way, chatting in the car when Nick's phone rang.

'It's my mum,' he said. 'I better get it. She doesn't usually ring at this time.' He took the call on his hands-free device.

'Hi, Mum, I'm in the car with Lily,' he said.

'Hello, Lily, I'm Maureen. Nick talks about you all the time. He says you have a lovely voice. We're looking forward to hearing you sing in the show.'

Lily grinned at Nick, knowing she was blushing. 'Thank you, Maureen, that's so nice to hear.'

'How can I help, Mum?' Nick said firmly, clearly trying to keep his mum on track.

'It's your father,' Maureen said, frustration in her voice.

'Okay, what about him?'

'He says he's going to get up the ladder,' Maureen said.

'Why?'

'Because the smoke alarm is beeping and the man can't come until tomorrow and he said if it doesn't stop he'll go and sleep in the garden if I don't let him change it.'

Nick shook his head, 'No, he's not getting up a ladder. Do you know how many people go to hospital being up ladders over fifty?'

'Yes, you and your sister are always telling me. That's why I'm calling you now.'

'We're on our way to a movie,' Nick said.

'It won't take long, I promise,' said Maureen. 'Otherwise he'll get up that ladder and you know he's a bit wobbly because of his tinnitus.'

Nick sighed and looked at Lily and mouthed the word 'sorry' to her but she stifled a giggle.

'Go,' she whispered.

'Okay, we'll be there soon,' he said and hung up the call.

'I'm so sorry,' he said. 'My dad can be a bit gung-ho and he's not quite as athletic as he thinks he is.'

'Don't stress about it. Family comes first; apart from that, this seems considerably more fun than any movie. I want to meet the family that raised this man.'

Nick laughed, relief clearly on his face. 'Oh God, this might be more than I bargained for. But thank you. You're fantastic.'

Lily was both excited and nervous as they travelled to Nick's parents' place. They drove through Silverton and to a residential area and stopped at the front of a suburban home, with a car in the driveway and a very busy garden filled with flowers, sweet art projects and wind chimes.

'Can you tell my mother is a nursery school teacher?' he asked as they walked up the path past a collection of wooden spoons stuck in a pot, each one representing someone in the family, all painted and decorated.

'That's very cute though,' said Lily, looking at the Nick the Nurse likeness. 'It's basically your mirror image.' She giggled.

'Rude,' he said and rang the bell. She heard dogs barking.

'That's Ziggy and Zola – Norwich terrors,' he said.

'You mean terriers,' she corrected.

'Nope, terrors,' he said as the door opened.

Maureen opened the door and hugged Nick and then hugged Lily.

'Oh okay, hi,' she said.

'This is so lovely. Come in, your dad is upstairs. Lily and I can have tea.'

'Mum, we're supposed to be going to a movie,' he said as two very cute small brown dogs jumped up at his legs.

Maureen looked disappointed at this news.

'It's fine, Nick. Let's not rush. You help your dad and maybe check the other alarms and I can find out everything about you from your mum.'

'Oh God, this might have been a mistake,' said Nick as he went upstairs.

Lily followed Maureen through the very eccentrically decorated house. Each room was painted a different colour and there was art on every wall, with indoor plants trailing down from hanging macramé holders.

'Your house is amazing,' said Lily looking around. 'I love it.'

'Oh that's nice to hear, Lily. Not everyone likes it. Jessica hated it,' she said and then made a face. 'Sorry, I shouldn't have mentioned her. I think I'm nervous. Nick doesn't bring his girlfriends home often.'

'I'm not really his girlfriend. I'm just here for the summer,' she said. The mention of Jess had deflated her mood. 'Did you like Jess?' she asked Maureen, wishing she didn't care but she did.

'I don't think she was possible to like,' whispered Maureen. 'She was very intimidating.'

Lily nodded. 'She's in the play. She doesn't like me very much.'

Maureen rolled her eyes as she poured hot water from the kettle into a brown teapot and put a knitted cosy in the shape of a strawberry on top of it. 'She doesn't like anyone very much,' Maureen said. 'Don't you worry about her.'

'How long did…' Lily was about to ask when Nick came into the kitchen.

'I need batteries. I'll check the others,' he said to his mum.

'I'll get some from the laundry,' she said and they left Lily alone in the kitchen.

She walked around the room, looking at Maureen's art and photos of the family.

Nick's sisters were very beautiful, she noticed. One of them was newly married and Nick looked handsome in the photo, wearing a suit.

She picked up another photo from the wedding of Nick and his sisters together. Jessica was in the background, looking at them with a furious expression on her face.

They had gone out long enough for her to go to his sister's wedding, she thought, and she put down the frame as Maureen came back into the kitchen.

'All sorted,' she said cheerfully.

'Now, tell me all about you,' Maureen asked and Lily paused.

'There's not much to tell,' she said but Maureen shook her head.

'No, not having that. Nick won't stop chatting about you: Lily does this, Lily said that. I want to know about the this and the that.'

Maureen opened a tin and put some lemon slices on a plate. 'Now let's take these into the living room, and I'm going to ask you fifty questions.'

'Only fifty?' joked Lily and soon she was sitting down, drinking tea and eating a slice, being grilled by Maureen about everything from her early childhood diseases to her favourite cocktail.

Nick came into the living room. 'Okay, all done,' he said, looking slightly harried.

'We need to head off soon,' he said to Lily.

'Do we?' she asked. 'We've missed the movie.'

'There's a later time,' he said. 'At a different cinema, and we can still make dinner after.'

'You could come back here for dinner,' said Maureen hopefully.

'Thanks, Mum, but we'll do it another time,' he said.

Lily put down her mug and plate as Nick's father came into the living room.

'Who's this then?' he asked. 'A new one? You go through them like socks.' The man laughed.

'Dad,' Nick said sharply.

'Only joking,' he said. 'I'm Mike, Mike Stafford.'

'Hi, I'm Lily,' she said trying to keep her tone light.

Nick went through girlfriends like socks. Was that a joke? It wasn't very funny.

'I know. He told me all about you,' he said with a warm smile and Lily felt herself relax a little but wondered what his sisters would think of her. *Don't worry about impressing them; you're only here for the summer*, she told herself. But the voice of doubt was in her head.

After she and Nick had left and they went to the movies, they sat through the film and she felt him reach for her hand.

She wondered if just spending the summer with Nick was realistic. She knew she was caring too much about what his family thought. It wasn't serious, she reminded herself. It was just a bit of fun.

At dinner, Nick looked at her. 'You know my father was joking about me having lots of girlfriends,' he said.

'It was a bit off-putting, I will admit,' she conceded.

'I know. He thinks he's funny. He's not,' Nick said with a sigh.

'And your mum brought up Jess,' she said.

'Oh God, was it about how she didn't like Mum's decorating?'

Lily nodded.

'I took Jess there once, before a rehearsal to pick something up, and she insisted on coming inside with me, even though I was only going to be a few minutes, and then she proceeded to walk about the house and tell Mum how bad the feng shui was with all of her plants and art.'

'That's so rude,' said Lily, aghast.

'I know. It was awful and Mum cried, and Jess couldn't understand what the fuss was about. Needless to say she never went back there.' He closed his eyes and shook his head.

'But she was at your sister's wedding,' she said. 'I saw her in the background of a picture, looking unhappy by the way.'

'Yes, do you know why?'

'Because she was invited?' she said.

'No, because she turned up at the church. She wasn't invited. We weren't even going out. She turned up, all dressed up, and I think she was expecting to then come to the wedding dinner with me.'

'Oh my God,' said Lily in shock.

'And she tried to get into the family pictures. When that one was taken of me and my sisters, I had just asked her to step out, as she'd joined in uninvited.'

'That's so embarrassing,' said Lily. 'And sort of sad.'

Nick nodded. 'I know, it's awful and weird. But in all honesty I haven't taken anyone home to meet Mum and Dad since university, I promise. I had a lovely girlfriend then, but she went to live in Australia and is now married to an Aussie, and it's all lovely and good for them. Jess and I were together for six months, then I realised she wasn't right for me and I broke it off.'

'Which she wasn't happy with.' The waiter brought them some bread and Lily picked some up and broke it into pieces and put it on her plate.

'No', Nick sighed. 'I'm sorry Lily,' He said but she waved her hand at him.

'No, I shouldn't have mentioned her, now let's order and talk about anything else but her, okay?' she said firmly.

Nick smiled. 'Yes. That sounds perfect.'

Twenty-one

Nick and Lily slipped into a routine with him coming over once a week to see Gran for dinner and rehearsing and ignoring Jessica's glares and snide asides. They went on little drives or did the grocery shopping together and mostly Nick was at Pippin Cottage.

'You're so kind to be here so much. I just can't leave Gran for long periods,' she said to Nick as they sat outside one day after he had visited Gran, and they drank tea in the garden together while Gran napped in her chair.

'It's fine, but I will admit I should have discharged her two weeks ago,' Nick said. 'I just come and check on her and then get to see you.'

Lily made a face. 'Oh no, I hope you don't get into trouble.'

'She's ninety-seven; she needs someone to check on her anyway. I just wrote in my notes that the granddaughter is very unreliable and skittish and Mrs Baxter needs a regular welfare visitor.'

Lily flicked a tea towel at him as Mr Mistoffelees jumped onto his lap, looking for attention.

'Oh finally he's decided to like me,' said Nick as he scratched behind the cat's ears.

Lily watched him, with his mug of tea and the cat, and wondered why she ever thought this life seemed so terrible.

Later that night, when she was talking to Nigel on one of their FaceTime calls, she told him about spending her days with Nick.

It was so wholesome she wondered if she wasn't living a fantasy, she told Nigel.

'He sounds perfect. Shame he's not in London.'

'I know. I have kind of hedged around it but he's not interested. He loves the country; in fact, I think this cottage and the way Gran lives is his secret fantasy life,' she half joked.

'Is it yours?' Nigel asked. She was about to laugh until she realised he was serious.

'Maybe when I was small,' she said. 'Life is very easy here, but it could get boring. Sometimes I love it and sometimes, it's just routine, looking after Gran.'

'But if you could have both? Doing shows and living in the country?'

Lily was silent. 'What's going on, Nigel? Why are you so encouraging for me to be here?'

Nigel sighed. 'I'm taking the extension on the tour. It's going to North America. I've signed on for another two years.'

'Wow, okay, wow,' Lily said. 'Gosh, that's a long time.'

'I know, but I've met someone,' he said.

'Oh, Nigel, that's lovely. Who is he?' Lily asked, feeling happy and sad at the same time.

'His name is Marcus and he's in makeup and I adore him and he me. He makes me laugh and I just want to be with him for the rest of my life. Corny?'

Lily shook her head. 'No, it's not. It's lovely and I'm so happy for you,' she said and she felt a tear fall. 'But I will be sad you're not here and I guess you'll move out? I'll have to rent your room out?'

Nigel nodded. 'Yes, I know. I can get my sister and brother-in-law to come over and get everything when the sublet finishes.'

'Okay,' said Lily. 'The end of an era – we have lived together for so long.'

'I know,' he said. 'But you can come and see me, come and have a holiday.'

Lily smiled. 'I will need to get a job first. The restaurant is closing and the call centre hasn't even offered me a shift.'

'You need to teach again. I heard how good some of those students got at the flat.'

Lily shrugged. 'Maybe, but it feels like failing.'

'Oh screw those stupid lecturers; that was their bitterness, not ours. The irony of being told you're a failure if you teach from a teacher is next-level nuts. I thought you realised that?'

Lily thought for a moment. 'You know, I didn't. I was so convinced I would be a failure, and there was so much pressure...' She didn't finish the sentence.

'You mean Denise?' Nigel rolled his eyes. 'You have to tell her to pop back in her box. If she wants to be famous so much she should have gone to college.'

'I know,' Lily said. 'I just don't know what I want to be honest. This break here has been lovely, even without the show and Nick.'

'Have you told Denise you're doing an am dram show?' he asked.

'No, and I'm not going to. I won't hear the end of it,' she said. 'As long I'm here she won't come over, which is good. She's got too many activities of her own to do; she's just joined a bonsai club.' Lily giggled.

'Not a surprising choice, considering she loves control,' Nigel said. 'Sorry, that was mean.'

'You're not wrong though,' said Lily. 'I need to stand up to her more.'

'No, you need to decide what you want your life to look like, not how Denise thinks it should look.'

Lily nodded. She knew he was right but she wasn't even sure what she wanted her life to look like.

'I have to go. I have rehearsals,' she said to her best friend. 'I love you and I'm so happy for you.'

'Love you too, babe. Speak soon.'

She thought about what Nigel said as she drove to rehearsals, arriving early to run lines with Henry Higgins.

Opening the door, she saw that Nick was already there, assisting Jasper and one of the set builders in the process of setting up the makeshift stage.

When she approached him with a smile, she enquired, 'Do you require any assistance there? I can't say I would be very helpful but I'm good at pointing where things should go.'

Nick beamed, and his eyes lit up as he caught sight of her. He was carrying a flat with Jasper. 'Always,' he said and they smiled and Lily blushed.

'Excuse me, lovebirds,' Jasper yelled out from the opposite side of the hallway. 'Less flirting, more working! I don't want to drop this. These flats are expensive.'

As she and Nick exchanged apologetic glances, Lily noticed that her cheeks were beginning to grow even pinker. So much for being discreet, she thought.

'Righto, we are doing a run-through with the start of the set, so I can see if the blocking is working.'

Jessica had entered the rehearsal at some point. Lily hadn't seen her come in but she was there, arms crossed, staring at Nick who was standing close to Lily.

Jasper started with a scene without Lily, so she took her script outside to practise lines with a cup of tea.

It was such a lovely afternoon, she thought as she sat under a tree on a little seat. She could hear music coming from the hall and she sipped her tea and sighed with contentment.

And then she heard a scream.

Dropping her script to the ground, she ran inside and saw Jess on the floor, clutching her ankle.

'Call an ambulance,' called Jasper but Jess shook her head.

'I don't need an ambulance. It needs to be iced, maybe strapped?' She looked at Nick with sad eyes and Lily looked at him and raised her eyebrows.

'Have we got any ice?' he called. 'I don't have my work bag on me.'

Sheila shook her head. 'We don't, I'm so sorry.'

Jess moaned on the floor, 'Help me, Nick,' she said.

Lily watched as Nick and David helped her up and she wrapped her arms around Nick's neck.

'You'll have to carry me,' she said. 'Can you take me home?'

Nick looked at Jasper who nodded.

Nick glanced at her, as he swung Jessica into his arms.

'Lily, I'll call you later,' he said loudly.

'Thanks, I hope your ankle is okay, Jess.'

But Jess ignored her and cuddled in closer to Nick's neck, as though she hadn't heard a word from Lily; in fact as though she didn't even exist.

Twenty-two

Lily woke to a text from Nick.

Ended up taking Jessica to the hospital for x-rays. They couldn't see anything, said it was a mild sprain. She's acting as though she's broken it. I'm tired since it was a long wait at the hospital. Can we catch up Friday night?'

Lily typed back quickly.

You're so kind. I hope Jess is okay. What did she fall over?

His text came back quickly.

Nothing as far as I could see. One minute she was standing, next she was on the floor.

Lily said nothing but it was clear Jess wasn't being entirely honest. She typed back:

Have a good sleep and I'll see you on Friday.

Then she went downstairs to set up breakfast.

When Gran was up, she filled her in on the rehearsals and Jess's injury.

'It's a reverse Beatrice Hawthorne situation,' said Gran with a furrowed brow. 'You watch her. She's up to no good.'

'Oh I'm not worried. She and Nick were never serious,' she said as her phone pinged with a message.

She picked up her phone as Gran sniffed. 'If it's your mother and father, tell them I've run away to Spain with my new lover and won't be back until I'm one hundred,' Gran said as she buttered her toast.

'No, it's Jasper,' she said, as she read aloud. 'Cast bonding session Friday night, at The Crumpetty Tree pub for a night of laughs and karaoke.' She made a face. 'Mandatory fun – I hate things like this.' She wanted to see Nick alone on Friday night and now they had to go and sing for their supper, as it were.

'Don't be a bad sport,' said Gran.

'I'm not,' Lily said as she poured their tea from the pot but she couldn't tell Gran about her and Nick in the field on their picnic. She couldn't stop thinking about him, his mouth, his hands, their passion. Lily bit her lip. 'I don't want to leave you at home alone on a Friday night.'

'Oh rubbish, don't use me as an excuse. I've been at home alone on a Friday night for the past thirty years. Another one isn't going to ruin anything. What are you avoiding? You've been lost in your own head since your picnic with Nick. Are you smitten, my love?'

Lily blushed. 'I do really like him,' she said. 'But it's not serious. I mean I'm heading back to London at the end of summer. It's not a forever thing.'

'It's London, not Vancouver. Go out with him for goodness' sake. Go tonight and have some fun and sing your heart out and see what happens. Take a chance, Lily.'

'But—' Lily began to resist.

'No buts,' Gran said, her eyes gleaming. 'You are only young once. And it might be good for you to see if Jessica has stopped sticking pins into the doll she made of you in her spare time.'

Lily sighed, realising she had been out-argued. 'Okay, I'll go for a little while but not too long, and we have rehearsals the next day so we can't go too mad.'

On Friday night, Lily stood outside The Crumpetty Tree, her palm resting on the tarnished brass door handle.

She adjusted her pink linen dress and ran her finger over her teeth to wipe off any pink lip gloss she might have on there and glanced inside the old pub.

The light from inside the pub's windows was casting a warm glow onto the street and she could hear laughter and music drifting out into the night before she even opened the door. She took a deep breath and pushed it open, stepping inside.

She had never spent any time in the pub at Appleton Green. Neither of her parents were drinkers and she and Gran preferred to be outside on adventures by the creek or pottering in the garden than sitting in a pub.

Lily looked around at the interiors. It was an eighteenth-century pub, with low-beamed ceilings and the original aged wooden floors, recently refurbished, she noticed, and she wondered about the generations of village gatherings. Had Beatrice, her grandmother's nemesis, come here for a drink? Or Raymond, her grandmother's spurned suitor? The pub was busier than she had seen before, but then again she wasn't usually roaming the village on Friday nights.

'Lily!' Jasper's voice echoed throughout the room. He motioned her over to a large table where the majority of the cast had already congregated – well, everyone except for Jessica. Hopefully she had a prior engagement so Lily didn't have to worry about her. 'So glad you could make it, darling!'

As Lily pushed her way through the crowd, she spotted Nick at the bar. Their eyes locked briefly, and Lily felt a flutter in her gut and he gave her a wink, which made her knees weak before returning to his talk with Sean.

'Here,' Sheila replied, placing a glass of wine in Lily's hand as she sat down. 'Liquid courage for later.'

Lily laughed uncomfortably. 'Oh, I doubt I'll need that. I'm not planning to sing tonight.'

'We'll see about that,' David, their Henry Higgins, remarked with a wink. 'I've got twenty quid riding on you being the first to take the stage.'

Before Lily could resist any further, the pub door flung wide and Jessica limped in. She was dressed to the nines in a slinky black outfit that looked more appropriate for a London nightclub than a country bar. She had an ornate walking stick with a silver topper, but still wore heels as she tottered into the bar. Despite her injury, she still oozed a sexuality that the likes of The Crumpetty Tree regulars had probably never seen before, and Lily watched as every man in the bar watched her move. Jess's eyes narrowed when she saw Lily and she came straight up to her.

'Well, well,' Jessica remarked, approaching the table. 'If this isn't our star. Hopefully you don't forget the words tonight. You'll have to show us all how it's done.'

Lily forced a smile. 'Just here for a drink and some fun, like everyone else.'

Jessica lifted her eyebrow. 'Of course you are.' She looked across at Nick, who was now observing them with a wary look on his face. 'I'm sure we all want to hear you sing. That is, if your voice doesn't disappear. Hate to see that happen, here or on opening night.'

'What do you mean?' Lily frowned. How did Jessica know she had lost her voice once? She hadn't told anyone at the play, unless Nick had told Jessica that her voice had been tricky.

The harsh remark stung, but Lily refused to let it show. 'Maybe later,' she replied carelessly.

As Jessica approached the bar, sidling up to Nick, Jasper clapped his hands to draw everyone's attention. 'Okay, my darlings! Let's get the party started. Who is daring enough to kick off our karaoke extravaganza?'

There was a small audience already in the karaoke room when Lily walked into it and found a seat, as Nick came to her side and sat down in the chair next to her.

'Hello, you,' he said with a smile and Lily smiled back, knowing she was blushing but unsure why. It was just a simple hello, not a marriage proposal.

'I've been looking forward to seeing you,' he said in her ear. 'I can't stop thinking about us, in the field… ' He left the rest of the sentence hanging and she felt herself almost faint with need for him.

'What are you doing to me?' she said back.

'I couldn't wait to see you,' he added.

'You would have seen me at rehearsals tomorrow,' she said, turning slightly to him, so his mouth was so close to her skin that she felt a shiver run through her.

'I know, but I can't stop thinking about you,' he said, closer again. 'I want to kiss you again.'

She felt desire rush through her body and for a moment, she thought about kissing him then and there in the pub until she glanced around and saw Jessica glaring at them and her desire dissipated.

'Why does she hate me so much?' she said shaking her head.

Before Nick could answer, David, their Henry Higgins, was up at the microphone, singing a beautiful version of 'Hallelujah' by Leonard Cohen, and the tavern exploded with applause when he had finished.

Sheila took to the stage next and sang 'My Baby Just Cares for Me' by Nina Simone.

'She's a bit more relaxed with a few wines,' Lily whispered to Nick, who giggled as Sheila danced around the small stage.

As the night progressed, more cast members took turns at the microphone. Lily found herself unwinding, enjoying the company and the slightly off-key but enthusiastic performances. When Jessica took the stage, she was just beginning to believe she might be able to avoid singing altogether.

'This one's for you, Nick,' Jessica said into the microphone as the opening chords began to play and then she started to sing 'Nothing Compares 2 U'.

It was mesmerising and Jessica was surprisingly good. Her voice was better in this register and she certainly had passion, but she sang the entire song to Nick, her eyes on him with every word.

Lily felt her cheeks heat and had a gnawing in her stomach as she watched Jessica's gaze fixed on Nick throughout the performance and at the end, Lily saw a single tear fall down her cheek, just like Sinéad O'Connor did in the film clip. When she finished, the pub applauded respectfully, but there was an awkward atmosphere in the room.

Nick stood up and left the room and Lily looked around, as Jessica came down off the small stage and walked out, following him.

'Oh dear, it's all very difficult, isn't it?' Sheila said to Lily.

'What is?'

'Jess and Nick. They were engaged, and then he broke it off when she said she would be going to London. I don't think she's over him.'

Lily sat in silence. 'All right,' the karaoke host said, 'how about a duet? Any volunteers?'

Before Lily knew it, Sean had taken her hand and raised it in the air. 'Lily!' he exclaimed.

Lily froze, her heart racing as Nick came back into the bar, his jaw set in an almost angry way.

'And Nick,' said David who was coming back from the bar and he grabbed Nick's hand and put it up. 'A duet.'

Nick looked a Lily, but she couldn't say anything and he came towards her.

'Shall we?' he asked, but there was no smile.

'I don't want to,' she said quietly.

'Come on,' called Jasper and he turned to the room. 'This is our leading lady and gent from the production of *My Fair Lady*, which is soon to be staged in the village. Please come and see these wonderful performers.'

Jasper hissed at Lily, 'It's marketing. Now get up there.'

Lily looked at Nick and shook her head but he grabbed her hand and led her to the stage.

As if in a dream, she found herself standing next to Nick in front of the karaoke machine.

'What should we sing?' she muttered, suddenly conscious of the waiting audience.

Nick looked through the song list and smiled. 'How about "Suddenly, Seymour" from *Little Shop of Horrors*?'

She shook her head.

'"All I Ask of You"?'

A classic duet from *Phantom of the Opera*, one she could sing in her sleep, she thought. Actually, she wished she was asleep and this was all a nightmare. 'Okay.' She nodded and took the microphone.

Lily's anxiousness dissipated as the opening chords sounded. This was neither an audition nor a performance; it was simply a song to sing, and as she looked at Nick and sang, everything else slipped away.

Their vocals melded perfectly, Nick's warm tenor complementing Lily's crystalline soprano. As they approached the chorus, Lily felt a rush of excitement race through her. This was why she enjoyed singing: the pure delight of creating something beautiful with another person.

Except Nick had lied to her. They had been engaged. She somehow managed to get to the end of the song but once it was over, she handed him the microphone.

The tavern had gone silent, with all eyes fixed on the pair on stage. Even Jessica was transfixed, her smugness replaced by a look of shock at their duet.

'That was—' he started to say, but she cut him off.

'I don't want to hear it,' she said and stepped down off the stage and went to the table, people still applauding. She drained her wine and picked up her bag, left the pub and stepped outside into the night to make her way back to Gran.

Twenty-three

As Lily raced out from The Crumpetty Tree, she felt like she wanted to scream and cry all at once. How dare he lie to her? Why wouldn't he tell her?

God she was so stupid. She ran to her car, her feet pounding the pavement as she made her escape. The humiliation. God, no wonder Jessica hated her so much.

An engagement! He said it wasn't serious, so who was lying here?

She could hear Nick's voice calling out after her, 'Lily, wait!'

As he came up behind her, he put his hand on her shoulder and she spun around and slapped it off.

'Do not touch me,' she said.

'What's wrong? What's happened?' His face was confused and she wondered how the hell did he not get what he had done.

'What's wrong? Are you serious? Did you think I wouldn't find out?'

'Find out what?' he asked looking genuinely confused at her words and anger.

She threw her hands up in the air, gesturing at him.

'The fact that you were engaged to Jessica, when you told me it was nothing serious. Why would you lie to me? I'm so embarrassed. This was clearly a joke to you and you have taken me for a fool.' She opened the car door.

'Engaged?' he asked. His voice was loud and shocked.

'Yes, Sheila told me,' she said. 'She said everyone knew.'

'Well I would have liked to have known since I was supposed to be the one getting married.' His voice rose.

'Don't yell at me,' she yelled at him and felt herself starting to cry. 'And I'm not crying because I'm sad, I'm crying because I'm angry. You wouldn't understand,' she said to him, furious.

'You can cry, even though I don't want you to cry, but honestly, I don't know what you're talking about. Jess and I were never engaged.' He did look genuinely confused but, still, why would Sheila say that if it wasn't true?

'But Sheila said,' she said.

Nick's expression was one of remorse and irritation at the same time. 'I was not engaged to her. She's making it up.'

They were both silent for a moment.

'Why wouldn't you ask me? Why would you assume that I lied to you, Lily? That's the worst part of this,' he said looking furious.

'Is it? That's the worst part?' she scoffed. 'Well, I don't know who to believe now, so unless she comes to me and tells me you weren't engaged, consider me out of the picture and out of the show.' She got into the car and slammed the car door and started the engine.

Nick stood by the side of the road as Lily took off, and not once did she look back in her rear-view mirror.

Gran was in bed when she made her way up the stairs, for which she was thankful. She needed to think and she didn't want to have to explain anything to her yet.

Why would Sheila say they were engaged? Jess was certainly acting appallingly for someone who was only in a brief and casual thing with Nick.

She was still in her clothes when she collapsed onto the bed in her room and lay there, the curtains still open. The sound of the owls calling made Mr Mistoffelees jump onto the windowsill and investigate the darkness.

'No mice for you, my friend. They belong to the owls,' she said to the cat and he jumped from the sill and onto her bed, and snuggled up next to her. For the first time in a long time, Lily buried her face in his velvety fur and cried for being so overemotional, for yelling at Nick and for Jessica making her doubt herself.

Lily awoke the following morning with a feeling of dread in her stomach. There was a rehearsal today and she wasn't sure what to expect.

She went downstairs to set things up for breakfast and sat outside with her tea and the cat, looking around at the garden. She should have worked on the garden instead of getting mixed up in this stupid amateur drama show.

'Morning, love, you going to rehearsals today?' Gran was at the door with her frame.

Lily smiled at her ruefully. 'Actually, I think I'm going to drop out. Jessica won,' she said. 'It's over.'

'What do you mean? What's over?' Gran scoffed.

Lily came inside and poured Gran a mug of tea.

'Last night Sheila told me that Nick and Jess had been engaged. He has told me all along it wasn't serious and he says it's not true, but I said if that's correct then Jess needs to tell me that. I don't know who to believe.'

Gran gasped. 'Why would he lie? Surely this is just that Jessica woman causing trouble?'

Lily shrugged. 'Maybe, but whatever it is, I don't want to be a part of it.'

'But leaving the show is poor form, darling. You have worked so hard and so has everyone else. It's only a few weeks until it's on. Don't be a bad sport.'

Lily put her head in her hands and leaned her elbows on the table. 'I know, but I feel sick at the thought of seeing them all. I ran away last night; it was all so overly dramatic.'

'It's not dramatic. You are being told inconsistencies, so you left to see what time will reveal. But I think not going to rehearsal is unprofessional, even in an amateur show.'

Lily knew Gran was right and she sighed. 'Okay, I'll go, but now I'm just embarrassed and if it is true, then I will be even more embarrassed,' she said.

'You need to go. You can't let everyone down – you know that,' Gran said firmly and Lily knew she was right, but the dread in her stomach was telling her to stay at home.

At the village hall, there was a palpable sense of tension when Lily arrived. She could sense people looking at her, and as she got closer, whispers were swiftly silenced. Jasper was already there, and Nick was in the middle of a very heated discussion with him. He saw Lily and he gave her a hopeful smile.

She looked around and saw Sheila looking at her, her face concerned. The rest of the cast were there, except for Jessica, which made it somewhat more bearable, but also didn't solve the mystery of whether she and Nick had been engaged or not.

'Right, places everyone!' The call came from Jasper, who was clapping his hands and walking away from Nick. 'Let's take it from the top of Act Two.'

As Lily took her place on stage, she turned and caught a glimpse of Jessica, who was standing in the wings and watching her with a smirk of triumph on her lips. So she was here, she thought as her stomach dropped.

Lily lifted her chin. She was resolute in her determination to conceal how she felt from her and listened to the introduction to the music.

The scene started after Higgins, Eliza and Pickering come back from the ball, and Eliza is furious and worried about her future, feeling taken advantage of by Higgins.

It wasn't a hard scene to portray, she thought as she started her lines. The fury and betrayal were something she didn't even need to act.

Lily turned into Eliza, expressing her gratitude for the opportunity to temporarily escape and at the end of the scene, the cast and crew clapped.

'Bloody marvellous, all of you, honestly. And Eliza, you were marvellous,' Jasper called. 'I want to see that passion more. Whatever is driving you today, harness it and ride it into the performances.'

As all eyes turned on Lily, she felt a burning sensation in her cheeks and she walked off the stage to where Jessica was.

'What happened last night? You ran out of the pub like you'd seen a ghost. Are you okay? Did you lose your voice again?'

Lily stared at her. 'Have you spoken to Nick?'

'No, I left when you did. I did see some missed calls from Nick though. I haven't caught up with him yet.'

Lily paused. 'Were you engaged to Nick?' she asked finally.

Jessica made a sad face. 'Yes, we were engaged, but he didn't want to move to London. He's very selfish, so I broke it off. He doesn't support his partner's dreams.'

Lily felt as though the world was falling out from under her feet.

'He told me that you weren't engaged,' she said.

Jessica shrugged. 'Well we were, not for long but we were. He's lying because he's embarrassed that I broke it off.'

Lily walked back onto the stage and looked out for Nick. 'Nick, can you come here please?'

She walked back to where Jessica was, as Nick came to them, and Jasper and a few of the cast came closer. Nothing like a potential scene off stage to get a committed audience, she thought.

Nick walked up to Jessica and Lily.

'I've been trying to call you,' he said to Jessica who smiled sweetly.

'I'm sorry, I was busy this morning and my ankle was playing up.'

'There's nothing wrong with your ankle. You're an attention-seeker,' Nick said. 'Now tell Lily that we were never engaged.'

Jessica looked at Nick and gasped. 'What? Why would I do that? We were engaged.'

'We were not engaged,' said Nick, exasperated. 'We went out for six months, and then you went to London.'

Jessica shook her head. 'We had discussed you moving to London and then you said you couldn't so I broke it off.'

'That doesn't mean we were engaged.' Nick looked at Lily, his face in shock. 'She's lying,' and he turned to Jessica. 'I don't know what's wrong with you, but you're either seriously unwell or vicious to the point of being cruel. We never were engaged. You and I were never going to be anything long term. We are completely different people and I'm glad, because you're not a nice person.'

Lily put her hand on Nick's arm. 'It's okay,' she said to him softly.

Now the entire cast and crew were watching them but it was too late to try and get any privacy, and Lily was somewhat relieved that there were witnesses.

'Is it okay?' Jessica snapped and turned to the cast, walking out onto the stage. 'You know I have met our leading lady before this show.'

Lily was confused. She had never met Jess. She really was making up lies with every word she spoke.

'I've never met you before,' said Lily loudly so everyone could hear.

But Jessica turned around. 'I was the person who gave you a tissue as you were lying in a heap backstage at the Theatre Royal after you lost your nerve and your voice during your audition.'

She looked at Jasper. 'And you cast her, even after I told you that she was unreliable and too emotional for the show. The girl can't even do am dram. How is she going to make it as a professional?'

Lily grabbed Nick's arm to steady herself.

'You told Jasper?' she asked her.

'I told everyone. Everyone should know what a flake you are.'

Lily took a moment to compose herself and then looked at Jessica.

'I was so grateful to you that day when you came to me to see if I was okay. It meant a lot. I see now I was wrong to think you and that woman you pretended to be were decent people.'

She walked downstage and then jumped off onto the floor.

'Jessica, the role is all yours now. I'm sorry, Jasper, but under these circumstances, I can't stay on. I will not work with her; she is truly horrendous. I wish you the very best with the show.'

'Lily,' she heard Nick call out from behind her but she kept walking away from the Appleton Green Amateur Drama Society and her broken and betrayed heart.

To my sweet Lily, aged twelve,

I'm sitting in the cottage with the window open, listening to the rain fall outside. We need this rain so I welcome it with open arms.

You left in a huff I noticed. You seemed to be very cross with your mum about something. I didn't ask because I am sure it will blow over, but you were very harsh on her. I know mums can be annoying; I remember your dad being annoyed with me often, but us parents mean well. Try to give her a little grace.

Now that you're home, Pippin Cottage is quiet again.

I can see the changes in you, Lily – perhaps the cottage isn't as fun as it used to be anymore. Twelve is an age where your friends are your world and your gran and parents are a bit of a boring time. I understand that. I was twelve too, you know.

I do understand how you feel and how it feels like everything around you is changing – including you yourself. Growing up is hard, and things that used to be simple or enjoyable may not seem the same as they did before.

We still had a lovely time, playing piano and singing. You have taken to Cole Porter this year and I have enjoyed hearing his music again. He was a wonderful composer, and you sing his songs so well.

I know what it's like to feel like your body is changing and your mind is filling up with new ideas and thoughts. In fact, it's normal to not know what to do with yourself sometimes. Twelve is a funny age because it's neither a child nor a teenager. Your feelings change quickly, like the wind. One minute you're happy and laughing, and the next you're sad and quiet. And I want you to know that it's okay to feel this way. I saw it this summer. That's how you grow up, and it's not always fun.

As always we did some gardening, planting flowers, pulling weeds and gathering herbs, but we have decided to leave the apple tree this year. Perhaps we are all apple-d out. Now Mr Wilkinson is gone, we have no one to give the apple sauce to.

Lily, remember that these changes are a part of becoming the person you were meant to be. You don't have to know everything now; this is time to get to know yourself. There will be good days and bad days. Both are very important. You're taking care of yourself, even if it doesn't always feel like it.

With all my love,
Gran

Twenty-four

Lily Baxter had always been a master at retreat. The repeated feedback she got when performing at college was she was too self-effacing, as though she didn't think she belonged on the stage. Any conflict, on or off the stage, and she would pull back, raising her drawbridge and battening down the hatches of her heart.

It was safer that way, she told herself. Lying on the sofa at the flat was her main mode of avoidance, but at Gran's she didn't have that opportunity. She still had to care for her and make sure everything was running smoothly at the cottage.

Her mother told her it was because she was a Cancer and crabs liked to be in their shells to stay safe, which could have been true, but Lily knew it was because she was so easily bruised.

Things that other people brushed off about feedback or lovers betraying them or nasty comments or reviews hurt her deeply. She had tried not to care but she did. She cared too much about everything, and thinking that everyone was laughing about her behind her back in the show broke her heart. So she stopped answering her phone or texts from anyone in the show and most of all Nick.

He had even come to the house and Gran had told him Lily didn't want to see him, which she felt bad about, making her ninety-seven-year-old grandmother do her gatekeeping, but Gran seemed to enjoy it, even lecturing Nick to be patient and give Lily time to think.

But the show would go on, she told herself, and no doubt, Jess would play the role of Eliza now and Lily would just go on with her life. So why couldn't she stop thinking about Nick?

Instead she threw herself into the garden. Despite Gran saying it was a waste of time Lily needed to be busy.

The garden was a mess and it was the perfect distraction from thinking about Nick and Jess.

For a week she had been pulling weeds with a force that even Gran had commented on.

'You'll pull the foundations of the cottage up the way you're yanking at that weed,' she said to Lily one day, but Lily said nothing. She viewed every weed as Jessica and was pulling her out of her life and out of Appleton Green.

This particular morning, Lily wiped the sweat from her forehead, leaving a smudge of dirt as she accomplished her work. It had been good to be outside, using her body. She was even enjoying the feeling in her body when she woke each morning, her muscles stretched and becoming more toned. Despite the fact that she was working in the overgrown garden with her hands buried in the earth, and the sun was beating down on her, she pulled each weed with her gloved hands, thinking about everything in her life for the past twenty-nine years. Each weed was a moment in her life, a decision, a choice, and she wondered how much she had been in charge of her own garden in life. Denise seemed to loom large in everything Lily had done up to now. In fact, the only independent decision she had made in the past three years was pack up and move to Gran's.

As she pruned the apple tree, according to the instructions she found online, she thought about what she wanted to prune from her own life, and it was terrifying. Whatever had happened over the past six weeks had changed her and being at Pippin Cottage had given her time to think, and perhaps, reevaluate her life.

'You're doing a wonderful job,' said Gran, wearing a large straw sunhat, as she came to the door with her walking frame.

Lily took a seat back on her heels and reflected on the accomplishments that she had achieved. As the flower beds began to take shape, there were indications of order emerging from the chaos that had come before. She reached for her water bottle and took a long gulp.

'You know,' Gran said from the back door, 'your mother called once more this morning. She's interested in knowing when you will be returning to London again.'

Lily made a face as she got up and helped guide Violet to the chair where she had put a cushion for Gran to sit on when she was outside. Gran enjoyed sitting outside and was spending more time in the garden, watching while Lily worked.

'That looks better,' said Gran, looking at the apple tree.

'Yes, it had some unsafe branches and some areas where the fruit was too heavy. It's a small sacrifice to make to lose some fruit to keep the tree.'

'You sound like a gardener,' said Gran with a smile.

'I feel like one each morning when I wake and my bones creak.' Lily laughed.

'Welcome to my world,' said Gran. 'But it's still a waste of time since you won't be here after the summer. I can't manage the upkeep.'

Lily was silent for a moment as she watched a worm move through the rich soil and underneath the ground, away from the sun.

'I'm actually thinking of staying, Gran,' she said slowly. 'If that's okay with you?'

Gran was quiet. 'Why?' She paused for a moment. 'It's not that I don't like you being here – you have been a lifesaver in every way – but you have a life in London: friends, work, a career.'

Lily sat on the ground from where she was kneeling.

'But I don't, Gran. I don't like London. It's too busy, too chaotic. My best friend is going away for a few years and he's met someone, so I would have to find a roommate, which makes me want to cry. My jobs have dried up, and I don't have a career, really. I was teaching in London from my flat and making more from doing that. It was the only thing I really liked, if I'm honest.'

'Teaching?' Gran nodded, as though it made sense. 'Does your mother know?'

Lily's stomach tightened up. She had been avoiding Denise's calls along with everyone else's, because she didn't know how to face the disappointment and bewilderment from her mum.

Lily shook her head. 'What did you say to her when you spoke?'

Gran gave a shrug. 'I told her that you were busy figuring out what you wanted to do and I wasn't quite well enough to be alone yet.'

As always, Lily was grateful for Gran's support. 'Thanks, Gran,' she said as she picked some weeds around the edges of the bricks. 'I looked in the local paper. There are piano and teaching jobs over in Silverton, which would be close. I mean maybe I just need to do it for a year and rethink. The thought of auditioning again, doing shows – I just don't want to.' She paused. 'I don't think I ever wanted to, but because I had this voice, I felt it was wrong of me not to pursue it.'

'And in doing so, you betrayed yourself and what you wanted,' Gran said, gently waving a bee away from her face. 'You know when you were younger, you always told me you wanted to be a teacher; that was the one consistent thing you said as you grew up.'

Lily nodded. 'I know. And I think being here, at Appleton Green, well it's reminded me of who I was then and how much I was truly myself. I needed to trust my younger self more.' She sighed.

Mr Mistoffelees wandered past and then lay on top of the earth she had been digging up.

'Really?' she said to the cat who gave a flick of his tail in reply.

'And what about the show?' asked Gran.

But Lily was adamant. 'No, it's done. I am happy to sing for you anytime, Gran, but not for them and not with Jess in the cast.'

And Lily knew it would take a miracle for her to ever go back on a stage again.

Twenty-five

Lily adjusted her black jacket and made sure her shirt was smoothed down as she walked into the school office and up to the reception desk.

A woman behind the desk was on the phone and she gestured to Lily that she needed to wait a moment.

Lily looked around the private school's reception area, which was rather tiny but well organised. There was a combination of student artwork and framed awards that highlighted the accomplishments of the students at the school that were displayed on the walls. She liked that it was more about the students than the school patting themselves on the back for their success.

Near the entryway, there was a large bulletin board that was covered in colourful posters that advertised forthcoming events, club meetings, and extracurricular activities, and Lily was pleased to see there was a selection of music groups, choirs and shows for the children to participate in.

There was a row of seats that lined the wall to her left, and the cushions on those chairs were clean but slightly worn. There was a modest table in front of the chairs that contained a carefully arranged stack of prospectuses as well as a few copies of the school magazine. The bell rang and through the large windows Lily could see the children in their red and blue uniforms rushing outside to play. The other side of the window looked out into a courtyard that had been meticulously maintained with spring flowers and a small bird stand. Next to the window there was a trophy cabinet that proudly displayed a variety of gleaming cups and plaques that were awarded to winners of various music, academic and athletic events.

Lily looked at the old-fashioned clock displayed over the reception desk, and she saw that its face had the crest of the institution. It ticked slowly every minute. It was past her interview time now at eleven o'clock with the head of music and she wondered if the receptionist would ever finish her call.

As though she heard Lily's thoughts, she put down the phone. 'How can I help you?'

'I'm Lily Baxter. I'm here for an interview with John McBride,' she said, suddenly feeling nervous.

'Of course, come through and John will be here in a moment,' said the woman with a smile and led the way to a room with a lounge and two armchairs.

'Can I get you tea or coffee or water?' she asked Lily.

'Water would be great, thank you.'

After the water had been delivered in a lovely jug with two glasses, Lily relaxed for a moment and then the door opened and a large man in his fifties beamed at her. 'You must be Lily Baxter?'

She nodded, instantly buoyed by his energy.

'I'm John McBride, head of music, father, new grandfather and mad jazz fan. Now tell me why you want to teach at this lovely little school.'

Lily sat in the car outside the school and breathed a sigh of relief. She could have twenty hours teaching a week for the rest of the year in a part-time position and if she liked it and they liked her, then they would look at making her permanent.

She couldn't believe how well the interview had gone. John was so lovely and funny and encouraging and told her there was a lack of good teachers in the area and that there were lots of children on the waiting list.

Lily drove back to Appleton Green singing along to the soundtrack of *Into the Woods*, relishing the feeling of relief from the sadness that had been ailing her since she had left the show and Nick.

But she was wise enough to know this was a fleeting reprise, because she was thinking about Nick every other moment of the day, still unsure what to believe.

Lily arrived back at Pippin Cottage and walked through the door. 'Good news, Gran,' she said and saw Gran sitting at the table instead of her armchair and next to her was Jasper, with a mug of tea in hand and Bernadette on his lap.

Mr Mistoffelees was sitting on the windowsill, staring at the dog with disdain, and the dog was snarling in return.

'Jasper,' Lily said, feeling the joy vanish at the sight of him in the cottage.

'Lily,' he said with an elaborate nod and half rising from his seat as though he was a character in a historical novel.

'Why are you here?' she asked putting down her handbag on the sofa.

'We need you in the show,' he said.

'No. You know why,' she said crossing her arms.

'Listen to him, Lily,' Gran said in a tone that meant no nonsense and one which Lily never disobeyed.

She sat down at the table, her hands clasped in her lap.

'Jessica has left,' Jasper said.

'What? Why?'

'Two things: the cast decided they wouldn't do the show with her. Sheila was actually the start of the movement and Nick, of course.'

Lily looked at Gran in shock.

'They said they wouldn't do the show with her and only you.'

'How did Jessica cope with that news?' asked Lily.

Jasper shook his head. 'She claims she had a role on *EastEnders* now, and was going to leave anyway. A sexy villain, she claims,' Jasper said with a wry tone and a raised eyebrow.

'Apt casting it seems,' said Gran.

'Has she?' asked Lily.

Jasper shrugged. 'I have no idea. I doubt it. She's a wild storyteller. She says whatever she needs in the moment to seem superior. It's because she's so beautiful that people forgive her, but I have had her number for years. I didn't even want her in the show, but Sheila insisted. Except now Sheila seems to have come to her senses.'

Lily swallowed, listening to his news. How different today had been from what she had expected when she woke up. Sometimes the best news comes on what seems to be an ordinary day. Perhaps that's why it seems so special, because it was such an ordinary day. First she had the job offer and now this news.

Jasper was patting Bernadette, who had stopped snarling and who was now closing her eyes, looking Zen in the warmth of the cottage.

'And we need to do this show, because we have to earn our money back. We were given some money by the council to do the show – an arts grant – and we have to put it on. It's part of the rules, and if we don't we have to pay it back and that would mean we, as individuals, would have to pay.'

He took a deep breath and Lily could see the anxiety on his face. 'And it's rather a lot of money, you see. Because we have fabulous costumes and sets. Some of Eliza's costumes and hats have been hired from the National Theatre,' he said, in a reverent manner.

Lily was silent.

'I know it's all been terrible,' Jasper said. 'And Jessica broke your trust and Nick might have seemed to have broken your trust, but for the record, I don't think they were engaged. I've known them both, having done many shows with them. Jessica likes drama and she likes Nick and she didn't want anyone to have him, even if she didn't want him.'

'I thought as much,' sniffed Gran. 'She reminded me of Beatrice Hawthorne. Similar types, the pair of them.'

Jasper looked confused for a moment and then kept going.

'I am begging you to please consider coming back for the show. We can't afford to repay the grant and we can't put it on without an Eliza. Please,' he said and for a brief moment, Lily saw tears in his eyes.

'Okay, I'll do it,' she said. 'For the society and the grant but not for any other reason.'

But deep down, she knew she was lying to herself. She wanted to see Nick and understand what the truth was.

Twenty-six

Lily's heart was beating so fast that she could feel the rhythm in her throat as she stood outside the village hall. It was a warm summer evening, and she wondered if she was ready to return, but she knew she couldn't leave the cast and crew with that debt.

After she had finished smoothing down her bright yellow sundress, which she had worn in an attempt to lift her mood and now seemed to be at odds with her fear, she pushed open the door.

As soon as she stepped inside, she was greeted with the familiar sounds and smells of rehearsal. Andrew on the piano, the smell of coffee and cake, and the scent of the old room and Sheila's perfume.

She stood watching the room, unnoticed by anyone for a brief moment, and she took in the surroundings. At the same time a group of chorus members were working on perfecting a dance routine for 'Get Me To the Church on Time', Sheila was trying on a hat in the costume area and then Nick appeared on the stage to the left.

The conversation he was having with David ended in the middle of a sentence when he noticed her, and Lily took a quick breath. He was still handsome but was he a liar? The expression of surprise appeared on his face, and then a gentle smile started to form.

The piano came to a sudden halt as Jasper followed Nick's gaze throughout the room. 'Lily!' he yelled out, his voice stealing the attention of everyone else in the room. 'Thank God you're here!'

Instantaneously, everyone's attention was focused on her. As a calm descended upon the gathering, Lily noticed that her cheeks had become red. Her throat cleared, and she managed to summon a smile as Sheila rushed up to her and some of the cast and Jasper hugged her.

She hugged people warmly and Sheila took a step forward with her arms extended, after which there was a brief pause in the conversation.

'Oh, Lily, I owe you an apology. I was far too swayed by Jessica and when I look back so many of her stories didn't make sense. I am deeply sorry,' she said, and as far as Lily could tell, she was sincere.

Lily nodded. 'It's okay, Sheila, forget about it. We can just move on,' she said. 'We just need to get the show on.'

Sheila looked crestfallen but Lily couldn't let her guard down and she wasn't sure why. Jessica had damaged her reputation but more than that, she was worried if she got too close again to anyone, she might lose her nerve, or worse, her voice.

Lily's eyes made their way back to Nick amidst the crowd. He stood tall at the back of the group observing everyone with a look that was difficult to understand. He had not moved towards her and she was grateful yet also disappointed. God the heart was so confusing.

'Okay, everyone, let's get to work. We have to find some more time to schedule rehearsals, and Lily now you are here, what is your schedule looking like? I know you care for your grandmother.'

Lily paused. 'I also have a job now. I'm working a few days a week teaching.'

She saw a look of surprise cross his face.

'Do you? Well done. Okay tell me your days and we can work out a schedule. We can do nights if it's easier for you and your grandmother.'

Sheila scurried off to get a clipboard and came back to look at the times with Jasper as Lily went and put down her bag and then stood with David who was practising his Henry Higgins accent.

'Glad you're back,' he said to her. 'It's been a nightmare.'

Lily smiled. 'I've heard. Do you want to walk me through any new blocking?'

As she and David worked, she noticed Nick kept himself busy, but she was acutely aware of him as she practised, and she knew he was aware of her.

Jasper called out, 'Act One, Scene Seven, Ascot. Actor please.'

Lily walked to the stage as Nick came over to her.

'Hello,' he said.

'Hi,' she answered.

'Can we talk after rehearsals?' he asked, his face hopeful.

She nodded. 'Yes,' she said as Jasper called for places and then she put Nick out of her mind and suddenly she was Eliza again, trying to fit in, shocking the Ascot crowd and making Freddy laugh uproariously and, for that moment, she forgot everything that had happened and was in the moment again.

At the end of the scene, Jasper clapped wildly. 'That was as good as anything I have seen professionally – all of you, exceptional work,' he said. 'Let's do it again with the chorus at the start, singing the "Ascot Gavotte". Places, everyone.'

'You were bloomin' marvellous,' said Nick as he walked past her and it took every ounce of willpower not to kiss him in the middle of the stage.

Nick was waiting outside for Lily when she left rehearsals.

'Sorry, I had to get measured for a hat,' she said to him.

'Do you want to walk down to the river?' he asked. Lily noticed Sheila looking at them from the doorway and Lily nodded.

'Yes please. Away from prying eyes,' she said with a rueful laugh.

They walked down the little, twisting path towards the river. After the stifling hall, the late afternoon air was refreshing as they walked in sync, their footsteps sounding lightly on the road.

Their view widened out before them as they rounded a mild curve, where a thin stone wall, its aged surface studded with tiny wildflowers and moss, ran beside the road. There weren't many tourists today, for which Lily was thankful, and Nick pointed to a quiet area somewhat off from the other groups. 'Shall we?' he asked, his voice matched in anxiousness to Lily's own sensations.

Lily nodded, inhaled deeply, and followed them down to the river, prepared to meet the truth that lay ahead.

'How have you been?' he asked her after they were seated.

'I'm okay,' she said, and it was the truth. 'I feel like my world has been shaken, but it had to be. I had to have some time to think about what I wanted, without any interference of promises.'

Nick was silent for a moment. The sound of the water was soothing, and Lily could see the late sun dappled in the trees over the river and some dragonflies darting about amongst the grasses.

'Do you mean me?' he asked.

'Somewhat, but also, I had to decide what I wanted to do for me, not for you or for my mum or for anyone really.'

'And you are teaching?'

'I start on Monday, at a school in Silverton. It's only part-time but that's fine for now,' she said.

'I love that. I'm so happy for you. You will be amazing,' he said.

'Thank you.' They were quiet for a while.

'Lily, listen,' he said and turned to her.

She turned to face him.

'I wasn't engaged to Jessica. We went out for six months but she was so intense, so quickly, and she spoke about marriage and children, but I told her that it was a bit soon. It was kind of weird actually, and she just went on and on about it, and when I said something she would fly off the handle. So I stopped saying anything and broke it off. I told her I wasn't ready for a relationship but then I met you and I was, I really was ready for one with you, and she became nasty. I can deny it till the end of days but it's true and you have to decide if I'm of good character or not and you believe me.'

Lily brushed her dress of invisible lint.

'I don't think it matters anymore,' she said. 'I just want to do the show and help Jasper out. And then I will just live my little life, which I am actually looking forward to. I don't want to restart anything while we're in the show. I need to be focused and I can't go through any drama again.'

'So you're saying we might be able to maybe start again after the show?' Nick asked, his eyes hopeful.

'I don't know – maybe, maybe not. You might be sick of me by then,' she half joked.

Nick gave a short laugh. 'I doubt it. I have missed you every day,' he said. 'And Gran also. Gee she was firm with me when I came to the cottage. She might be ninety-seven but she's still terrifying.'

Lily couldn't help but laugh. 'Yes, she keeps me in my place.'

'Is she well?' he asked.

'She's good,' said Lily with a sigh. 'Speaking of which, I need to get back to her.' She stood up. 'Friends?' she asked. 'For now?'

Nick nodded and smiled at her. 'I will never not be your friend, Lily, now and forever.'

She smiled and then walked back to her car at the village hall, wondering why she felt so deeply sad, as if something she had was lost and she knew it was never coming back.

Twenty-seven

Her alarm went at six thirty in the morning, jolting her awake from a very nice dream about Nick and a picnic blanket under a tree. She sighed as Mr Mistoffelees clawed her legs through the covers, looked furious at Lily.

'Ouch, don't,' she told him off and hopped out of bed and opened the curtains.

It was her first week of teaching and she was getting used to the new routine and early starts.

'Don't look at me like that. You can nap all day; I have to go to work,' she told the cat. 'This is my first week and I want to be there early to make a good impression.'

But Lily couldn't lie that it was tiring. Between getting up early and making sure everything was ready for Gran, and her lunch was made and ready for her in the fridge and breakfast was set out, plus then coming home and making dinner or going to rehearsals, Lily was so tired, she had no time to even think about anything else.

Lily showered and dressed and then went downstairs, fed the cat and let him out for a while in garden, which had been left neglected again since she had started back at the show and working.

She boiled the kettle and set the table when she heard the sound of Gran's cough reverberating throughout the cottage. Over the course of the last few days, it had become increasingly severe, a recurrent rumble that caused Lily more anxiety than she would have liked to admit.

She walked upstairs and tapped on the door and opened it and saw Gran sitting up in bed, in her pale blue nightgown, her grey hair tousled.

'Morning, love,' Gran said and then burst into another spasm of coughing.

'That sounds terrible,' she said.

But Gran flicked her hand at her. 'Null and void. A tickle is all that it is.'

Lily put her hand on Violet's forehead.

It was warm, but not in a frightening way. 'I think you should spend the day in bed. I'll bring breakfast up to you and then you can rest and nap. And I will come home straight away after work, no dilly-dallying.'

'You fuss too much,' said Violet but Lily noticed she didn't protest about breakfast in bed.

After Gran was set up in bed with tea and a crumpet and her newspaper, Lily gave her some paracetamol and her phone. 'You call me if anything changes, okay?'

Violet rolled her eyes. 'Be off with you,' she said gruffly. 'And drive safely.'

The first two days she had been doing training and learning the school and its routines but now she was ready to teach.

A mixture of nervousness and excitement greeted Lily as she entered the Silverton School music room for her first proper day of teaching. She set up in the music room and set the books up on her desk. She was really nervous. She heard a hesitant knock on the door as she was arranging some sheet music and setting up the piano.

The door opened and a small girl with red hair stood there.

'Hi. I'm Emma. I'm learning piano,' she said.

She gave a warm smile to the child, who looked to be as nervous as she was.

'Well hi, Emma. I'm Miss Baxter, or Lily. I don't mind what you call me, and I am your new teacher. Let's get going. Show me where you're up to.'

Emma sat down at the piano and looked at the exercises on the music stand on the piano and looked at Lily.

'You want me to play these?'

Lily nodded. 'Just as a warm-up, get those fingers moving.'

Emma started to play and Lily relaxed. This is what made her happy, she remembered, as she gave Emma gentle encouragement as she led her through some basic exercises and scales. Lily took her time going over each passage with Emma when she was having trouble with it.

'Watch my fingers,' she told her. 'See how I'm crossing under with my thumb? You try now.'

Emma's face lit up when she got the difficult fingering down pat. She cried, 'I did it!'

As the morning went on, she changed between piano and singing lessons and each of the children brought with them their own talents and enthusiasm, making Lily laugh and remember how fun it was to learn with no other expectations.

'Do you live in Silverton?' one of the children asked her.

'No, in a village not far from here,' she said.

'With your husband?'

'No, with my granny,' she said, finally having time to think of her for the first time all morning.

She wondered how she was going at home. That cough was worrying.

She would call her at lunchtime, she thought, as she went back to teaching.

She had called Gran but she hadn't answered, and Lily hoped she was just napping.

She settled into her last afternoon lessons when her phone rang with an unknown number.

'Excuse me,' she said to her student who was learning the 'Moonlight Sonata'.

'I have to take this,' she said to the student and she picked up the phone and answered it.

'Hello, Lily Baxter speaking,' she said.

'Lily, it's Mrs Douglas. I just came to see Gran with her orders for the day, and she's not well. The front door was open and she was downstairs but she's got a temperature and is a little delirious. What do you want me to do?'

'Call an ambulance,' she said and: 'I'll be right there as soon as I can.' She turned to the student. 'I have to speak to Mr McBride for a moment,' she said and rushed to his office and knocked on the door.

'Come in, Lily, is everything okay?'

'Hi, I'm so sorry, but my gran is sick. Someone in her village just called. I think she needs a doctor but I'm in the middle of a lesson.'

But Mr McBride was already on his feet. 'Go, family first. I'll finish the lesson,' he said firmly and soon Lily was out the door with her things and heading to her car, calling the only person she knew who could help right now.

'Lily? Are you okay?' Nick answered almost immediately and the relief at hearing his voice made her burst into tears.

'It's Gran. She's sick and I'm at work and it's a thirty-minute drive home and Mrs Douglas has called an ambulance but I worry it will be too long for them to get there. It might get diverted.'

'I'm on my way. I'm nearby. I'll assess her and wait for you and if I think she needs an ambulance, I can get one faster, okay? Drive home carefully and I will be there with her, so don't worry about that part.' Nick's voice instantly calmed her and she took a deep breath and wiped her eyes with her hands.

'Okay, thank you,' she said and she started the car.

'I'll see you soon,' he said. 'If anything happens I'll call and you can pull over, okay?'

'Yes, thank you again,' she said and hung up from the call and made her way back to Pippin Cottage.

It seemed like an eternity on the drive to Appleton Green but when she got there, an ambulance was out the front and Lily ran inside where two paramedics were with Gran, and Nick was standing to the side.

Gran was wearing an oxygen mask and was wheezing and looked very pallid.

'Oh, Gran,' she said, feeling the tears coming again as she rushed to her side.

'I'm fine,' Gran persisted in a feeble voice as a paramedic looked at Lily.

'I'm going to have to ask you to move. We need to put a heart monitor on her,' he said and Lily stood up and went to Nick.

'What is it?' she whispered.

Nick shook his head. 'I'm not sure, definitely a chest infection but maybe something with her heart; they are doing all the tests but she will need to go to hospital,' he whispered.

'I heard that,' Gran said loudly summoning up energy from God knows where. 'I'm not going there again.'

Gran was watching them with an expression of exhausted resignation, and Lily turned to look at her. 'You don't have a choice, my love,' said one of the paramedics. 'You're in heart failure.' He stood up and looked at Lily. 'We need to move fast.'

Lily blurted out, 'Oh, Gran,' as tears began to build up in her eyes.

Gran closed her eyes, and for a moment Lily wondered if she was even alive and then she sighed.

'Bugger, bugger, bugger,' she said and Lily laughed and cried simultaneously.

While they prepared Gran for the ambulance trip, Nick took command of the situation and made sure that the cottage was locked and secured.

'I'll pack a bag for her,' he said to Lily and he ran upstairs while Lily sat next to Gran, holding her hand.

'Righto, we're moving,' said a paramedic and they wheeled her out and up the path and onto the road, where they opened the back of the ambulance.

'Do you want to follow in your car?' the paramedic asked Lily.

'Okay, yes, I need to ring my parents first,' she said to him.

'Bye, Gran, I'll see you in a bit,' she said.

Violet lifted her hand up to touch Lily's cheek and gave her a little smile beneath the oxygen mask and then she was pushed on the trolley into the back of the ambulance. The doors were closed and they were driving away with flashing lights. As the vehicle disappeared from sight, Lily felt her composure disintegrate and sobs came from her that she didn't know existed while she stood in the centre of the country road.

And then she felt Nick's arms encircle her and she turned to bury her face in his chest, allowing herself to feel the pain and fear.

'They'll do everything they can,' he said as he stroked her hair and held her close. 'Your Gran's tough – don't forget that.'

She gathered herself and reluctantly pulled herself away from his shirt.

'I've ruined your shirt,' she said to him, looking at the mess she'd left on his chest.

'I've had worse,' he said with a grin and she laughed despite herself.

He handed her a tissue and she wiped her eyes. 'I need to call my parents,' she said, trying to think clearly. 'And then I need to go to the hospital.'

'Why don't I drive us up to St Vincent's, and you can call your parents from the car?'

'Don't you have to work?' she asked him but he shook his head. 'This is my work, Lily. This is what I do.'

She nodded and grabbed her bag from the cottage, locked up and met Nick in the car, where he had Gran's overnight bag on the back seat.

'I just grabbed some nightgowns and some things from the bathroom and some smalls,' he said. 'We can get anything else she needs in town. And I left some food and fresh water for the cat.'

'Thank you,' she said, meaning it. 'I don't know if I'm very good in a crisis. I seem to panic.'

'It's not panic, and it's not about being good or bad. It's happening and you called me and this is what I do, so call your parents and we can be on our way,' he said as he started the car and took off.

Lily's fingers were shaking as she dialled her mother's number and on the second ring, Denise answered.

'Oh you've finally decided to call have you? I've been asking Gran where you are and she said you are busy but no one can tell me with what. Are you coming back? There are auditions for *Wicked* at the end of September.'

'Mum,' Lily said, her voice breaking slightly. 'It's Gran. They think she's in heart failure. She's been taken to hospital.'

Denise gasped. 'What happened? Did you wake up and find her like that? Did you call the ambulance?'

Lily paused. This was it; she would have to tell her mother what she had been doing.

'No, I was at work,' she said.

'Work? Where are you working? You're supposed to be with Gran.'

Lily swallowed. 'I'm teaching music three days a week in Silverton.'

'Teaching? Why? You're not a teacher,' Denise screeched.

'Mum, this isn't the time to have this conversation. Gran's really unwell, so I'm telling you and Dad to get to the hospital as soon as you can and we can talk about the other stuff later. We are just driving behind the ambulance now.'

'Who is we?' Denise snapped.

'My friend Nick, who has also been looking after Gran. He's a district nurse.'

Denise made a dismissive sound. 'I don't know what has been going on there but it seems like you have lost your mind and have left Gran to fend for herself. Your father and I are coming and whether she likes it or not, Gran will be moving into care and you will be moving back to London, where your real career is.'

Denise ended the call and Lily looked at Nick.

'How was that?' he asked.

'It went as expected,' Lily said shaking her head. 'But there's one thing my mother doesn't realise about me and it's something I just recently realised.'

'What's that?' asked Nick, glancing at her as he drove.

'That I'm more like Violet Baxter than she knows and neither of us will be easily persuaded to do anything we don't want to.'

Nick laughed as he nodded. 'Isn't that the truth. You Baxter women are formidable and that's what I love about you both.'

And as they drove, Lily put her hand on his knee, grateful he was by her side, and he patted it as he sped towards the hospital.

Twenty-eight

The accident and emergency department was busy when Lily and Nick walked inside with paramedics and nurses bustling about, and people on stretchers and patients with various maladies.

A few staff walked past Nick and said hello and he greeted them in return.

'Wait here and I'll speak to the triage nurse,' Nick said. Lily stood to the side and people milled about. A young child with her arm in a sling came into the hospital with her mum.

'Do you think it's broken?' asked the child of her parent.

'I don't know, darling, but the x-ray will tell us,' the mum said and leaned down and kissed the child on the head.

Denise would be here soon, thought Lily. There would be no kisses on the forehead for her with the news she had just broken to her.

Nick came back to Lily's side. 'Gran is with the doctors now,' he said.

'Can I go in?' She looked around.

'Not yet, they'll come and get you. You'll just be in the way.'

Lily nodded and crossed her arms and leaned against the wall.

'My parents should be here soon,' she said. 'My mother is a lot. I think you should know that.'

The automatic doors opened and Lily's parents came through and looked around and then saw Lily.

'Hello, darling, any news?' asked her father as he kissed her cheek. He looked pale and worried and she felt his fear. Gran had always been in excellent health, remarkable really considering her age.

Lily shook her head. 'Hi, Dad, I'm so sorry this is so tough.'

Denise kissed her daughter's cheek and turned to Nick. 'You must be the nurse?' she said.

'Mum and Dad, this is Nick Stafford. Nick, this is Peter and Denise. Nick's been looking after Gran and he's in the amateur show we're both performing in.'

'An amateur show? What on earth have you been up to in Appleton?' asked Denise, looking extremely displeased.

Before Lily could answer, a nurse came out into the waiting room. 'Family of Violet Baxter?'

The four stepped forward but the nurse held up her hand. 'Only two at a time please.'

Lily stepped forward but her parents were already through the door, leaving her to stand next to Nick.

'God she's going to hate that they're first in.' Lily sighed.

'Do you want to get a coffee or a tea?' Nick asked. 'There's a café in the hospital.'

Lily shook her head. 'No thanks.'

Lily's mother came out of the door, her arms crossed as she walked up to Lily.

'She's asking for you,' she said.

'Oh God, is she...?'

Denise rolled her eyes. 'No, she's not dying. She's eating an egg and cress and asking for another teabag as her tea isn't strong enough.'

'They said she was in heart failure,' Lily said.

'Well if she is, it hasn't affected her appetite,' Denise said. 'Now I need a coffee.' She turned to Nick. 'Now, you're a nurse. Where's the café?'

'This way,' said Nick in his charming way and Lily was sure she could sense Denise's mood shift.

'Go on then, Gran's waiting,' said Denise to Lily, who made her escape to inside the doors, after being let in by the nurse at the desk.

Lily walked around the department, trying not to stare at people in the cubicles while looking for Gran.

'There you are,' she said to her dad who was standing outside a cubicle with the curtains drawn.

'How is she?' she asked in a quiet voice.

Her dad shrugged and sighed. 'She has a chest infection. Her heart is being tricky. It's not in full failure as they thought, but she needs to stay and have antibiotics and some more tests.'

She could hear voices from behind the curtain and then it was pulled back and Gran was sitting up in bed, with a gown on and wired up to a machine.

'They're doing a heart test,' she said. 'I'm fine but it's the chest that's bothering me more. I have a chest infection,' she said to Lily. 'Where's Nick?' she said looking behind Lily and into the walk-through.

'He's taken Mum to the café,' said Lily and Violet raised her eyebrows.

'That's brave of him, although if anyone can manage Denise, it's Nick.'

'Mum,' said Lily's dad. 'Don't be rude. Denise is very good to you.'

'She is, Peter, I agree, and she certainly lets me know about it.' Gran picked up a sandwich and took a bite in defiance.

'Mrs Baxter.' A nurse came into the cubicle. 'We are sending you up to the heart ward in a little while. We're just waiting for a few tests to come back.'

Gran smiled sweetly. 'Thank you, dear.'

She looked at Peter. 'Don't get any ideas about me going to a nursing home. I will be here and then home again.'

Peter glanced at Lily who avoided his glance. It was clear the teaching job wouldn't work if she couldn't leave Gran, but that was a problem for another day.

'Nick packed a bag for you, but I'll see what else you need,' Lily said, looking in the overnight bag on the chair.

'I'm not going to need much,' she said to Lily. 'I can let you know if I need anything else.'

The nurse returned with an orderly. 'Righto, Mrs Baxter, we're heading upstairs. We can take your things but you're having some tests so...' She turned to Lily and her father. 'How about you head off and we will call you later and let you know when you can come and see her. We'll be a long while.'

Violet waved her hand at Lily and Peter. 'Go home, come back tomorrow unless I'm dying. I'm tired and I don't want to have to make small talk.'

Lily saw the nurse try and smother a smile and she looked at her dad. 'I think we have been told,' she said and she went to Gran's side and kissed her cheek.

'I'll come back tomorrow,' she said.

'I'll be here, God willing,' Violet said. 'You have rehearsals tomorrow, so don't forget to go.'

Peter looked at Lily. 'Yes, I heard you mention that. What show is it?'

'*My Fair Lady*,' said Lily, knowing that this would be interrogated later in detail.

The orderly kicked up the brakes on the bed and started to wheel Gran slowly to the door, making his point known.

'Okay, Mum, we'll see you later,' said Peter as Lily waved.

'Come and see me tomorrow,' Gran instructed Lily and she looked at her son. 'You can stay at home. I'll let you know if I need anything.'

And then Gran was wheeled away with a wave of her birdlike arm at them both.

Twenty-nine

Nick and Denise were sitting opposite each other in the hospital café, surrounded by the indoor plants and serenaded by the noise of trays crashing and messages over the PA system, as Lily and Peter approached them. Nick was speaking with intensity, half leaning over the table, and Denise looked to be almost snarling with her fingers securely wrapped around a takeaway cup of coffee, while Nick had an unopened bottle of water in front of him.

As they were getting closer, Lily managed to catch the last few words of Nick's sentence.

While he was speaking, his tone was soft but authoritative. '...consider what Lily wants,' he said.

Oh no, this isn't good, she thought as she rushed up to the table.

'Hello, Gran's up to the heart ward, to have some tests,' she said trying to add some cheer to her voice.

'Oh good, you're here.' The tone of her mother's voice was abrupt. 'Perhaps you can explain to Nick why your grandmother can't possibly go back to that cottage and why you are teaching in a school and doing a silly amateur drama show.'

Lily saw Nick react to her mother's words but thankfully he said nothing.

Peter grabbed the chair next to his wife, and Lily slid into the seat next to Nick. 'Mum, I don't think we should have this conversation here. None of that is as important as Gran right now.'

'Then where will we have it?' Denise asked. 'I've been trying to call you for the past ten days. If Gran hadn't told me you were busy, I would have filed a missing person's report.'

Nick shifted his attention to Lily, his face displaying a mixture of compassion and exasperation. 'I can leave if you want. This feels like a family matter.'

'Yes that's probably for the best,' said Denise.

But Lily grabbed his hand. 'No, Nick is my friend and he is supporting me.'

Denise rolled her eyes. 'Supporting you? He hardly knows you.'

Anger caused Lily's cheeks to flush, and she felt her voice rise. 'He knows me better than you do right now. He knows what I want and he encourages me to live my life the way I want to live it.'

'And what you want is to throw away years of training and hard work to play teacher in some village school?' Denise's voice was filled with contempt.

'Denise,' Peter said. 'Now is not the time.'

But Denise put her hand up. 'You have an extraordinary talent, Lily. Why are you not honouring it?'

'I am honouring it, Mum. I love teaching. I've always wanted to teach, but you told me to go to performing college, you told me not to waste my time teaching, and yet, I knew I wanted it all along.'

'You have never said as much to me,' she said looking at her husband. 'Has she?'

Peter sort of mumbled and Lily shook her head at them both.

'Dad, when are you going to stand up to her?' She turned her attention to Denise. 'I know you think you know what's best for me but I'm nearly thirty and I don't want what you wanted for me. I don't think I ever did but I was too afraid to say so. Stop bullying me and stop henpecking Dad. It's exhausting to be around you.'

Denise's face crumpled, and she started to cry.

Lily put her hand on her mother's, across the table. 'Mum, you just don't listen to me, and I know you love the theatre and all it entails but I want a different role in it. I've only been teaching for a short while but I can't wait to get to work. I like having a weekly pay in my account. I like watching children see what they're capable of.'

Lily noticed her father give a little smile and for a moment she was back at Pippin Cottage.

She was eight years old, and kneeling next to her grandmother in the garden. The air was filled with the aroma of freshly turned soil as they carefully distributed carrot seeds from a packet into the ground. Even though Gran's hands were wrinkled, they were so strong back then, and they guided Lily's smaller hands as they patted earth over the seeds.

'Carrots don't like to be moved, so we have to plant the seeds where they will stay. They don't do well if you move them; they die from the shock.'

Lily felt sad for the little carrots who might die and she shook her head. 'Oh we don't want them to die,' she said and looked up at her. 'Gran, how do you know so much about carrots, and cooking and... well, everything?'

Lily remembered the pleased look on Gran's face. 'Darling, I'm sorry to say that I don't know everything but I do like to learn and I read a lot. There are teachers everywhere if you look.'

'Teachers?' Lily became more alert. 'Like at school?'

'Sometimes.' She nodded. 'But a teacher can also be the lady up the road who has chickens, who can tell you what to do when your chooks stop laying, or the bin man who might know how to stop snails from eating your cabbages. People know lots of things; you just have to ask them.'

'I would like to be a teacher. My piano teacher, Miss Weston, is so pretty and she wears pink nail polish when she plays, and she smells like roses.'

Gran gave a little laugh. 'She sounds lovely,' she said.

'But I don't know what I would teach?' Lily pondered out loud.

'Well, what do you love most?' Gran enquired.

'Singing!' Lily responded without any hesitation. 'Singing yes, and playing the piano.'

'Then teach that,' said Gran. 'Now come on, let's water these so they can have a drink and get growing. They need all the help they can get.'

Lily was back in the present as her mother cried.

'I have wanted this for so long, Mum, and I didn't know how to tell anyone, but being at the cottage with Gran – I can't explain it – it's like I'm my truest self.'

'And you can't be that with me?' Denise asked. 'You can't be that in London?'

'No, Mum, I can't.'

Peter leaned into them. 'I understand this is important, but we do have to discuss Gran,' he said. 'She can't go home. We do need to consider a nursing home,' he said.

Lily glared at her father. 'She's not going to a nursing home,' she said. 'She wants to be in her own home.'

'She can't be. It's out of our hands,' he said. 'You've seen how she looks and if you're working, who will be there to care for her if this happens again? No, she needs to go to a home.'

Lily felt the rage returning. 'No, she will be at Pippin Cottage.'

'And you will give up your new job to care for her? And not do the show, which we haven't even discussed,' Denise snapped.

Lily looked at Nick who was silent. 'Do you think she needs to be in a home?' she asked him.

'No,' he said. 'I think she needs to be in her home because older people don't like to be moved.'

'Like the carrots,' Lily burst out. 'They don't do well if you move them. They die from the shock.'

Her parents looked at her as though she was insane and turned to Nick.

'You honestly think she will cope at home?' Peter asked Nick. 'She's ninety-seven.'

Nick took Lily's hand in his and held it tightly and she paused before he spoke.

'We have a while before she can be home. They'll do everything they can to help her but you have to be prepared. She will need an oxygen tank and lots of support.'

Lily nodded but looked at her parents. 'We can arrange things at the cottage, I'm sure of it.'

But Denise shook her head. 'She won't be able to make it up the stairs.'

Lily looked to Nick. 'What do you think?'

'I think we have to do what she wants, which is to return home. We'll have to make it as easy as possible for her but they'll be able to work out what's wrong with her heart and if they can improve the blood flow.'

'We have to do this,' Lily said. 'We have to get her home again.'

Everyone was silent.

Lily went on. 'She wanted to see me sing one more time on stage,' she said firmly. 'We open in two weeks. Can we get her to the show?'

'They will do everything they can,' said Nick. 'But she'll be in here for at least a week, I think, and then we'll see.'

Lily turned to Nick. 'We have to make this show the best it can be.'

He nodded. 'We will,' he said as Lily looked to her parents.

'And you can bring her, and I don't want to hear anything about the show from you, Mum, about what's wrong with it or why it's not good enough for me. The people in this show are working so hard, for nothing more than putting on a great show. So come, enjoy it and I don't want to hear a single bad thing, okay?'

Denise's eyes were wide and she nodded her consent.

Lily stood up. 'We have to go,' she said to her parents. 'We have a rehearsal tomorrow night and I am working tomorrow, but I will come and see Gran after work because I'm right near her now.'

Nick stood up with her. 'Nice to meet you both,' he said. 'I'm sorry it's under such difficult circumstances.'

Denise and Peter nodded at him and Peter outstretched his hand for Nick to shake.

'Thank you, for everything,' her father said.

Lily leaned down and kissed both her parents on the cheek. 'I'll speak to you tomorrow. If you hear anything from the doctors before me, please let me know.'

And then she turned and walked out of the hospital with Nick, no longer a child but finally feeling like an adult.

To my sweet Lily, aged fifteen,

I'm sitting at the kitchen table and writing this. Ever since you left, I've been thinking about your goodbye. It felt more poignant than before and I think I know that your world is so much bigger than mine and so it should be.

No matter how close you were to me this summer, I could tell your mind wasn't always with me, in the cottage, on our adventures.

You talked about your friends so much and yet when I asked you if you wanted to go back early to see them you said no. I wouldn't have minded. I know you're torn between them and still being a child.

Fifteen is hard.

I know that being here, away from your friends and the boys you've been talking about, hasn't been easy for you. The house was enough when you were younger. It was enough to have the yard, the walks, and the baking. Now I see that pull – the one that makes you want to go back to the life you're making outside of here. It's true that this summer wasn't quite the same for you, but I'm so proud of the young woman you're becoming.

You were torn this summer between the slow, peaceful days at the farm and the fast-paced, fun life you had with your friends back home. I could see it in the way you'd sit in the garden and look at the trees. Your mind was somewhere else, but I know you were trying to be present here and that was so sweet. You don't owe me anything, Lily. You have shown me more love than twelve grandchildren. I'm excited for you and what's next for you because you're becoming an adult and finding out who you are.

With all the fun that comes with being fifteen, there's nothing wrong with wanting to be where the action is with your friends. You should have a great time and enjoy every second of it as we are only young once. Also, don't forget that it's okay to slow down every once in a while. After the busy life you have now, the house may seem quiet. But there's something special about that quiet that I hope you'll remember even when you're not here.

You're at an age where everything is exciting and new, where friendships are strong, and where feelings are strong. I've seen how happy you get when you talk about your friends and how much you care about them. They care about you and share your laughs and secrets.

You're lucky to have them in your life. My friendships in this village are everything to me.

I'm so proud of how much you're growing up, my love. There is a lot to see and do in the world ahead of you. You have a big heart, and I'm sure you'll enjoy every trip that comes your way. Also, don't forget that you can come back here if you need to. You will always have a connection to Pippin Cottage. It's in your heart and soul. Even if you don't come back as often as you once did, it will be here whenever you need to remember who you really are.

With all my love,
Gran

Thirty

As Lily entered the cottage, she was struck by a deafening silence. Everywhere you looked, Gran's absence was like a physical slap. No glasses on her table, no music playing, no paper half read. Gran's little but imposing figure typically inhabited the armchair, but today it seemed empty and abandoned. The quiet room was filled with the loud echo of the old clock on the mantel, which had formerly provided solace as background noise but now seemed like a timpani.

She noticed Mr Mistoffelees sitting on Gran's armchair. 'She won't be happy seeing you there,' said Lily with a false enthusiasm as she walked through the room and opened the back door. As she watched the sun set, Nick cleaned up the mess the paramedics had left in the living room and put the rubbish in the kitchen bin and tied up the bag.

'I'll take this out and then head off if you want,' said Nick to Lily.

She turned around. 'Can you stay a while?' she asked.

He nodded. 'Of course,' he said and went outside to dispose of the rubbish and returned to her and washed his hands.

Lily wandered about, looking for something to do. The cottage always looked its best when the morning sun came through the front windows and when the sunset came through the back windows and doors.

The sunset light flowed through the back windows and door, bathing everything in rich, amber tones that appeared to make the house glow from within.

The few copper pans hanging above the old cooker in the kitchen seemed to smoulder in the light, reminding Lily of the many days she spent baking with Gran. The old wooden table, its surface scarred by years of usage, was bathed in a gentle, honey-coloured light and Lily could see her father's initials in the wood, and her own and then Gran's and those of Gran's father. Four generations of vandalism, Gran used to say. Lily wondered if she would have a child one day who might carve their initials into the wood. She could only hope, she thought.

Lily could just see Gran sitting there with her wrinkled hands wrapped around a steaming mug of tea and the paper spread out in front of her, as she read from it, giving opinions and remarks on anything that she thought deserved attention.

The living room was a tapestry of recollections in the dying light. Shadows swirled across Gran's old flowered wallpaper, which she had always intended to change but never did. The armchair, Gran's favourite seat, with the cat on it, a king for a day while the queen was away from the palace, but Lily could still imagine her there, remembering when she used to knit, the needles clicking softly as she worked on another jumper for Lily for winter.

One wall was lined with bookshelves and photo albums, each one filled with a favourite book of Gran's or Lily's favourite childhood stories. Lily stroked her fingers along them.

'You okay?' she heard Nick ask and she turned to him.

'When I was young, Gran would call out, row three, number five from the left, page 45, third paragraph, and I would have to pick the book and open it and read from that exact place.' She smiled at him.

'That sounds fun,' he said.

'Well it was a great way to get me to read. Because I would often want to know the context of the paragraph or the characters and so on. Unless it was one of Grandad's books on air force fighter planes from the Second World War.'

Nick laughed. 'Yes, not really scintillating material for a young girl.'

She looked at the piano. She had been avoiding it the entire time she had been at Pippin Cottage. Lifting the lid, even the faded keys appeared to shine in the failing light. Lily could almost hear the echoes of the songs they'd performed together, Gran's rich alto mixing with her soprano.

She opened the piano stool and saw all the sheet music inside it, and she picked up a copy of Cole Porter's songbook and sat at the piano and placed it on the stand. She played the first opening bars of 'I Concentrate On You' and then started to sing.

As she sang, a song she knew by heart, she closed her eyes, and saw her gran through the years. She opened her eyes and looked up as the mantelpiece captured the final rays of sunlight. The framed photos reinforced what she had been seeing in her mind. Images of Gran over the years – as a young lady, on her wedding day, cradling baby Lily – appeared to come to life during the golden hour. Each was a frozen moment in time, and now Lily was starting the process of saying goodbye. She felt a sob catch in her throat as she sang and Nick joined in, taking over the melody as she played until she came to the last chorus of the song and they sang together, their voices blending perfectly in the small room.

Lily turned to look at Nick. 'I haven't played that piano for years and yet it's still in tune. I think she's been getting it tuned, just in case. She kept asking me to play and I didn't and now I feel terrible.'

She started to cry and Nick pulled her into his arms, lifted her from the stool and held her on his lap.

'It's okay. You weren't to know. You had things happening; stop being so hard on yourself.'

Lily relaxed into his chest, feeling his arms around her.

'All my life, Gran was my safe place,' she said. 'Mum and Dad aren't terrible people but Dad's kind of henpecked and Mum is the biggest mother hen in the world, sort of suffocating me under all those feathers,' she said.

Nick gave a little laugh.

'I could be myself here. I think I've been closer to my true self since I've been back.'

Nick held her close. 'That's good,' he said and she moved her head so she could see his face and then she smiled and kissed him on the mouth.

A slow kiss, and she felt him kiss her in return. She moved her body so she was sitting facing him now, and he kissed her again and she felt his hands on her back and then lower. She pushed into him as his hands went under her shirt and she started to unbutton it and he held her hands.

'Are you sure?' he asked.

'Never been more certain,' she said as the sun finally dipped below the horizon.

The next morning, Lily was up before Nick, asleep in the little bed, which they had somehow managed to get some sleep in, despite the owls calling, the cat trying to dig his claws into Nick's feet, and the fact they simply couldn't keep their hands off each other. But Lily woke feeling invigorated and she showered and set about getting ready for work.

'Morning,' said Nick, when she came back into the bedroom to dress, wrapped in a towel.

'Hello.' She smiled at him.

'Any chance of that towel dropping and you running away from work today?' he asked.

'Nope, I have a very busy day. Don't you have work today?'

He shook his head. 'No, but I did promise Jasper to help with the sets.'

Lily dressed quickly in jeans and a linen blouse and pulled her hair up into a ponytail.

'I'm going to work, then I'll see Gran and then be at rehearsals,' she said, checking her phone. 'I haven't heard from Dad or Mum so I assume no change in Gran's condition overnight.' She slipped the phone into her pocket. 'Okay, I'm going to go and get coffee before work. Stay here for the day between helping Jasper and rehearsals if you like,' she said and she leaned down and kissed him, feeling the butterflies come back. 'I'll see you at rehearsals?'

'See you then,' he said with that beautiful smile of his, and Lily rushed out of the house before she could stop herself and stay in bed with him all day.

Thirty-one

Lily pushed open the heavy door to the cardiac unit, the unfamiliar antiseptic smell filling her senses and making her feel a little nauseous.

All day at school she had been counting down the hours until she saw Gran and now she was here. There was no update yet. Her father had told her via text message, which she took to be a good sign for Gran's health, for now.

'Hi, Gran,' Lily said quietly as she entered Gran's room. Her heart clenched when she saw her so small and fragile-looking in the hospital bed, dressed in a pale pink hospital gown, her eyes closed. Her hair was messy and her face was dry from the air, Lily noticed.

Gran's eyes flickered open. 'Lily, my darling,' she said softly, her voice shaky. 'You're here. How was school?'

Of course, Gran's first question would be about her and how she was.

'Never mind about me, how are you?' Lily said as she pulled up a chair beside the bed.

'Oh I'm fine, same as ever, but please tell me about your day. It's so boring here.'

'Okay, we can trade question for question,' Lily said. 'School was fine. I'm teaching some of the girls who are getting singing lessons the Andrews Sisters songs so they can learn harmonies. They're enjoying them.'

'"Boogie Woogie Bugle Boy" or "Apple Tree"?' asked Gran, a little breathlessly.

'"Don't Sit Under the Apple Tree",' Lily answered.

'A good choice,' Gran said and hummed a little until she was well out of breath.

'Less singing, more breathing,' Lily said to her and Gran gave a little giggle.

Lily observed the oxygen tube in Gran's nose, and the monitors beeping constantly beside her. She appeared paler than she had ever seen her, almost translucent against the bright white hospital linens.

'Has the doctor been in today?' Lily enquired, attempting to keep her voice light.

Gran nodded slowly. 'Dr Thompson arrived early. A lot of big words and concerned looks.'

Lily's stomach twisted as she tried to keep her voice and tone light. 'What did he say?'

'Nothing I didn't already know, love,' Gran murmured, patting Lily's hand lightly. 'This old heart of mine is tired.'

Lily felt tears forming in the corners of her eyes. She blinked them back, determined to be strong for Gran. 'Do not talk like that. You'll be back at Pippin Cottage before you know it!'

Gran's gaze appeared to be directed away from Lily, towards someplace distant. 'Pippin Cottage,' she mumbled. 'I do miss it so much.'

'It's waiting for you,' Lily informed her. 'Although Mr Mistoffelees has been sitting on your chair.'

'The impudence of that cat,' said Gran, not sounding the least bit cross.

Gran's gaze refocused on Lily. 'How is Nick?'

Lily smiled, and Gran raised her eyes to the heavens.

'Oh you are in love. I can see it now.'

Lily was silent for a moment, thinking of her night with Nick.

'I think I am, Gran.'

Gran smiled and closed her eyes. 'Perfect.' She was quiet for a moment. 'Rehearsals tonight?'

'Yes, not long now. We open in two weeks,' she said trying to keep her voice cheerful. 'I really hope you can come and see it, but I understand if you can't, you know, if things are beyond your control,' she said leaving the unspoken between them.

'I'll be there,' Gran whispered. 'I'm just a bit tired now but I'll perk up.'

'You should rest,' Lily stated, straightening up and adjusting Gran's bed linen. She leaned down and kissed Gran's forehead. 'I'll be back tomorrow.'

'Lily.' Gran grabbed her hand. Her grip was strong, despite her weak appearance. 'Don't do anything you don't feel passionate about in life, you know, the big things. Just try everything that speaks to you,' she said, her eyes bright. 'Don't waste your time here living another person's life. Live your own.'

Lily nodded, her eyes stinging with unshed tears. 'I won't, I promise,' she said as Gran then let go of her hand.

'Now go, I need my beauty sleep.'

Lily left the room, closed the door and leaned against the wall outside Gran's room. Her chest was tight and tears fell. She had never seen Gran look so vulnerable and she knew what Nick was saying was true. The realisation struck her like a physical blow: Gran was dying. This was it, and the question was: would she get to see her sing one last time?

Lily walked out of the hospital in a fog, not noticing the busy reception area or the sliding doors that opened for her. As she stepped outside, she felt the fresh air on her face and took a deep, trembling breath.

Her phone vibrated in her pocket. Sheila sent a text:

Rehearsal in thirty minutes. Do not be late!

Lily looked at the message, her eyesight blurring. How was she meant to attend rehearsal now? How could she sing and dance while Gran lay in a hospital bed looking so unwell?

But she knew exactly what Gran would say. 'The show must go on,' she would insist, her blue eyes gleaming. Lily could almost hear her own voice.

It felt like she was walking through tar as she headed to her car. *Keep it together*, she said to herself as she started the drive to Appleton Green. *Concentrate on the show, concentrate on Nick*, she told herself, and she thought of them singing the Cole Porter classic together, the way their voices sounded so perfect together, the way they kissed, the way their bodies fitted together.

'Concentrate, Lily,' she said loudly in the car, attempting to collect herself. 'Onwards,' and she drove to rehearsals.

When she arrived, she could see some of the cast members approaching the hall, chatting and laughing. She envied them and their moods and she took a moment. *Don't bring bad energy into the rehearsal space*, was one of the biggest lessons she had learned at university and never had it been more apt than this moment.

She took a deep breath and exited the car, walking towards the entrance. She smiled as she pushed the door open and walked inside and gasped.

The makeshift stage that she had become accustomed to was gone and in its place was a beautifully built set that could have been used in a professional show. The entire hall had been transformed, in fact, with the old walls now hidden behind carefully painted sets of London streets in the 1800s.

The stage was lined with intricately designed shopfronts and lampposts, making a lively, three-dimensional cityscape, and there were even lampposts along the aisle, carefully placed so they didn't disrupt the view of the audience but still lent ambience to the room.

On stage was the Covent Garden flower market, complete with flower carts and vendor stands with lots of artificial flowers. The attention to detail was amazing, from the floor that looked like it was made of worn-down cobblestones to the lighting that was meant to look like gas lights. Lily could almost smell the scent from the pretend flowers and hear the city's noise.

She stood in shock, as she realised that this amateur show had all of a sudden become very professional. The set wasn't just a background; it was a live, breathing part of their show that made it better than she had imagined.

'Jasper, it's incredible,' she cried out. 'It's absolutely incredible.'

Jasper turned to see her and he beamed. 'You wouldn't expect anything less would you, Miss Baxter? Now, we will run Act One from the top.'

Lily nodded, still in awe of her surroundings, and made her way to the stage. As she looked around, she almost prayed that Gran would get to see this.

Sheila cried out, 'All right, places, everyone. Lily, centre stage please.'

Lily took her place on the stage, and as the scene ran through, she heard her name.

'Lily, it's your line,' yelled Jasper from the seats below and she realised she was still mentally back in the hospital room with Gran.

'Oh God, I'm so sorry.' She let out a sob as David, in his Henry Higgins hat, put his arm around her.

'Lily?' Sheila's voice sounded anxious. 'Are you all right?' She came onto the stage as Jasper came up and Nick came rushing from backstage.

'God I'm so sorry, I'm such a sook,' she said.

'You're not a sook. Your grandmother is in hospital,' Nick said to her.

'Oh no,' said Jasper. 'Is she okay?'

Lily shook her head, tears falling freely down her cheeks. 'I don't know,' she choked out. 'I couldn't... I can't do it today and I want to because I want her to see it, but I can't seem to focus.'

Nick held her close and helped her off the stage and down into the chairs on the floor as Jasper came and sat beside her.

'That's very sad, Lily. She's a marvellous woman – very wise,' he said.

Lily nodded, attempting to get herself together, but Jasper's words just made her cry again. 'I'm sorry,' she reiterated. 'I shouldn't have come.'

'Nonsense.' Sheila was standing in front of her. 'You're right where you should be. We are a family here, Lily. We support one another through thick and thin. That's what a company does.'

Lily looked up, astonished to find the rest of the cast gathering around, their expressions filled with concern and pity.

'Why don't we take a break?' Sheila proposed. 'David, turn on the urn. I believe we could all use a cup of tea and I have a lovely sponge cake and some of Mrs Douglas's shortbreads for everyone.'

Lily started to cry again and shook her head, as though trying to set all the pieces in place in her brain.

As the cast dispersed, Sheila returned her attention to Lily. 'What do you need?'

'Why are you being nice to me? You're Jessica's aunt. I know what you think of me.'

Sheila swallowed. 'I am not a terrible person, and yes, I will support Jessica, but I also know she might have misrepresented the truth recently and I have been unfair, blinkered by familial loyalty instead of common sense. And for that I am very sorry.' She lifted her head proudly.

Lily nodded. 'I understand,' she said with a sigh.

'I am very capable in a crisis, so why don't you tell me everything and we can all work it out as a team, because that's what we are, a team. The Appleton Green Amateur Drama Society.'

She spoke with a sense of kindness and also practicality that Lily admired. Sheila might be many things, but Lily had the sense she was someone you could rely on in a crisis.

And there, in the centre of the village hall, surrounded by the aroma of greasepaint and the distant sound of a kettle, Lily let it all out. Her anxieties, shame, and overpowering love for Gran all came spilling out.

Sheila listened carefully, her arm never leaving Lily's shoulders and when Lily eventually became silent, Sheila murmured softly, 'Your grandmother and I were not ever friends but she is a remarkable woman, and she raised an equally remarkable granddaughter.'

Lily managed a teary smile. 'Thank you,' she muttered.

'Now,' Sheila replied, her tone brisk. 'This is what we are going to do. You'll drink a cup of tea and then run through Act One. Not because we have to rehearse, but because music heals, Lily. It'll serve you well and who knows, your grandmother might just make it to the show in time.'

Lily nodded, feeling a warm sensation in her chest for the first time since leaving the hospital. As David approached with a warm mug of tea, Lily realised that even if her world was shifting beneath her feet, she was not alone. She had her grandmother's love, the love of Nick, her newfound family in the cast, and the healing power of music to help her get through.

Thirty-two

Holding her leather satchel tightly, Lily walked through the gates of Silverton School. Less than one week to go to opening and she felt a chill in the air as she noticed the long shadows fall across the well-kept lawns in the morning sun. The air was cooler and crisper than it had been all summer and Lily knew autumn was on its way. Some people love summer for its heat or spring for the new growth but Lily and Gran's most favourite season at Pippin Cottage had always been autumn. As September turned into October, the scenery around Derbyshire turned into a beautiful quilt of burnt oranges, golds and reds. The old apple tree in the garden, which was twisted but still bearing fruit, dropped its apples on the grass, filling the air with the sweet smell of apples that were about to ripen.

When Lily visited Gran during autumn when she was younger, she and Gran would sit on the little bench by the cottage door on cold mornings, wrapped up in woollen jumpers and drinking hot tea. They would watch the mist rise from the fields nearby.

In the cosy afternoons, they would make apple crumbles and blackberry pies. The old cooker would keep the house warm, and the smell of cinnamon and nutmeg was still one of Lily's favourite smells. As night fell, they would start the fire in the hearth and the crackling flames would cast a warm glow over the living room, where they would read or listen to Radio 4. Sometimes Lily would lie in bed at night and hear the sound of the wind blowing through trees, whose leaves were changing colour, where the owls would call, the wind carrying their messages into the next village.

Maybe she would make a blackberry pie for Gran and take it into the hospital, she thought, and then had a reality check. She had rehearsals every night before opening and was teaching; she could hardly visit Gran let alone bake a pie.

She felt the weight of everything as she walked through the halls to the music department. Then there was Nick...

Thinking of him made her smile as she came to the room where she taught. He had stayed every night since the first and he had even found a bigger bed for them and somehow managed to get it upstairs and into her room.

In the middle of all the chaos, their relationship was growing – a bright spot in the storm of uncertainty and anticipatory grief.

'Good morning, Miss Baxter,' someone chirped, bringing Lily to the present, and she saw a young student waiting for her piano lesson.

'Good morning, Emma,' Lily said as she opened the door to her classroom. 'Ready for your lesson?'

With a happy nod, the girl followed Lily into the room. Lily felt calm as they sat down at the piano. She was meant to be here.

Scales, arpeggios, and soft words of support made the morning go by quickly. As Lily watched her students make progress, she was still in awe of how much she enjoyed teaching and was surprised at how quickly the time had gone by when the lunch bell rang.

Lily called the hospital to check on Gran during her break. The nurse said Violet was steady, but she was still weak. The nurse also said, 'She's been asking when you'll be back.'

Would the guilt ever leave her?

She texted her parents:

Have you seen Gran today?

Her father responded:

We're here now. She seems well, on a new heart medication they said. She has a bit of colour in her cheeks today.

She texted her father:

Great news.

She felt relief. Maybe Gran wasn't ready to leave just yet. If there was a new drug then it meant there was hope, she told herself.

As the afternoon went on, Lily's mind kept going back to Gran and Nick. Time seemed to drag compared to the morning lessons and now she had to visit Gran and then rush to rehearsals.

She hurried to her car because she knew she only had a short time to see her grandmother before rehearsals. The hospital halls were quiet as she walked to Gran's room.

Violet was lying on her back in bed and looked weak but awake and she did have a little more colour than before.

When Lily walked in, her face lit up. 'There's my girl,' she said in a soft, warm voice.

Lily said, 'Hi, Gran,' and kissed her on the cheek. 'How are you feeling? You look a bit better. Dad said you're on a new medication.'

'Oh, yes apparently it's doing what it's supposed to do. So don't worry about me. How was your day? How are things with the little music monsters?'

Lily had to laugh. Gran's spirit was unbreakable even though she was weak. She told her about her day, keeping things light and easy.

'How are rehearsals?' she asked.

'Really good,' Lily said. 'The set is incredible. We're doing a dress rehearsal tonight, which is exciting.'

'Black and white for Ascot scenes?' asked Gran.

'Absolutely,' confirmed Lily.

'I am so looking forward to seeing it,' said Gran, but as Lily looked at the almost one-hundred-year-old woman, she wondered if she would even make it out of hospital, let alone to the show.

She glanced at the time and knew she had to go, and as much as she didn't want to leave she didn't want to let the show down.

'I have to go to rehearsal now, Gran. I promise I'll be back tomorrow.

Gran agreed with a knowing look in her eye. She winked and said, 'Give that handsome nurse of yours my love.'

Lily kissed her goodbye and then ran to her car. She got to the village hall just as Jasper was outside adjusting some posters.

'Cutting it fine, aren't we?' he joked in a friendly way. 'It's a dress rehearsal don't forget.'

'I know,' she said.

The cast was already getting ready inside. Nick smiled at her from across the room, which made her heart skip a beat.

'All right, everyone!' Jasper spoke up. 'Let's take it from the top of Act Two!'

The moment Lily walked out, she felt the usual thrill of being on stage. She was excited to forgot about her problems for a while as she got lost in the world of Eliza Doolittle for the next few hours.

As the *My Fair Lady* company plunged into their first full dress rehearsal, the village hall hummed with excitement as they wore their costumes for the first time.

Lily stepped out on stage in Eliza's flower girl costume, which was a masterpiece of shabby charm, painstakingly created by the National Theatre to mirror Eliza Doolittle's modest origins in Edwardian London.

Lily twirled in the dress, which consisted of a long, voluminous skirt made from rough, dark brown cloth that had been creatively damaged to highlight years of use. The hem seemed to have been hurriedly repaired several times, with fraying and patches.

She wore a ragged shirt in faded cream over the skirt; its once-crisp collar now limp and greying. And one of the makeup women had streaked Lily's arms with plausible stage dirt on the skin, showing where her sleeves were rolled up to her elbows. Her otherwise austere outfit was given a flash of colour by a ragged shawl in subdued green flung loosely over her shoulders and in her hat was a red fabric rose, a little battered and defeated but, like Eliza, it still showed its beauty.

As the actors took their places for the opening number, the hall echoed with a loud crack then a thundering smash and Lily jumped back with Higgins and Pickering as gasps and shrieks burst forth from everyone.

'What the bloody hell was that?' Jasper's voice sliced through the tumult.

Lily turned around and saw that a good portion of the background for the Covent Garden street scene had fallen free from its moorings and now lay crumpled on the stage floor.

'Oh dear,' she said.

'Is everyone okay? Lily?' Rushing from the wings came Nick.

'I'm fine,' she said, feeling a little shaky. 'But that was close. Lucky I wasn't standing there.'

Jasper rushed onto the platform. 'How did this happen?' he asked, his arms sweeping frantically at the dropped backdrop.

The harried-looking stage manager moved forward. 'Jasper, I'm not sure. This morning, we examined all the rigging; everything seemed stable.'

'Well, obviously it wasn't!' Jasper snapped, his typical flamboyance replaced with real wrath.

The actors and crew stood around the dropped set piece as the first shock subsided. Sheila whistled and studied the backdrop's edge. 'Look here,' she replied, pointing to a torn edge. 'This is an old canvas. You can see where it's faded and where it was joined. Most likely, it has been weakening for weeks. We should have checked this. We'll have to check them all now.'

Jasper ran a hand through his hair and looked strangely depressed. 'This is a disaster,' he said softly. 'We open in less than one week. So now I have to check, reorder, which can take weeks for these lengths to come in and then repaint. We don't have time.'

The gathering sank into an uncomfortable quiet. Lily turned to look at Nick and saw her same anxiety in his eyes.

Lily drew a long breath and moved forward. Her voice more forceful than she felt, she added, 'We'll fix it together. Remember, we are a team. You told us that, Jasper.'

Her comments seemed to release the people from the spell of hopelessness. Still sporting his Higgins costume, David nodded confidently.

'Lily's right. This is just the canvases. We can check them all as a team. It's not up to only you, Jasper. We have come too far to allow a setback like this to stop us.'

'I can sew that tear,' Sheila said. 'It will hold although it won't be perfect.'

'And I can help to reinforce the rigging,' David said. 'We will check and triple-check everything.'

Cast and crew members started to volunteer one at a time. They sorted themselves into groups to check, sew, reinforce and repaint where needed.

Jasper stood with his mouth open at everyone speaking at once, and sharing ideas. At last he clapped his hands, the glitter returning to his eye. 'I have never seen a cast come together like this before, ever in my years of directing. Thank you.'

Lily heard his voice crack and then he pulled himself together. 'What are we waiting for? Let's get right to it!'

The rehearsal descended into an unplanned repair session.

Lily was clutching one end of the backdrop while Sheila deftly sewed the tear as the rest of the cast got on with their tasks. Lily looked over at Nick who was working with the stagehands to check the rigging.

As Lily helped Sheila, she heard Andrew start to play the first chorus song – 'Get Me to the Church on Time' – and Alfred Doolittle started to sing and then the chorus joined in, followed by the rest of the cast and crew.

Lily looked around as she sang. This was what she loved about the theatre. Not the applause or the fame or ambition. This pulling together for something bigger than all of them.

At the end of the rehearsal Jasper stood on the stage and looked down at everyone in the show.

'I want to thank you all,' he said, his voice choked with feeling. 'Tonight you have displayed professionalism and cooperation far beyond anything I have seen in professional shows. The essence of theatre is overcoming challenges together, and you have all done that in spades. Bravo! Now we will have our run tomorrow night instead. I hope that is possible, and if it's not, be here anyway.'

Lily looked at Nick and smiled. He gave her a wink and she thought, if only Gran was well, this would have been the happiest she had ever been in her life.

Thirty-three

With her head full of the lessons for the day, Lily ran down the Silverton Grammar hallway, her arms stuffed with sheet music that she had just copied for the choir.

As she turned the corner, she crashed into someone and her music went flying.

'Oh, I'm so sorry!' With a start, Lily scrambled to pick up the paper.

'No damage done, sweetheart,' a voice said. Looking up, Lily was taken aback to see Maureen there, wearing a bright blue apron with badges on it and a painted peacock on the front.

'Maureen? Hello,' she said, shocked to see Nick's mum here.

Maureen laughed and her eyes gleamed. 'Hello, what are you doing here?' She gave Lily a hug.

'I'm the new music teacher, just part-time,' she said.

'Oh, love, that's great, how fantastic. Nick didn't tell me you were working here.'

'He didn't tell me you were working here either.' Lily laughed.

'You think he might have mentioned it,' Maureen said. 'Honestly, these men sometimes.'

Lily laughed. 'I know, but at least we know now.'

'I wish we had spent more time together the other day. How was the movie?'

'It was fun and we had a nice dinner after,' said Lily.

The bell that announced the beginning of classes rang.

'Oh, must dash!' said Maureen. 'But how about we catch up over lunch? Midday in the junior school staffroom?'

Lily nodded, still a little taken aback by the chance meeting. There was a tiny spark of enthusiasm that she couldn't resist as she made her way to her classroom. Having a pleasant, familiar face at work would be good, especially if it was Nick's mum. She had such a great, creative energy, it was infectious.

Lily went to the choir room, where the senior students were sitting, looking uninspired.

'Hello, everyone, I'm Lily Baxter, your new choir teacher. Now if we can get into groups of sopranos, altos, tenors, baritones please?'

The students shuffled about, and finally they were settled and Lily handed out the music to them.

'We are doing a song from a musical called *Rent*. Do you know it?'

There were a few glances and smiles and nods.

'Okay, everyone. Let's talk about the song we're going to sing. The song starts the second act of the show *Rent*. It's called 'Seasons of Love'. We should really think about how we value a year in someone's life because this song makes us do that.' She looked around the room.

'The words ask this question and talk about how we might measure time in different ways, such as by minutes or miles or by more general ideas. In the end, though, the song seems to say that love is the most important way to measure a year.'

One of the students put her hand up.

'Yes?' she asked her.

'We usually sing old songs, like Latin and God music,' she said.

'Who was your choir teacher?' she asked.

'Mrs Hughes, she's really old. She was doing it until they found someone new.'

'Oh, okay,' said Lily. Mrs Hughes lived in Appleton Green, right near Gran. What a small world, she thought. The woman must be close to eighty. They must have been desperate if she was taking choir.

'Well, we will be singing more contemporary music now. We will sing it as a group a few times to learn the melody for those who aren't familiar and then we can start on the harmonies,' she said and sat down at the piano and played a few chords and then started to sing with the students.

As midday approached, Lily was looking forward to seeing Maureen and having a friend to spend time with at lunchtime. Not that people hadn't been welcoming, but many were busy and she was looking forward to a catch-up.

Maureen was already in the staffroom when she arrived, setting up her prepared lunch at one of the little tables. Maureen smiled warmly and waved her over.

'How was your morning?'

Lily felt some of her tension begin to release as she took a seat across from Maureen.

Lily said, 'It's been good,' and opened her own meal. 'I took choir for the first time. I didn't know my gran's neighbour had been teaching it – small world.'

'Mrs Hughes? Yes, she's a sweetheart but terribly old-fashioned,' she said.

Lily smiled as she opened her container of last night's leftover chicken that she had added to a salad.

'Now I hope you didn't pay any attention to Nick's dad thinking he was funny. Nick never brings anyone home, except for Jessica but she barged her way in.'

Lily paused, her fork halfway to her mouth. 'What do you mean Jessica barged her way in?'

Maureen sighed, shaking her head. 'Oh, that girl. She's always been a bit... intense. She and Nick dated but it was nothing serious. At least, not on Nick's part.'

'She told people they were engaged,' Lily said, watching Maureen's face for a reaction.

She laughed. 'Oh, love, no. That's just another of Jessica's tall tales. She's been spreading that rumour around, but it's simply not true.'

Lily felt a mix of relief and confusion wash over her. 'How can you be sure?'

'Because I'm Nick's mother, dear,' Maureen said with a gentle laugh. 'Don't you think I'd know if my only son was engaged? Besides, Nick was never that serious about her. He cares for people, you see, and I think Jessica mistook his kindness for something more. I think they went out a few times over a few weeks but he wasn't serious.'

Lily sat back in her chair. 'You know, he told me that but I needed confirmation, not that I didn't truly believe him, but she's so beautiful, I wondered.'

Maureen patted Lily's hand. 'Jessica can be very convincing when she wants to be. But let me tell you, I've never seen Nick as happy as he is when he's with you. All he does is talk about you. His sisters are dying to meet you.'

Lily felt her cheeks warm at Maureen's words. 'Really?'

'Really,' Maureen confirmed with a nod. 'Now, why don't you tell me about this choir you're leading? I bet you're shaking things up a bit, aren't you?'

As they continued their lunch, chatting about music and the school, Lily felt a weight lifting from her shoulders.

'I'll see you at opening night,' said Maureen as they finished their lunch. 'I'm bringing the whole tribe. Will I meet your family there?' she asked.

Lily shook her head. 'It depends on Gran. We need to see how she is. Mum and Dad will come with her, hopefully on the last night so she has more time to rest and recover.'

'Wonderful,' said Maureen as they packed up their lunch containers.

'I can't wait to see you and Nick in it, the dynamic duo!' she said, and gave Lily another hug and then was gone to class and Lily headed back to the music school to shake things up a little more. On the way she texted Nick.

I just had lunch with your mum.

What? Why? How?

You didn't tell either of us that we worked at the same school. We bumped into each other.

> Oh wow, how funny. I was going to tell you
> but all the stuff with Gran meant it just
> went out of my brain. She loved you.

She was great, very enlightening.

> Oh no, what did she say?

That's between her and I. Gotta go teach piano!

And she laughed all the way to class.

Thirty-four

The morning of opening night was clear and crisp and Lily made her tea and went into the garden. Nick was at his flat and she was alone in Pippin Cottage.

The garden of Pippin Cottage was awash in soft morning light, and the leaves of the old apple tree were a riot of reds and oranges. It was the sort of morning that Gran would have cherished and she felt the sadness come back. She wiped tears from her eyes with the sleeve of her robe.

As though the world was listening, she heard her phone in her pocket signal a text message and she opened it and saw her dad's name. Fear ran through her. When would she stop being anxious at text messages? she wondered as she opened it.

> Gran had a good night. Nurse said if she continues like this she can come to closing night. Hope we can come then too.

Despite Lily's best efforts to keep her optimism in check, her heart soared at the prospect of Gran coming, but she was also aware of how rapidly things could shift in relation to Gran's condition. It was disappointing her parents weren't coming tonight but her mother was barely speaking to her, so she wasn't about to beg her to come to the show.

'That's good news about Gran, isn't it?' she said to Mr Mistoffelees as he wandered about the grounds. The garden was still half done and Lily wondered if she could fix it in time for Gran's return and then gave up the thought.

One thing at a time, she told herself. She had moved here to slow down, not to fill every moment with activities.

She had the day to herself, alone, and it felt almost surreal. Nick had been here every night since Gran had been in hospital but they had agreed they would get proper sleep the night before the show.

After breakfast, Lily cleaned the cottage to keep herself busy and pulled a few weeds out and then sat in the sun with the cat and enjoyed the morning.

At lunchtime, she contacted the hospital, but Gran was asleep, and she didn't want to wake her up.

How is Gran? came a text from Nick.

She's asleep but Dad said she's a bit better and might come to closing night, she said.

That was five shows away. Would Gran make it to then?

Want a pickup on the way to the show? texted Nick.

Yes please.

Lily sat at the piano and played a few notes, and then started to play a 'Nocturne in B-Flat Minor' by Chopin and felt herself relax into the music as she played. How long had it been since she had spent time playing for no reason other than for pleasure?

It was so peaceful in the cottage as she played. Mr Mistoffelees came and jumped up onto the stool beside her and sat purring, listening to the music.

She glanced down and smiled at the cat. Everything was okay, she reminded herself. Not perfect but it was okay.

Late afternoon, Lily arrived at an already bustling village hall, with the orchestra warming up and the final touches to the lights and sound being tested.

The members of the cast were seen moving around in a variety of costumes and makeup styles. All the while Jasper's voice could be heard booming directions.

'Lily!' Immediately after he saw her, Jasper called out, 'I'm very happy to see you, my dear, but please, please, let's get you ready.'

Lily knew she had plenty of time but she wasn't about to tell him that. Jasper seemed to do best when he was in panic mode.

During the process of being led into a makeshift dressing room, Lily caught a glimpse of herself in the mirror. Her face was pale, and her eyes were wide with nervousness.

'Deep breaths,' Sheila murmured as she appeared next to her with a smile. 'You're going to be wonderful.'

In the hour that followed, Lily had been converted into Eliza Doolittle by the makeup girl, who was also Sheila's granddaughter. Lily was in her costume, standing in the wings and looking out at the hall, which was fast filling up. The rapid beating of her heart was so loud that she was certain everyone could hear it.

Suddenly, Nick was there by her side, looking absolutely stunning in his Freddy Eynsford-Hill costume. He put his hands on her shoulders and she felt herself relax at his touch.

'Are you okay?' he asked.

'I was wondering where you were,' she said with a smile. 'I'd kiss you but I would put coal on your face and suit and that isn't in the script.' She laughed.

Nick kissed her shoulder. 'You're going to be amazing.'

'Do you have anyone in tonight?' she asked, peeping through the curtain at the audience.

'Yes, my parents, sisters and their partners and my neighbour at the flat and some friends,' he said casually.

'God, that's terrifying,' said Lily.

'What about you?' he asked.

'No one,' she said.

'Not even your parents?' he asked, surprised.

She shook her head. 'They might come with Gran but let's just say, Mum isn't happy with me and this show.'

Nick shook his head. 'Her loss. You're amazing in it.'

'Five minutes to curtain!' In his call, Jasper's voice had a little quiver, which was a clear indication of his own uneasiness.

She felt Nick's breath on her neck.

'Lily,' he said in his low voice. 'You were born for this moment. This includes not only the performance but also teaching, being at Appleton Green, and everything else. You have arrived just where you were supposed to be. Take it all in.'

Lily's eyes began to well up with tears, but she blinked them back.

'Thank you,' she said as she left.

'Places everyone!' Jasper's voice could be heard again.

Nick gave her hands one final squeeze before leaving. Lily drew in a long breath and closed her eyes for a brief period.

'This is for you, Gran,' she whispered. 'Thank you for everything, even if you don't get to see this, thank you. I love you.'

As soon as the curtain began to rise, Lily experienced a peculiar sense of serenity that engulfed her as she looked out into the audience, and there, in the front row, with her parents sitting either side of her, was Gran, all three beaming with pride.

Thirty-five

Lily took her fourth bow to a standing ovation, as she saw Gran standing up, using her walking frame, and she noticed she was wearing nasal prongs for the oxygen tank that was attached to the side of the wheelchair.

Denise was wiping her eyes between clapping and Lily took the final bow with Henry Higgins and hugged him on stage. Finally she left the stage to where Nick was standing and she fell into his arms and kissed him.

'They loved it,' she said.

'They loved you,' he returned and spun her around.

'Gran is here,' she said. 'I have to get changed and go and meet you at the dressing room and we can see her together,' she said.

'I'll be out soon,' Nick said and Lily rushed to the dressing room to undress and take off her makeup.

It was so exhilarating as people came and said well done to her and she returned the excited greetings and congratulations. Finally she was dressed and ready to see Gran.

Lily picked up her bag and gathered some of the flowers and cards from well-wishers, laughing and smiling as she made her way out of the dressing room and into the space at the back of the hall. There were so many people around and she looked for Nick in the crowd.

Gran would be so happy to see them both, she thought, as she walked towards the male dressing rooms, but as she came closer, she could see Nick stood in the poorly illuminated hall and he was not alone. Jessica was there, her face vulnerable in a way Lily had never seen before, tear-stained and passionately talking about something. Nick then answered her, as subdued, low, anxious tones, his hand then was on her arm and she fell forward into his arms and he held her as she cried.

Lily stopped; the flowers in her arms became unexpectedly heavy and she knew whatever she was seeing wasn't for her. She couldn't hear their words, but the intimacy made her stomach fall away. Jessica nodded at something Nick said, then stretched up to touch his face in a movement too familiar.

What the hell was happening? Lily's brain ran wild as she watched them, knowing she should leave and not jump to conclusions but it was impossible. Was Nick just consoling an ex-Jessica, or was there more to it? Was Jessica back to her manipulative ways?

No one had ever made Lily feel quite so terrible as Jessica and she didn't want to feel it again.

Don't let her ruin this, she told herself and she stepped away quietly and through the back doors, around the side of the hall to meet Gran and her parents outside.

'Lily,' she heard from her mother as she came around the corner. 'Congratulations, darling,' Denise said. 'You were marvellous – all of you but especially you.'

Lily hugged her mum and dad and then leaned down to Gran.

'You being here is the best part of the night,' she said to her and Gran beamed at her.

'Darling girl, what a show, and what a voice you have. It's just so beautiful, Lil. I'm so proud of you. I have missed hearing you sing. I can die happy now,' Gran said and Lily laughed.

'Well don't die too soon. I still have five more shows to get through,' she said as she looked around for Nick but also for Jessica.

'Are you out for just the night or for good?' she asked Gran.

'Just the night.' Gran made a face. 'Maybe you can hide me in the cottage?'

Lily laughed. 'I don't think so, even if I do love you more than life itself. Dad and Mum would kill me.'

Gran peered over her shoulder. 'Here he comes, our Freddy,' she said. Lily stood up, feeling her body tense at his presence.

'Hello, I waited for you,' he said and put his arms around her shoulder.

She looked at him, 'I came to see you, but you were busy,' she said, looking him in the eye and lifting her chin.

Nick blinked a few times. 'Yes, I need to talk to you.'

Lily raised her eyebrows at him. 'I'm sure you do,' she said and turned back to Gran.

'Can I help you back to the hospital?' she asked her.

But Gran shook her head. 'No, you stay with Nick and celebrate. I have to get back or the nurses will send out a search party and give me cold tea and toast in the morning.'

'We can't have that,' said Lily, catching her father's eye who rolled his eyes at her.

'Let me speak to Nick,' Gran said and Lily turned to him.

'She wants you,' she said and she stood back and looked around for Jessica but she couldn't see her anywhere.

'You all right, darling?' Denise was by Lily's side, watching her face.

'Yes, fine,' she said, smiling brightly at her mother.

'No, you're distracted,' said Denise. 'I might not know what's right for you but I know you.'

Lily looked at her mother, and felt her eyes sting. 'Nick's ex is here. She's been really difficult. Like really difficult.'

'Well I know when a man is in love and that man adores you, and he's worth being here for. He's just lovely, Lily,' Denise said.

Lily sighed. 'I don't know. Why didn't he tell me she was coming?'

'Maybe he didn't know,' said Denise putting her arm around Lily. 'I feel like I've ruined you somehow.'

'What do you mean?' Lily asked.

'I think I put so much time into telling you what to do that I ended up stifling your ability to trust yourself,' Denise said.

Lily looked at her and saw her mother's face. 'You know, I did stand up to her a few times and I even quit the show for a while but seeing her tonight, it really threw me.'

Denise turned to her daughter and held her face in her hands. 'You have everything you want right now, Lily. Don't let your newfound freedom here get waylaid by anyone, least of all an ex-girlfriend.'

Lily nodded. 'You're right,' she said. 'Thanks, Mum. I needed that reminder.'

Nick stood up from talking to Gran and she smiled at Lily and she nodded at him. He came to her side and Denise stepped away.

'We're taking Gran back to the hospital,' Denise said to Lily.

Lily said her goodbye as Nick waited.

'My family are at the pub. Do you want to and come and see them? I didn't think now was the right time for them to meet your gran and parents.'

Lily was silent for a moment. 'What did Jessica want?' she asked.

Nick shook his head sadly. 'She wanted to talk to you, to say sorry, but I told her to leave you alone. That she'd done enough damage.'

'Why was she crying?' Lily asked, shaking her head in disbelief.

'Because I told her I loved you,' he said, his eyes searching hers.

Lily felt her mouth drop. 'Oh, Nick,' she said.

'If you don't feel that way, let me know. I mean I will still hang around anyway in case you change your mind; but Lily, I think you're so talented and I know you love it here but I do think you should try again in London, if you want to, that is.'

'But you hate London,' she said to him.

'No, I don't hate London. I don't have any opinion on it really but I love you, so if you said you wanted to be in Outer Somalia to pursue anything you wanted, I would follow.'

She leaned up and kissed him.

'I love you too, Nick, I do; but I don't think I want that. I want to be here. I just need to get Gran home and well.'

'Well we can do anything, as long as we're together,' he said.

Lily smiled at him. 'Okay, let's go and get a drink,' she said. 'I really hope Jessica won't be there.'

'And if she is, have a great time anyway. She's not an issue for us, okay?' Nick took the flowers and cards from her arms. 'Let me put these in the car and then I'll come back and walk you to the pub.'

Lily nodded as the crowd started to dissipate and she stood alone at the front of the hall.

'Lily?' she heard and she turned and saw Paul, her agent from London, standing to the side.

'Oh hi, how are you? Did you see the show?' she asked, surprised.

'Yes, a friend told me you were in it and I thought I would come up and see if you were still as good as I remembered.'

There was a cold breeze in the air, and Lily shivered and crossed her arms.

'I'm wondering when you're coming back to London, as you haven't called me back and I heard what happened at *Les Mis*, but they said they would see you again and, if not, there are several auditions coming up, closed ones, that I think we need to get you in to sing for, and there's also a tour with *Phantom of the Opera* through Asia. It would be wonderful for you. You'd be an amazing Christine, and you wouldn't need the wig.'

He laughed at his own joke but Lily forgot to smile.

This was everything she had once wanted, and now it was being handed to her, she wasn't sure what she thought. Paul was finally paying attention to her but did she want it?'

'You ready?' Nick was walking towards her and Lily stood between the agent and Nick.

And suddenly, everything she had been sure about didn't seem so clear anymore.

Act Three

Thirty-six

Lily stood still, stuck between Paul and Nick.

This couldn't be happening now, could it?

The cool night air felt sharp on her skin, bringing her back to reality. It really was happening.

'Lily?' Nick's voice interrupted her thoughts. 'Everything okay?'

He walked up to Paul and held his hand out. 'Hi, I'm Nick Stafford.'

'Hi, Paul Meadows, Lily's agent. I loved your performance tonight,' Paul said to Nick. 'Ever think about doing this professionally?'

Nick laughed. 'No, I have a job already.' He turned to Lily. 'You didn't tell me your agent was coming?'

'I didn't know,' she said with a raised brow at Nick.

'Nick's my boyfriend,' she said, and the confidence in her voice surprised her. That was one thing she was sure of, even though the end of the night had been weird with Jessica.

Paul sniffed at Lily. 'I was just telling Lily about some great chances in London. *Phantom of the Opera* is going on a tour through Asia that I think it would be great for her.'

Nick's hand around Lily's waist got tighter almost without her noticing. He kept his voice neutral and said, 'Wow, that sounds amazing.'

Lily felt a rush of love for him. Lily agreed, her mind still racing, 'It does sound amazing and thank you, but I've just started teaching here, and I need to help with my gran. I mean you don't need to know about that but still...' She was rambling. *Stop talking, Lily*, she told herself.

Paul gave a nod of agreement. 'Of course, but Lily, chances like this don't come up every day. You have had a quiet spell. It would be good to get back in the swing of things. You're a real talent. A voice like that is hard to come by. I think you could do Broadway as well,' he said.

'I remember this speech,' Lily said with a frown.

'What speech?' Paul snapped.

'What you just said, it's what you said when I graduated college. You said, I'm a real talent. A voice like that is hard to come by. And I could do Broadway as well.'

'It's the truth – that's why I'm saying it again,' Paul said, putting his hands deep in the pockets of his coat.

'And you said it to Nigel, when he graduated.'

'Nigel?'

'Never mind,' she said with a shiver. 'I have to go. I'll speak to you tomorrow.'

Paul nodded. 'I'll wait for your call.' And he walked away from Lily and Nick.

Lily turned to Nick. 'Let's go for a walk.'

They walked in silence for a while, the sounds of the village fading behind them. The moon hung low and full in the sky, casting a silvery glow over the landscape. It was beautiful, peaceful – everything London wasn't, she reminded herself.

'So,' Nick finally said as they reached the riverbank. 'London, huh?'

Lily let out a shaky laugh. 'Yeah. I don't know. I mean it feels too good to be true. Why now? It feels like déjà vu. It also feels like a test,' she said.

'It's an amazing opportunity, Lily. You should do it.'

She looked up at him, searching his face. 'But what about us? What about Gran? My teaching job? I can't just leave all that behind.'

Nick took her hands in his, his touch warm and comforting. 'Lily, listen to me. I love you. I want you to be happy. If that means going to London and doing some auditions, that's what you should do. Just try it. You don't know what might happen.'

'But what about you?' Lily pressed. 'You said you'd follow me anywhere, but I can't ask you to uproot your life for me.'

'You're not asking. I'm offering,' Nick said firmly. 'I can find nursing work anywhere. And as for Gran... well, we both know she'd be furious if you turned down an opportunity like this because of her.'

Lily laughed softly, knowing he was right. She could almost hear Gran's voice: *Don't you dare use me as an excuse, Lily Baxter!*

'But what if I don't want to go?' Lily whispered, voicing the thought that had been nagging at her since Paul approached her. 'What if I'm happy here, teaching and doing community theatre?'

Nick cupped her face gently. 'Then that's okay too. But Lily, I need you to be sure. I don't ever want you to resent staying here, to wonder "what if". If you don't at least audition, you might always regret it.'

Lily leaned into his touch, closing her eyes. He was right, of course. Even if she ultimately decided to stay in Appleton Green, she owed it to herself to at least try.

'Okay,' she said softly. 'I'll call him tomorrow.'

Nick smiled, pulling her into a tight embrace. 'That's my girl. And hey, who knows? Maybe you'll hate London and come running back to little old Appleton Green.'

Lily laughed, burying her face in his chest. 'Maybe. Or maybe you'll fall in love with the big city and never want to leave.'

'As long as I'm with you, I don't care where we are,' Nick said, his voice sincere.

They stood there for a long moment, holding each other under the moonlight. Lily felt a sense of peace.

'We should head back,' Lily said eventually, reluctantly pulling away. 'The others will be wondering where we are.'

As they walked back towards the village, hand in hand, Lily's mind was already racing with plans. She'd need to talk to Mr McBride at the school, arrange for someone to cover her classes. And Gran... how was she going to tell Gran?

'Stop,' Nick said suddenly, tugging on her hand.

'What?' Lily asked, shocked out of her thoughts.

'You're already miles away, planning and worrying,' Nick said, a fond smile on his face. 'We have time for all that tomorrow. Tonight, let's just celebrate your amazing show. Deal?'

Lily smiled, feeling the stress leave her shoulders. 'Deal.'

They entered The Crumpetty Tree to a chorus of cheers. The entire cast and crew were there, along with what looked like half the town. Jasper rushed over, pressing a glass of champagne into Lily's hand.

'There you are, my dear! We were about to send out a search party,' he shouted. 'Come, come, we're about to toast our marvellous Eliza!'

As Lily was swept into the crowd, taking congratulations and answering questions about her performance, she felt a surge of affection for these people. They had become her family over the past few months, helping her through ups and downs.

Could she really leave everything behind?

As she laughed and talked, the thought kept coming back to her, but she ignored it. Nick was right; tonight was a good night to party. She could worry about London, auditions, and big choices that might change her life tomorrow.

As the night went on, Lily stopped by the bar to catch her breath. Nick showed up next to her with two new drinks in his hands.

Someone raised a glass and said, 'To Eliza and Freddy!'

'To Lily and Nick!' Jasper added, and everyone in the crowd cheered.

Lily felt a sour pang as she looked around at all the happy faces. Now this was her home and these were her people. It hurt her heart to think about leaving them, even for a short time.

However, when Nick squeezed her hand, she too felt excited. London was calling, giving her the chance to make a dream come true. She felt like she could do anything with Nick by her side but did she really want that dream anymore? Just because it was offered didn't mean she had to take it, she reminded herself.

Tomorrow would bring choices and plans, as well as endings and starts. But tonight, when she was with people she loved and who made her laugh, Lily let herself enjoy the moment, enjoying her victory and the bright, unknown future that lay ahead.

Thirty-seven

Lily was in the solitude of Pippin Cottage, her shaky fingers hovering over her phone, and the last curtain call of *My Fair Lady* had finally faded. She had been avoiding what she was about to do. Most people would have been on the phone the next day but Lily couldn't do it. She knew she had to but couldn't make the call. Finally, she took three deep breaths, straightening her shoulders, then dialled Paul Meadows's number.

'Paul Meadows,' she heard him answer.

'It's Lily Baxter,' she said.

'Oh how wonderful, I'm so glad you called. I thought we might have lost you to the am dram world.' He laughed, somewhat meanly she thought, but maybe she was imagining it. 'Now tell me you are heading to London.'

Lily looked at Mr Mistoffelees sitting on the windowsill. 'Yes, I would like to audition. If that's okay?'

She wasn't sure why she was so nervous but she was.

'Oh that's the best news I've had since Nicole Scherzinger pivoted and took on *Sunset Boulevard*.' He laughed loudly. 'Although that's gone a bit south now. I will be truthful with you and tell you I already have *Phantom* pencilled in for you. Still, listen; while I have you, we should investigate a few more possibilities. How's your belt? Any issues?'

Her brain whirled by the time Lily hung up. Apart from *Phantom of the Opera*, she now had scheduled auditions for *Les Misérables, An American in Paris*, and a workshop for a fresh musical creating buzz on the West End.

'Right,' she said to herself, 'then no pressure.'

She would have to be in London for a week and she still had subletters in the flat. Nigel's things hadn't been cleaned out and Lily would have to deal with that also when the tenants left. She felt like her head was spinning when she heard a soft knock at the door and Nick, in his work uniform, peered around the corner with a bag of pastries.

'Sweet treats and a cup of tea?' he asked.

'Oh yes please. I just got off the phone with Paul. It's too much to take in,' she said.

'Let me make some tea and then tell me everything,' he said.

Soon Lily was sitting with a mug of tea and she inhaled the reassuring scent of Earl Grey. 'I have to go to London next week.'

'Okay,' he said. 'That's great.'

'And not only am I auditioning for *Phantom*, but I'm also trying out for three other shows.'

Nick's eyebrows shot higher. 'That's amazing, four auditions in a week. You will get something for sure, probably all of them and then you'll have to choose. What will you sing?'

'Well, naturally, there is *Phantom*. For that "Think of Me" and "Wishing You Were Somehow Here Again". *Les Mis* then is searching for a new Éponine, hence "On My Own" is good. Oh, and "The Man I Love" for *An American in Paris*, but I don't think that one is really me, as Lise is supposed to be able to do ballet and I am not really ballet trained.'

Nick whistled. 'That's a lot to prepare for in a week,' he said.

'I know,' she said and sighed.

Her phone buzzed with a flurry of alerts before Lily could reply. She looked down to watch the am dram society WhatsApp group come alive.

'Oh no. How do they already know?' she let out.

Nick made a face. 'I might have told Sheila about it when I hurried out for the pastries. In my defence, I wouldn't have expected her to tell the whole village.'

'You might as well have given her a bell and asked her to roam the village and say "Hear Ye, Hear Ye" to all and sunder,' she snapped at him.

She stood up and went into the kitchen and started to read the messages and then smiled.

'I'm sorry. I was rude then – these messages are so sweet,' she said to Nick.

'What do they say?'

'Sheila has offered to care for Mr Mistoffelees while I'm away, and David has said he's happy to do anything around the cottage before Gran comes home, and Jasper has offered me his "lucky audition cufflinks".' She looked up and laughed. 'Bless them all.'

'Everyone just wants you to be happy and share your talent with the world,' Nick said.

His work phone buzzed. 'Sorry, let me get this quickly,' he said and answered. Lily rinsed out her cup and then glanced at him.

'Hi? Sure, yes, I'm here now,' he said and as he listened, Lily noticed his face become serious. A frown covered his brow and he ran his hand through his hair.

'Okay, yes, thanks, I see. I'll let her know.'

His voice faded off, the final note hanging in the air. 'What is it?' she asked, but somehow she knew the answer.

'It's Gran. She's had a heart attack,' he said. 'That was the ward. I asked the nurse to let me know any change.'

'I'll lock up,' she said. 'Call Dad from my phone. Can you drive?'

Just as she said it, her phone rang and she saw it was her father.

'I know, I'm on my way,' she said, as she put out food for the cat and locked the house.

'Let's go,' she said to Nick and suddenly London didn't seem so important anymore.

The trip to the hospital was silent as Lily's head spun with options, each one less appealing than the next. Nick stretched across and gently squeezed her hand.

'Don't try and solve everything right now. One moment at a time,' he said to her and she nodded.

'You're right, you know. I am trying to solve everything. I'm going from London to Gran to the village, to the school, to Mum and Dad and the flat. It's all too much,' she admitted.

As they pulled up to the hospital, Nick stopped the car out the front.

'You go up and I'll find a park,' he said.

Lily leaned over and kissed his cheek.

'Thank you,' she said and then she was out of the car and running inside and up to the ward where her parents were in the hallway with a doctor.

'Hi, what did I miss?' asked Lily, breathless from running.

The doctor looked at her. 'I was just explaining that Mrs Baxter has had a significant heart attack,' he said. 'Although her situation is critical, we have stabilised her for now. The next twenty-four hours will be absolutely vital.'

Lily felt as though her world was slipping away from her and she couldn't hang on for much longer. 'Can we see her?'

Nodding, the doctor said, 'Yes, but she's sedated and in ICU. She's in and out of consciousness. I would try and keep it calm. She can't be stressed at this point.'

A nurse came to them and gave them a sad smile, and Lily wanted to scream at her that this was all a huge mistake, but the nurse kept walking and then went through large glass doors that made a hissing sound as they opened and then through to a small room to the side.

They went silently into the room. Gran reclined in the bed, smaller and more fragile than Lily had ever seen her. She had wires and drips hooked up to her and the heart rate monitor was ticking over in the background. Her eyes, when they opened, were as keen as they had always been.

Gran spoke. 'There you are,' her voice soft yet kind. 'I started to think you would have forgotten about your old gran.'

Lily hurried forward to grab her hand. 'Never.'

Her father came to the other side of Gran and held her other hand, as Denise stood to the side.

'You know I'm going soon,' said Gran, her pupils dilated and her words slurred.

'Where's that, Mum?' asked Peter.

'Home,' said Violet with a smile.

Lily nodded. 'Yes, home again, Gran – the cottage is waiting for you.'

Violet smiled and for a moment, she looked like a little girl.

'Sing for me, Lily, one more time.'

'Oh, Gran, there will be plenty of singing in the cottage when you're home. I've been playing the piano again,' she said to her but Gran shook her head.

'Sing Cole Porter, one more time,' she said, almost fervently.

Lily felt her voice tighten in her throat but then she took a deep breath and started to sing 'Ev'ry Time We Say Goodbye', softly, the rhythm of the heart monitor being her only accompaniment.

The old woman closed her eyes and nodded, in time to the song, and gave a deep sigh, a smile on her face.

As Lily came to the end of the song, she felt Nick's hand on her shoulder.

'She's gone, Lil,' she heard him say and she looked at Gran, so still, with the smile on her face, her features softened, without pain or worry. And the heart monitor was still, a single line, sounding like an oboe note playing in the background.

She looked to her father who was hugging Denise and crying.

'Gran? Gran?' she said. She looked at Nick. 'Do something. Can't you restart her heart, do CPR, something?'

Nick shook his head. 'No, she signed an order, no heroic measures, Lily. She was tired; she was ready to go.'

Lily put her head on Gran's hand.

'I love you so much,' she said to her grandmother for the last time in her presence.

Thirty-eight

Violet's thin body was propped up by pillows as she lay on the hospital bed, and her breath came out in short, uneven gasps. She was surrounded by a continuous beep from the heart monitor, which rang around her like a distant rhythm, as well as the sterile air of the room, combined with the slight scent of antiseptic that clung to the sheets and made her feel ill. She was able to hear it, but it seemed to be very far away, as if it had lost its connection to her for some reason. Why couldn't she get back?

A deep, unrelenting pressure caused her chest to ache with each and every breath that she took.

Her body was dying. This was it, the end, curtains, show's over. For months she had been aware it was coming, and this was why she couldn't go to a nursing home. She had to do things, set them right before she left. Now they were as right as they were going to be, she thought.

It was a strange feeling, this dying business. It sounded like there was a party happening in another room, talking and laughing and some music playing, but she was too drowsy to join. She didn't mind. She had been to enough parties in her time; she was happy to lie here and listen for a while.

But it felt as though the world around her was slipping away from her, becoming something less concrete, or less certain. It was almost impossible to explain, just like a baby can't explain what being born is like. It was the same thing, she realised.

She opened her eyes and the room flickered in and out of focus. She saw that the bright lights of the hospital were gradually dimming, and in their place, she saw her cottage, so snug, so perfect, where she had spent most of her adult life. There were the flowered curtains, the wooden beams, her armchair by the heater, the kitchen table, the initials carved into the wood, the windowsill where she had sat for countless mornings, watching the garden and its creatures.

She could see the garden as it used to be. The flowers swaying in the breeze and the apple trees laden with fruit. Martin was visible in the distance, standing just beyond the tree line. He was there, hands in his pockets, smiling at her, waiting. He had been waiting a long time, she thought. She should apologise for living so long but then she wouldn't have had all this time with Lily.

She smiled at him, and lifted her hand in a wave. 'In a minute,' she said to him.

His smile was clear, warm, and full of love. His body was blurry at the borders, but his smile was distinct.

'Not long now,' he called back to her, and his voice carried on a gentle breeze.

Nevertheless, there was something that prevented her from moving forward; it was something that bound her to the bed, to the hospital room, and to the world that she was leaving behind.

Lily.

Where is she? Is she still around? Violet's eyelids opened with a flutter, and the harsh fluorescent lights came back into focus for a brief time. The weight of the hospital bed pressing in around her caused her to feel chilled, and the place was too bright and too sterile for her convenience. It became increasingly difficult for her to breathe as the agony in her chest became more intense. It was a heavy, persistent pressure.

'Gran. I'm here.'

Even though it seemed like it was coming from a vast distance, Violet was drawn back to the present moment by the voice, though only for a brief moment.

When Violet slowly turned her head, her eyes were having trouble focusing, but she was able to see her granddaughter sitting by the bedside. Her granddaughter's face was pale, and her eyes were red from sobbing. The hand that Lily was clutching was warm and steady, and it was gripping hers. On the other side her son, such a good man, so much like his father.

The words 'I'm here, Gran' were spoken softly by Lily as she wrapped her fingers more tightly around Violet's fragile hand. 'Look, I'm right here.'

Violet felt a flood of warmth sweep over her as she heard the sound of her voice, which was so reassuring.

A brief moment later, she found herself back in the garden. Lily was there. She was young, laughing, singing, her curls tangled in the wind. She could hear her voice, no older than ten.

★

'Gran! Listen to me sing.'

Violet flashed a grin in response to the recollection, but it was short and disappeared just as fast as it had appeared. In its stead, the cottage vanished, and the hospital room was brought back into existence. Now, the ache in her chest was intolerable, and her breathing was shallow, making it difficult for her to take a breath.

She needed something, and then she heard it.

Lily was singing once more, the final time. She listened, feeling her breathing slow down and the pain began to go. It was sweet relief, both the pain going and Lily's singing.

The hospital room began to fade. She wasn't there anymore. She was back at the cottage once more. Martin was standing at the window, and she was indeed at home. His hand was extended ahead of him, and his grin was filled with love and patience. He was getting closer.

'It's time to go,' he said, his voice quiet but insistent to get his point across. 'You've been here so long. You must be so tired.'

Violet smiled. 'I am a little weary,' she said and took his hand, and they opened the back door and walked out together.

Thirty-nine

Lily felt the air change as soon as she left Pippin Cottage. As if nature herself was grieving Gran's death. The clear, brilliant days of summer were gone and it hadn't stopped raining in the four days since she passed.

Just days earlier, the trees that had been a riot of reds and golds now stood naked, their skeletal branches pointing towards a leaden sky. A stinging wind carrying the promise of cold murmured through the village. Feeling the cold sink into her bones, Lily tightened her cardigan around her as she sat looking at Gran's empty armchair.

The funeral had to be organised and everyone in the village wanted to come, and Gran, never one for religion, would have wanted everyone to be welcome and have some of Mrs Douglas's shortbread and a cup of tea, so it was agreed with Peter and Denise it was to be held in the village hall.

But now she felt so alone. Even though the heater was on and Mr Mistoffelees was sitting on Gran's chair, purring happily, the cottage, once so vibrant and cosy, now seemed empty and chilly.

That morning her phone buzzed for the umpteenth time. Lily turned it over, as she had been doing for the preceding few days. She grudgingly grabbed it when it started ringing, though, seeing Paul's name on the screen. She had been avoiding his calls but she knew she had to answer now.

'Hello?' Even to her own ears her speech sounded hollow.

'Lily! At last!' Paul's speech seemed way too cheerful for her present state of mind. 'I've tried to get in touch to you. Listen, we should discuss the auditions.'

Lily closed her eyes, feeling like a headache was developing. 'Paul, my grandmother passed away and I have the funeral, so I won't be able to come next week. I know it's inconvenient but it's important.'

There was a pause. 'Was that the old lady at the show? With the oxygen tank?' he asked.

'Yes,' Lily said rolling her eyes at how rude he was.

'How old was she?' he asked.

'Ninety-seven.'

'So it's not a surprise then,' he said.

'Pardon?' Lily wondered if she had just heard that correctly. 'She might have been ninety-seven but she was still—'

Paul interrupted, 'Listen, I get you loved her and so on, I do, but understand – these auditions, they don't happen every day. The directors of *Phantom* and *Les Mis* have committed to seeing you next week and they're looking forward to it. I've been talking you up. This is a huge opportunity for you.'

'I can't not be at my grandmother's funeral,' she said, feeling firmer in her decision. His voice was exasperated as he spoke.

'I'm not sure you understand, Lily. If you don't come to these auditions, then I can't represent you anymore.'

Lily thought she had been slapped.

'Paul,' she said, her voice quivering with restrained feeling. 'I appreciate everything you have done, but my grandmother was everything to me, so I will be here, not in London.'

She could hear him draw a sharp intake of breath.

'You know when Jessica told me to come and see you, I said that I was worried you were a flake. I was going to let you go as I heard the rumours about *Les Mis*, but she insisted you were still a talent and she was right. I mean she just wanted you to get out of the village so she could get back with that nurse you're both fighting over, but I remembered that talent I saw when you left college, and you are talented – unlike Jessica. She can't sing for shit but now, you want to throw this chance away? I don't understand it.'

Lily held the phone to her ear, her mind going at one hundred miles an hour.

'Jessica told you to come?' she heard herself screech down the line.

'Yeah, she did,' Paul said. 'We dated for a while. I got her some auditions but she's not very good, terrific in other ways though.' He laughed and Lily looked at the phone and hung up.

'What a prick,' she said to the cat and then she dialled Nick's number. Her hands were shaking but from anger, and she was so mad, she started to punch the cushions on the sofa.

'Hey, how are you?' he answered immediately.

'I'm in shock,' she said with a punch to the cushion.

'I know, it's hard but it will become more bearable as time goes on,' he said in his kind way.

'Not about Gran,' said Lily quickly.

'What?' Nick seemed confused.

Lily was pacing now in the living room.

'Paul, he wanted me to skip Gran's service, said I should have seen it coming because she was so old, and come to London for the auditions and act like nothing happened.'

'Oh my God,' said Nick. 'What an absolute prick...'

'I just said that to the cat, but it gets worse,' she said.

'How?' Nick's voice was incredulous.

'He told me he and Jessica used to date and he got her some auditions. That's why she was at *Les Mis* when my voice went, and she wanted him to get me out of the village so Jessica could come back for you.'

'You can't be serious?' Nick's voice was furious.

'I am serious and I tell you that woman is such a liar. She's honestly like the villain in every show ever made.'

'She is out of control,' said Nick. 'I'm so sorry.'

'Don't be, it's not your fault,' she said, starting to calm down at the sound of his voice.

'So how did you leave it? Are you going to go to London?' he asked.

Lily laughed, her first real laugh since Gran had passed.

She went to the window and looked out at the half-done garden, the apples all over the ground, the blackbird dancing along the back fence.

'It just reminded me of everything I hate about that world. I know not every agent is like Paul and not every co-star is like Jessica, but I already have my happily ever after. Why would I throw it all away for a long-run eight shows a week in London?'

'Don't do it for me, Lily,' said Nick. 'You have to be sure this is what you want. I told you I would go anywhere with you.'

Lily looked up at the picture on the mantelpiece of her and Gran with their daisy chains on their heads and the piano net to the window and Mr Mistoffelees purring on the chair.

'I'm home, Nick, so hurry home to me as soon as you can. I want to get this show on the road. I have so much I want to do here in the cottage and in the garden. I want to make a life here.'

'Did Gran leave you the cottage?' Nick asked innocently and Lily stopped.

'I don't know,' she said. 'I hadn't even thought about it. God, what if Dad wants to sell it. I will have to try and buy it. Would he let me buy it?' she asked, feeling panic rise up in her throat at the thought of losing the cottage.

What if this was all for nothing? All these hopes and dreams and the cottage was never going to be hers?

She couldn't even bear to think about it.

Forty

Lily stood outside the village hall where she was holding a box of the order of service she'd had printed for the funeral the next day. She was waiting for Jasper to come so she could put them inside. The cold air producing little clouds from her breath was making her almost jump up and down on the spot to keep warm.

'Lily,' she heard and she turned and saw Jessica striding towards her.

'Please don't. I am not in the mood to hear anything from you, Jessica. I don't know what your issue is with me, but you need to leave me alone.'

'Why aren't you auditioning in London?'

'Because I don't want to,' said Lily. 'I know you sent Paul up to try and get me out of the village so you could be with Nick.'

Jessica laughed. 'No, I sent Paul up because you are better than this village and this stupid society. Why are you wasting your talent here?'

'What exactly is your problem with me?' Lily asked, putting the box on the ground.

'My problem with you is that you're wasting your talent, that you aren't meeting your potential,' Jessica said, throwing her hands up in the air.

Lily blew air out of her cheeks, not just because she was cold but also at Jessica's words.

'Do you know what the problem is with saying people aren't meeting their potential?'

Jessica crossed her arms. 'No. Enlighten me.'

'When people say things like that, it's not that they think the person has true potential, it's just that you think what you would do if you were me. This is only about you wanting to be able to sing, not actually about me at all.'

'That doesn't make any sense,' sneered Jessica.

'No it does – think about it. You want me to get away from here, from Nick, which means that you have won, except you didn't factor in two things.'

'What's that?' Jessica sniffed at her.

A light drizzle was starting to fall, making Jessica's hair glow in the light.

'One – Nick said he would come with me wherever I decided to go: London, Asia, Broadway. He only said he didn't want to leave because he didn't want to leave with you.'

Lily saw Jessica's face fall and part of her felt bad for a moment and then it disappeared.

'And two – you are acting as though he has no free will in this, as though you are some sort of siren who will sweep him up again. He's not your toy, Jessica, so stop playing with everyone and work out your own life. And stop lying and sabotaging people for your own benefit. Keep your acting for the stage, because that's the only place it belongs.'

'Everything all right?' Lily turned and saw Jasper at her side. Bernadette was on a leash, wearing a tiny pink fake fur coat with a hood and she didn't look thrilled about it either, Lily noticed.

'Yes, Jessica was just giving me her condolences for Gran,' she said, looking Jessica in the eye.

Jessica lifted her chin. 'Yes, it was very sad – lovely, though, that she was able to see you sing one last time, even if it was in the village hall.'

Jasper snorted at her. 'Be gone, Jessica, you have no powers here. Go and spread your bitchy ways somewhere else. We're tired of you.'

And Jasper picked up the box of the order of service for Gran and walked to the hall and opened the door with his key and Lily followed him, leaving Jessica stunned outside in the rain.

'You all right, pet?' he asked as he turned on the lights and dropped Bernadette's lead so she could wander.

Lily sat on a chair. 'She is like the wicked witch of Appleton Green,' she said in astonishment. 'I can't believe she's so relentless. If I told you what she had been up to you wouldn't believe it,' she said.

'Oh I would,' said Jasper with a laugh. 'I've seen her type before. After thirty years of directing shows, she's a dime a dozen. Too beautiful for her own good and not talented enough to be a star.'

Lily shrugged. 'She seems to hate me.'

'She hates anyone with talent,' he said and he sat down next to her.

'I know you think I am just a silly amateur drama director, who flits about and worries about ridiculous regional shows and how the costumes look,' he said, and as Lily protested he waved his hands. 'I know what some people think and say but, to be honest, I don't worry anymore,' he said. 'When I started my career, I was on the West End and for two years I went to Broadway with a show.'

'I did wonder, you have a great style of directing, much more professional than people realise,' said Lily.

'I don't talk about it, because it's not relevant now. My skills have grown from having to try and put a show together with three pounds and some enthusiasm.' He laughed.

She nodded. There was nothing like ingenuity in the theatre, especially amateur theatre.

'I was an assistant director to some very experienced people, with numerous Oliviers and Tonys amongst them all, but I knew it would be decades before I got to put on shows of my own and so much of their job was wooing the producers and investors, and I just wanted to put on a show.'

Bernadette padded over to them and put her paws up on Lily's legs to be picked up.

'She really does love you.' Jasper smiled. 'Everyone does.'

He went on with his story.

'And I thought about why I started directing theatre and I realised it wasn't for anything else but the rehearsal, the opening night, the closing night, all the problems to solve and how to put on a show that made people feel something. And I left it all. This is my job now and I love it,' he said. 'I make my living doing these sorts of things, and school shows and semi-professional shows, and it's always exciting and always rewarding. Not everything has to be at the top tier to be important.'

Lily nodded. 'I told the agent I couldn't come to the auditions and he basically told me I was finished before I started.'

Jasper sighed. 'There is a sort of expectation in the industry that you will do whatever it takes, the show must go on above everything else, but sometimes, the everything else is the most important thing.'

Lily patted Bernadette as she gave a comfortable sigh and nestled into her lap. 'I don't think I have that sort of energy in me,' she said. 'It was lovely to be asked but the anxiety started to rise in me and then when I was asked to choose, well... I couldn't. There was no choice.'

'I understand, dear, so much. You have built a life here in that sweet little cottage.'

'Now Gran has passed, I think Dad will sell the cottage though. We haven't found Gran's will yet, so it's hard to know.'

Jasper shook his head. 'Her will is at the post office.'

'What do you mean?'

'She kept it there. She told me when I went to see her and you to convince you to come back to the show.'

'Why did you talk about that?' Lily asked, confused.

'I don't know really. We were talking about the cottage and how old it was, and she said sometimes she worried about it burning down, which is why she got rid of the old open fire and put a heater in, and she told me she left her important papers with Mrs Harris. Has she not come and given them to you yet?'

Lily shook her head. 'No, she called me but I didn't take answer. There's been so many people calling and texting, you see.'

Jasper patted her hand. 'Well give her a call and pick it up and you can read it with your family when you're ready.'

'I can't. I have to get the hall ready for the funeral.' Lily looked around at the drab hall, the plastic chairs lined up in rows. 'I wish I had more time to make it nice, but I don't and there's too many people who want to come to have it in a church.'

'You never mind that. I'll take care of it,' Jasper said. 'This is what I do. Leave it with me. I'll call in the troops. Go and call Mrs Harris.'

'Okay, I'll call her now,' said Lily, her heart beating faster. 'Are you sure?'

'Surer than sure – now call her.' Jasper picked up Bernadette from Lily's lap and held her as she stood up and called Mrs Harris back.

'Hello, Mrs Harris? It's Lily Baxter,' she said.

'Oh, Lily, I am so sorry about Violet. What a woman she was.'

Lily nodded, not trusting herself to speak, as the tears came so easily, especially when people were nice about Gran to her.

'I've got some things she left for you here, if you want to come and get them.'

'Are you open?' asked Lily, looking at the time on the large clock on the wall.

'I am open for you, dear,' said Mrs Harris. 'See you soon.'

Lily slipped the phone into her pocket.

'I'm going to see her now,' she said to Jasper, who was taking the order of services out of the box and placing them on the chairs that were lined up in rows in the hall.

'Want me to walk with you?' Jasper asked.

'No, thank you though. I am grateful to you, Jasper,' she said and she hugged him.

'My darling, it is a pleasure. Now go and get Gran's things and I will see you tomorrow for the service.' He paused for a moment. 'Are you sure you're up to it?'

Lily nodded. 'Yes, I'm okay, I want to do my best.'

'And you will. I know whatever happens, you will always shine through, Lily Baxter.'

Forty-one

Lily hurried back to the cottage and turned on the heater and sat in front of it warming her hands, the papers in her lap.

Why on earth hadn't Violet told anyone in the family her will was at the post office? But Jasper and Mrs Harris knew? Honestly, she thought, and she dialled her father's number but he didn't answer so she left a voice message.

'Hi, the will was at the post office, apparently she told Jasper and said she was worried the cottage might burn down. Honestly, sometimes Gran's thinking was so bizarre. Anyway, she's left letters for us. I won't read the will; I'll leave it for you. Love you,' she said and put down her phone. Mrs Harris had given her a manilla envelope filled with letters and the will inside, each one marked with a different date.

For Lily. Please read in order.

Some of the letters were old, on older stationery. Fifteen letters, all with dates on the front.

She opened the first one and read. The first summer she had spent with Gran alone at Pippin Cottage. As she read it she started to cry, deep racking sobs that were both painful and healing. She read each one carefully, remembering things she hadn't thought of since they happened. Funny things, silly things, sad things, wonderful memories of a time that made Lily who she is.

She came to the one when she was fifteen. God she had been so torn that summer and Gran had seen it all. She had wanted to be with Gran but there was so much happening at home with her friends. What she would give to have that summer again and be more present with Gran.

And she came to the last one.

To my darling granddaughter, Lily, aged twenty-nine,

I am sitting at the kitchen table writing this to you when you're at rehearsals.

If you are reading this, then I have taken my final bow and finally get to join Grandad, if you believe such things. I am unsure if I do but it's helpful to think that there is something after all of this.

Try not to be too sad, darling, as we had such a wonderful time together, didn't we?

It has been a tremendous run for me, and the last few months that I have spent with you have been the most satisfying conclusion that I could have hoped for. It really is a wonderful final act, and I thank you for coming to be with me and for being so generous, kind, caring and for treating me like an adult. So many people seem to think we reverse in age when we get older. It is so annoying to be spoken to and treated as though I can't make my own decisions when I have been making them for over ninety years.

Lily smiled at Gran's obstinance to the very end.

As my time winds down, memories long since buried have returned. Most of them of you. When you would sing in the garden, your voice would rise with the birds, and I would know that you were destined for something extraordinary at that very moment. Nevertheless, I never in a million years would have guessed that it would be this – not the stages of the West End, but right here in Appleton Green, where you have finally discovered your voice. Never stop singing, Lily, never stop sharing your talent with the world.

During the past few months, I have been watching you grow, Lily, and I have witnessed you mature and how you have learned to tap into yourself and find out what you wanted. When you arrived, you were disorientated, and your beautiful voice was muffled by uncertainty and anticipation. I remember that feeling. However, by taking care of me, Pippin Cottage, and then immersing yourself in the society's show, you found your way. You found your personal purpose, which is to share. You are the most selfless person I know and people benefit from being around you. And now you are sharing it with your students at the school.

Lily wiped tears away that fell onto the paper. Gran had written this recently, in the last month. She knew she was dying. That's what she meant when she said it was the last summer and seeing her sing one last time.

If my time with you over the years has shown you anything, I hope it's that there is always a second act in life and the greatest applause you can get is the one you give yourself when you get through anything hard. If you're not giving yourself a standing ovation then what does it matter?

You are proud of yourself now, Lily, and it has been a joy to watch you come into your own. I watched how your eyes light up when you talk about your students, how you come alive after a rehearsal and how you've opened your heart to Nick and to this community. I see all of these things. This is the real Lily Baxter; not the one who is trying to keep anyone else happy. Rather, she is the one who is trying to create her own dreams here in Appleton Green.

And I know you will be tempted back to London again, and perhaps you will try again and maybe succeed. You certainly have the talent to do well anywhere you go, but I know, deep in the marrow of these old bones, that you will always have your heart here.

For this reason, I am leaving Pippin Cottage to you. This little village has always been a safe haven for people who are searching for who they are, and finding themselves, and I know how much you adore the house. I know you want to restore the garden and in all honesty the roof in the kitchen leaks and the wallpaper is peeling behind the bookshelf, but I know you will do what you want with the home now. Don't hang on to anything because of me; make it your own.

Lily, don't be frightened to put down your roots in Appleton Green. Nurture them like a garden and your voice, and know that wherever you are – on stage, teaching in a classroom, or just singing to yourself in the morning while you're making tea – I will be listening. You have done what you set out to do, my little girl, and I couldn't be prouder of you.

Have a happy life, love sincerely, and never, ever, ever be anything other than who you are.

Thank you for everything, Lily. You were the making of me as a grandmother and I cherished every moment of our time.

With all my love,
Gran

PS: Don't forget to give that handsome Nick a chance as well. I see the way he looks at you. It reminds me of the way Grandad used to look at me. And not to mention he does make an excellent brew, so perhaps he can move in and make you brews for as long as you both shall live.

Lily sat in silence. The wind outside was making an eerie wail and Mr Mistoffelees jumped from the windowsill and onto the back of Gran's chair.

'You were the making of me, Gran,' she said to the empty chair. 'The very best parts of me are from you and I thank you for everything I am because of you.'

There was a single crack of thunder and then the wind stopped and the cat was on the seat of Gran's chair clawing at it until it was ready for him to sit, and Lily knew then that Gran's spirit had left Pippin Cottage.

Forty-two

A hazy, soft rain seemed to shroud Appleton Green in a quiet solemnity on the morning of Gran's funeral. Watching water droplets make their way down the glass of Pippin Cottage, Lily stood there unable to force herself to cry a single tear. She had cried enough, she told herself, knowing that's what Gran would say to her.

She put her hand in the pocket of the black coat she was wearing, touching the letter from Gran. The weight of it seemed to tether her to this very time and this place. This was her house; this was her home. It had always been her home in many ways.

A soft tap on the door jolted her out of her daydream. It was Nick wearing a sombre black suit. He held out his hand and asked softly, 'Ready?'

Lily nodded, inhaled deeply, and then put her hand in his and they walked out to the car that was waiting for them to go to the village hall.

Her parents were in the car ahead of them and when they stopped at the hall, Lily alighted and hugged her parents.

'You ready?' said Peter.

Lily nodded and her hand trembled a little on the door handle; then she inhaled deeply before pushing the door open and going inside.

Her breath caught when she saw what was in front of her. Jasper had surpassed expectations, converting the hall into an amazing homage to Gran. The gentle flicker of electric candles took the place of the normal harsh overhead lights, which were dimmed. There was a small classical quartet playing as people sat waiting, and there were bunches of white anemones in vases on the tables at the side of the hall, where cups and saucers were lined up with plates and forks and a selection of fresh baked goods, covered by nets, lay ready for the wake.

Lily saw that the hall was already crowded as her eyes grew accustomed to the gentle light, and as Nick walked her to their seats at the front, she saw the cast from the show lined up with their partners. There was Sheila sitting with Mrs Harris, and Mrs Douglas wiping her eyes and giving a gentle nod to Lily as she caught her eye.

The soft hum of discussion died down as people became aware of her entrance, and all eyes were instantly fixed on her. Nick gave a gentle squeeze of her hand, a sort of silent reassurance of his presence, and they found their seats at the front.

Once Lily sat down, she looked around and saw what Jasper had done. He had somehow created a tapestry of Gran's life. Old programmes from shows, photos, and even some of her handwritten recipes covered the walls, printed onto them. There were photos of her and Gran, Gran and Peter, so much joy in her life, so many lovely memories, she thought.

Lily's eyes lingered on a faded picture of herself and Gran sitting at the piano when they were both laughing.

Jasper took to the podium, and smiled at Lily and her parents.

'Friends, family, esteemed guests and all who knew Violet Rose Baxter.' His background in theatre was clear in every word and Lily smiled at him. Gran would have loved this, she thought. Jasper was putting on a show for Gran and those who loved her, and Lily felt herself relax.

'Enjoy the show,' she was sure she heard Gran whisper in her ear. 'Tonight, we have come together to honour Violet Baxter's extraordinary life. A bright light on our small stage, a cornerstone of our neighbourhood, and a close friend to all of us.'

Lily let her eyes roam the room as Jasper went on and she saw Mr McBride from the school and the choir behind him, all in their school uniforms. Lily felt her eyes fill up with tears, genuinely moved by their presence, reminding her that she was in the right place.

'We will start this tribute to Violet with the choir from Silverton Grammar who will sing for her and us tonight.'

The students walked out onto the stage and stood in formation. Mr McBride stood in front of them and then the sound of Andrew playing the piano started and the choir sang 'Seasons of Love' from *Rent* and Lily felt happy tears fall as she turned to Nick, who was also wiping his eyes.

As the children sang, she mouthed the words with them and smiled and clapped along. She was taken aback to see her students, some of whom she had only known for a few weeks, honouring Gran in this manner, honouring her.

Lily felt a warmth rise across her chest as the young voices sang about measuring a year in love. It was so beautiful, she thought as she watched them.

The eulogy was next on the schedule. Peter, Lily's father, got up and walked over to the podium. He cleared his throat and unfolded a piece of paper, his hands trembling a little.

With a faltering voice, he said, 'My mother, Violet Baxter, was an incredible woman. However, she would have laughed at me if I had said that. She would say, "I'm just an ordinary woman who has lived a very long time." However, the truth is known by those of us who loved and knew her.' His voice broke at the end of the sentence and he stopped and composed himself.

'Mum had a talent for elevating the ordinary to the spectacular and making everyone feel special. As a child, a stroll around the garden could become an adventure, and a simple cup of tea could become a momentous occasion. Her intelligence was great, her laughter contagious, and her love, well, it seemed limitless.'

As he went on, Peter's voice got louder as he related tales of Gran's life, including her romance with Lily's grandfather, her time spent performing on stage with the amateur dramatics club, and her steadfast devotion to her friends and family.

'But her role as a grandmother was perhaps the greatest,' Peter remarked, his gaze falling on Lily. 'There was something quite unique about the relationship my mother and daughter shared. Mum used to say that Lily was the surprise gift that she loved more than a standing ovation.'

Lily sensed tears trickling down her cheeks, and Nick's fingers constricted around hers, offering silent comfort.

'In the past few months, since Lily moved back to Appleton Green, I've noticed a brightness in my mother's eyes that I hadn't noticed in years,' he went on. 'She enjoyed seeing Lily rediscover who she was and what her real calling in life was. She would proudly tell me over the phone, "Our Lily is blooming."'

He stopped and inhaled deeply. 'Mum showed love and faith in her last deed. She hung on to watch Lily play one more time, to watch her granddaughter take centre stage in life as well as on stage and knowing Lily was happy, settled with love and purpose in her life, Mum made her farewell bow.'

Upon finishing his sentence, Peter's voice broke as he firmly held on to the podium. 'Mum, words cannot express how much we will miss you. However, we will live in your memory by following your example of love, laughter, and a constant song in our hearts. Mum, I hope you rest well. You deserve it, all of it.'

There was not a dry eye in the church when Peter returned to his seat.

Jasper was back at the podium. 'And now we ask Lily, Violet's granddaughter, to sing her tribute to her.'

Lily stood up, and felt a sense of calm she had never felt before singing.

She smiled at Andrew who was at the piano and he nodded. He knew what song Lily was to sing and he started the introduction. Lily closed her eyes and 'Someone to Watch Over Me' flooded the room. Her voice was faint at first, but as she continued, it became louder. Gran seemed to be right there with her, singing along at the piano in the cottage. They loved to sing the standards and this was a favourite for them both.

There was a deep stillness in the room as the final note was heard, and then the room broke into soft cheers. Lily stood, tears on her cheeks that she was unaware she had wept, and then made her way back to her seat, where Nick waited for her.

Jasper spoke again. 'And as a final tribute to Violet, she told me how much she loved a particular song so we will sing it for her, in full chorus, so if you pick up your order of service, you will see the words on the back.'

The music started and the cast of *My Fair Lady* out the front, all ready to sing and off they went, encouraging the crowd to join into a rousing version of 'Get Me to the Church on Time'.

It was a perfect ending to a perfect service – irreverent, silly, loud and utterly mad – and Lily knew that Gran would have abso-blooming loved it.

The rest of the evening was a slow ebb and flow of music, stories, and conversation around cups of tea and cake, and Mrs Douglas's shortbread.

As the crowd began to thin out, Lily wandered the room, looking at the work Jasper had put into the service. It was better than any show she had ever been in, she thought.

Nick's arm slid around her waist as she took a step back. 'You okay?' he whispered.

Lily leaned closer to him and nodded. 'Yeah,' she answered, startled by how accurate that statement was. 'I think I am.'

Lily had a feeling of calm descend upon her as she took in the sights of her grandmother's life, commemorated down to the last detail, and the faces of both old and new acquaintances. Gran might have passed away, but she was everywhere in the village and now it was Lily's turn to create a life here.

She turned to Nick. 'So, when are you moving in?' she asked him. 'Gran said you had to make me cups of tea in her last will and testament. You can't let her down or she will haunt you from beyond.'

Nick laughed loudly. 'I have no doubt she would. Well I better make good on her instructions,' he said and he kissed her in front of the large photo of Gran and Grandad on their wedding day.

Finale

On a crisp spring morning, Lily Baxter pushed her daughter Daisy's pram along the river towards Appleton Green. The air smelt like new flowers and turned soil, and it was clean and sweet. Sunlight filtered through the new trees and warmed Lily's face gently as she walked, and she adjusted the hood of the pram to make sure Daisy's eyes were shielded from the light.

Daisy was happily cooing in her pram. She was only four months old, and her fat fingers reached out to grab the moving shadows of leaves. Lily smiled at her daughter discovering shadows. Being a mother was her most rewarding role yet, she had told Nick.

Watching Daisy discover the world was unlike anything Lily had known. She wondered why she hadn't seen how much she had wanted to be a mother before. Daisy was a surprise. She found out she was pregnant not long after Gran had passed, and it was bittersweet to know that Gran would have loved to have met her but couldn't.

They passed some tourists taking photos of the bridge and Lily waited for them to finish before she crossed it and stopped and leaned against the old wall to look down at the River Dove running below. There was a dark time when she had stood on the edge of a bridge and questioned her being in the world. Now she never wanted her life to end, if it was going to be this amazing.

The water in it was gurgling happily, matching Daisy's happy chatter, and she reached down and touched her daughter's soft cheek.

'You are so beautiful,' she said to the child.

She started her walk again and pushed Daisy towards the village, where she was stopped by Mrs Harris who had knitted Daisy a little cardigan and Mrs Douglas, who had more shortbread and a little book about a corgi for Daisy.

'You all spoil her,' Lily said to the women.

'We don't get many babies in the village,' said Mrs Harris. 'It's quite a novelty.'

Lily said her goodbyes and then crossed the road and came to the village hall.

The heavy door was held open for Lily by Sheila as she approached the building. Lily's feet were deliberate and unhurried as she approached.

'How is our future ingénue?' Sheila enquired while looking into the pram, cooing at the baby.

A grin appeared on Lily's face as she looked down at Daisy.

'To be honest, it's excellent. She slept for a total of eight hours last night.'

'Bravo, encore, encore, more of the same tonight please,' Sheila cooed as she reached out to softly stroke the baby's cheek. 'Hello, Miss Daisy,' she said. 'You should continue to work on your sleep so that your mother can get her beauty sleep.'

Daisy's eyes narrowed for a little minute as she looked at Sheila, her little face contorted in concentration, and then she made the decision to smile at her since she was so focused.

'Oh, did she give me a smile?' As Lily pushed the pushchair deeper into the hall, Sheila gloated, exclaiming, 'I feel so special.'

As Lily entered the village hall, she felt at home again. People were milling about, engaging in conversation, practising their lines, and setting up coffee and tea.

'Hello, sweetheart,' a familiar voice cried out and she looked up. She saw her mother, Denise, standing on stage, with Jasper next to her.

Denise was holding a script for *Auntie Mame*, in which she was playing the lead role.

Surprisingly Sheila hadn't taken umbrage at this news, insisting she was getting too old now and was happier in costumes.

Lily waved at her mum. She couldn't help but feel a surge of happiness at the sight of Denise so naturally at ease on the stage. She really was in her element.

Jasper entered the conversation before Denise could respond, and his voice was filled with adoration as he said, 'Your mother is wonderful. She is going to be an amazing Auntie Mame.'

'I have no doubt,' she said in return to them and she saw her mother preen.

It was Nick's idea to get Denise into the society and it was the best one he'd had, next to them getting married.

David came over to her with a cup of tea in his hand and said, 'She is doing great. She's very enthused and she and Sheila are getting on well.'

'I'm so glad,' Lily said. 'When Nick mentioned that she should join I thought he was mad, but now I see it was all a projection of what she wanted for herself onto me. I don't think I've ever seen her happier.'

'She does seem to love being the centre of attention,' David said, not unkindly.

'I think, because she didn't work, she never had a real passion or purpose. Between this and her coming to help with Daisy now I'm back at work two days a week, she's in her element.'

Andrew, the pianist for the society, played the first few bars of the song 'It's Today' from the show as if he had been given a cue, and people started to sing along, Lily included. She had missed this but Denise could have the limelight this year; Lily would be back next year. It was a reminder of the joy and mayhem that comes with living in the theatre that the familiar music filled the hall. Denise's voice sang out, crystal clear and full of vitality as Lily smiled at her proudly.

During the time that Lily was rocking Daisy back and forth, she was standing behind the pram and swaying slightly and then she felt Nick's arms slip around her waist from behind.

He came up to her and said, 'Hello, you,' as his breath warmed against her neck.

As she stared down at their daughter, she sank back into his arms and her heart grew larger. As she responded, her tone was gentle and filled with affection. 'Hello, yourself,' she said.

Nick cast a quick glance over to the stage, where Denise was performing, and he watched her as she sang and danced with an infectious enthusiasm. 'My parents are meeting us at the pub for dinner. Are yours going to join us?'

'I think so. I'll send Dad a text,' she said. 'But let's not rush. I want to watch Mum a little longer.'

'You love her being in this society, don't you?' Nick asked with a smile.

Lily gave a small laugh. 'Up there, Mum is having the time of her life, and to tell you the truth, while she's busy living out her West End fantasies, she's not bothering me, so I'm happy.' She laughed as she said this.

He leaned down to give her a gentle kiss on the top of the head. He teased: 'How happy are you right now?'

Lily muttered, 'Happier than I ever imagined possible,' she said as she leaned back into him.

There was a brief moment when they stood there, encircled by each other's arms, and the world around them seemed to recede into the background. The previous year had been a whirlwind; it had been a journey of rediscovery, of finding her voice once more, and of learning to strike a balance between her old goals and the new life she was constructing. There had been times when she had questioned her own abilities, situations in which the burden of children, career, and her own aspirations had appeared to be too much for her to bear. On the other hand, when she stood here with Nick and Daisy, surrounded by the theatre society that had become her second family, she experienced a sense of serenity that she had never experienced before.

As Lily watched her mother perform on stage, she felt as if the last piece of a jigsaw had been put into place.

It all made sense now, she thought, and she wondered if Gran would have seen this plot twist coming.

Her phone buzzed in her pocket and she took it and saw it was a video call from Nigel.

'Break, everyone,' called out Jasper.

'Hello, you,' she said to Nigel.

'Oh I thought Daisy would answer the phone,' he complained.

'She would but I said no phones till she's six months, and she's only four months,' she joked.

'Show me the baby,' he said in a kingly tone and she laughed as she flipped the screen and showed Nigel her daughter.

'Hello, darling, I have bought you so many fun things in Japan. I can't wait to see you, sweetie.'

'Stop buying her presents,' she said to him as she flipped the camera back to her. 'She won't fit into anything by the time you get to meet her.'

'About that,' he said, 'I'm coming back. I'm doing a new show, so we're coming back to the UK. I'm tired of being on the yellow brick road. I need to be on London's chaotic streets.'

'Oh yay, amazing, I cannot wait.'

'Yes, this show is terrible now. They have a new Dorothy and she's such a diva with no chops to back it up. I've no idea where they found her, but she's got a voice of an unoiled door and is so awful to everyone. People are leaving their contracts early just to get away from her.'

'Oh no, who is she. Do we know her?'

Nigel rustled some papers and then picked up a programme from the show and turned the page and showed Lily on the screen.

'Her, Jessica Wilcox. Do you know her?'

Lily looked at the picture of Jess and she shook her head. 'Oh I know her, and then some. I need to have a huge gossip with you and tell you everything. When are you back?'

'Next week. I'm coming to see you, and…' He paused. 'I'm engaged to Marcus,' he said.

'Oh my God, I love all of this news,' said Lily, jumping up and down in the hall as the sound of Daisy crying reverberated in the hall.

'I have to go,' she said to Nigel. 'I love you. Call me when you're in London.'

She turned to her daughter who stopped crying at the sight of her mother.

'Were you pretending to be sad then?' she asked and Nick laughed.

'She wants the spotlight more like it, I think,' said Nick with a laugh and she picked up her daughter and gave her a kiss.

'She can't help it. Show business is in her blood.'

Acknowledgements

THANK YOU to my editor, Aubrie Artiano for the continual guidance and collaboration. Thank you to Holly and the team at Head of Zeus and their support and hard work. It is noticed and appreciated. And to my agent, Tara Wynne, the best in the business, thank you for all you do.

About the Author

KATE FORSTER writes books filled with love, laughter, and the enchantment of everyday life. Kate, a Melbourne-based author, crafts realistic characters and touching stories that feel like you're catching up with old friends. When she is not writing, you can find her sharing glimpses of her creative life on social media, soaking up inspiration from her dynamic online community, or spending time with her loving dogs, who are constantly by her side (and occasionally steal the spotlight). Kate, who is tea-fueled and daydreaming on the beach, is all about finding joy in the little things and sharing them through her writing.

Stories to fall in love with.

Aria

Thanks for reading!

Want to receive exclusive author content, news on the latest Aria books and updates on offers and giveaways?

Follow us on X @AriaFiction and on Facebook and Instagram @HeadofZeus, and join our mailing list.